S.S.F. Public Library
West Orange
840 West Orange Ave.
South San Francisco, CA 94080

D0451637

TROUBLE IN THE TAROT

JAN 1 4

This Large Print Book carries the
Seal of Approval of N.A.V.H.

TROUBLE IN THE TAROT

KARI LEE TOWNSEND

WHEELER PUBLISHING
A part of Gale, Cengage Learning

GALE
CENGAGE Learning·

Detroit • New York • San Francisco • New Haven, Conn • Waterville, Maine • London

GALE
CENGAGE Learning®

Copyright © 2013 by Kari Townsend.
A Fortune Teller Mystery.
Wheeler Publishing, a part of Gale, Cengage Learning.

ALL RIGHTS RESERVED
This is a work of fiction. Names, characters, places, and incidents either are the product of the author's imagination or are used fictitiously, and any resemblance to actual persons, living or dead, business establishments, events, or locales is entirely coincidental. The publisher does not have any control over and does not assume any responsibility for author or third-party websites or their content.
Wheeler Publishing Large Print Cozy Mystery.
The text of this Large Print edition is unabridged.
Other aspects of the book may vary from the original edition.
Set in 16 pt. Plantin.

LIBRARY OF CONGRESS CATALOGING-IN-PUBLICATION DATA

Townsend, Kari Lee.
  Trouble in the Tarot / By Kari Lee Townsend. — Large Print edition.
    pages cm. — (A Fortune Teller Mystery) (Wheeler Publishing Large Print Cozy Mystery.)
    ISBN 978-1-4104-6187-2 (softcover) — ISBN 1-4104-6187-4 (softcover) 1. Women Psychics—Fiction. 2. Tarot (Game)—Fiction. 3. New York—Fiction. 4. Large type books. I. Title.
  PS3620.O9598T76 2013
  813'.6—dc23   2013032341

Published in 2013 by arrangement with The Berkley Publishing Group, a member of Penguin Group (USA) LLC, a Penguin Random House Company

Printed in the United States of America
1 2 3 4 5   17 16 15 14 13

This book is dedicated to my husband, Brian. The first book I ever published I dedicated to him, but this series is near and dear to my heart, and he is even more so. He deserves to have another book dedicated to him, because he is my rock. My soul mate. My everything. I met him when I was eighteen and married him when I was twenty-one. We have been married for twenty-three years and have four amazing children: Brandon, Josh, Matt, and Emily. I am so lucky to be able to work from home and do what I was born to do: write books. He has always supported me in anything I've ever wanted — stay home and raise our children, write books, live my dream even when it barely helped pay the bills. He understands what makes me happy, he still makes me laugh, and I truly can't imagine going through life without him by my side.

This one's for you, baby. I love you with all my heart.

ACKNOWLEDGMENTS

Once again, I have to thank my fabulous editor, Faith Black. I just love working with her. She's an amazing person, and she has a great eye. She, as well as the rest of the Berkley Prime Crime staff, have done a great job of making me look fabulous.

As always, I am forever indebted to my fantastic agent and partner in crime, Christine Witthohn of Book Cents Literary Agency, for standing by me and fighting for my best interest. She keeps me grounded yet makes me feel like a rock star. Love her to pieces and will never have another agent . . . just saying.☺

Of course I have to thank my original BC Babes: Barbara Witek, Danielle LaBue, and Liz Lipperman. You talented and fun ladies make it all worthwhile.

Then there are my beta readers: the fabulous Michelle McDonald, Matt Bourdon, and Joanne Russo, who always have my back. Thank you as always for making my stories shine. And my chiropractor Dr. Jeffrey Byrne along with his office manager Jane for helping me keep my butt planted in my chair and reading all of my books. Your office rocks!

And last but never least, my extended family: The Townsends, the Harmons, and the Russos (especially my niece Meghan and my sister Debbie, who just "get" me and always know exactly what to say). I have the best, most supportive family ever. You all rock. And a special thanks to my mom, Marion Harmon, who is a rock star herself. The woman is literally my biggest cheerleader, and I seriously couldn't do any of this without her. Love you, Mom. Thanks, everyone. Another one bites the dust.☺

1

"The cards predict a very long week ahead of us, Morty," I said as I laid out my fortune-telling supplies on a table inside the gazebo in Mini Central Park.

My big, white, beautiful, arrogant cat scowled and gave me a look — as much as a feline can give a look — that said, *Duh! Ya think?*

"*How* did I let her talk me into this?" I asked.

Cat or no cat, his scowl deepened, and I swore I could see the brow he didn't have arch sky-high.

"Fine. Not me, *us,*" I added, making a set of air quotes. "And don't give me that look, mister. You can't say no to her any more than I can."

I shook my head at the ridiculous traditional, turban-style fortune-teller hat she'd tied to his head because I'd refused to wear one. I was a real psychic and simply used

9

fortune-telling tools to help interpret my visions. I didn't care to add to the stigma already attached to my profession.

As usual, Granny was clueless and made it clear she thought I was being silly. She thought Morty looked adorable and that his attire added to our authenticity. I didn't have the energy to argue, so I'd let it go. At least it was an improvement over the godawful bow ties she usually dressed him up in.

Morty rolled his jet black eyes, leapt onto the railing, and stretched out in the early morning sunshine. I could see he would be absolutely no help whatsoever.

Just peachy.

The small town of Divinity, located in upstate New York, kicked off the summer every year with its Summer Solstice Carnival. This year June twenty-first fell on a Friday, so the carnival would start today, continue all week with an auction to boot, and end on Sunday, June thirtieth, with the widely popular bakeoff.

My grandmother Gertrude was a member of Trixie's Sewing Circle, and they were in charge of the carnival this year. Somehow, I'd let Granny Gert talk me into reading tarot cards under the gazebo. *All for a good cause, mind you,* she'd said, pointing out that the money the carnival raised would help the local animal shelter. The carnival committee chose a different charity every year to help support through the carnival proceeds, and this one just happened to be near and dear to my heart.

As cunning as my cat, Granny had pounced. *You find such joy in Morty. Why not help others find an animal to love? If we don't raise enough money to get Animal Angels going, they might have to shut down before they even get started. Just think of what might happen to those critters if they don't get adopted,* she'd said, knowing the word *euthanize* wasn't in my vocabulary. So here I was . . .

Nine A.M. on a Friday morning, setting up shop in the park.

I was *not* an early riser or a coffee drinker. Hot cocoa or tea for me. Only, neither one was doing the trick this morning. I yawned and tugged my belted blouse down over my flowy skirt, then proceeded to pull the rest of my supplies out of the fringed knapsack I carried.

In my line of work, I used all fortune-telling tools to help me interpret my visions. But wanting to keep the carnival readings as simple as possible, I'd chosen to read tarot cards this week.

I glanced around the park. Divinity was

an old-fashioned town with antique street-lamps and big, old Victorian houses. Mini Central Park was just as quaint with street-lamps, park benches, a gazebo, and even a swan pond.

The other venders were setting up their tents filled with food, crafts, and games, and the carnival workers were giving a final inspection to the rides. The swans in the pond were putting up their usual fuss at having their harmonious habitat invaded, but at least their babies had grown a lot in the last two months.

The sewing circle had been kind enough to assign the gazebo to me. It was right in the middle of the park, and it was big. I'd placed a rope across the entrance so only one person could enter at a time, affording us a bit of privacy for the readings, and I'd even hung my shingle from the roof.

SUNNY'S SANCTUARY.

Or, at least, I tried to hang my shingle. After it fell down five times, a tall, distinguished-looking older gentleman named Harry stopped and fixed it, giving me hope that this week might turn out okay after all. He seemed to be a really nice guy.

"Are you sure I can't pay you or give you a free reading in thanks?" I said.

He hesitated as though he was considering it, but then he looked around a little anxiously as more people arrived to set up. "I don't care much for crowds," he responded, clearing his throat. "Besides, I've got a date with this fishing pole." He smiled as he saluted me with his pole and then hurried away.

He'd said he was staying at Divine Inspiration — the charming inn where my parents always stayed, situated on the outskirts of town on Inspiration Lake. Oh, well, hopefully I'd see him again before he left and the rest of the carnival goers would be just as nice.

Normally, I did my readings from the comfort of Vicky, my distinguished, if slightly haunted, ancient Victorian house. But for the sake of the carnival, this gazebo would have to do.

The round wooden gazebo had a built-in table right in the center. I spread a lavender silk scarf over the top to protect the cards' energy from undesirable vibrations. Next, I placed elemental symbols around the table. I used a stone to represent the earth, a seashell to represent water, a candle to represent fire, and incense to represent the air. Finally, I turned on a soft-sounds-of-nature CD to try to drown out the noise

13

from the carnival and help create a tranquil space.

"Have you seen Granny?" Trixie Irving, a thin, short seamstress with black-and-gray-streaked hair secured in a tight bun, approached me looking a bit frazzled. "I need help with the Sewing Sisters' booth, and she's nowhere in sight."

"Sorry, Trixie, I have no clue. I was just wondering the same thing."

"Well, okay then. I guess I'll just have to figure it out myself. I swear, nothing is going right this morning. It's like a bunch of gremlins are on the loose. Anything that can go wrong *is* going wrong. If I didn't know better, I would think something was afoot." She bustled off, shaking her head and wringing her hands as she talked to herself.

Quincy Turner, the person in charge of the Parks and Rec Program, caught my eye. He kicked the Animal Angels sign over as he walked by their booth. The owner, Ozzie Zuckerman, saw him and came running out, waving his fist in the air. The two argued rather heatedly, and then Quincy huffed off.

I frowned, hoping nothing really was "afoot." Granny and the rest of the sisters had worked way too hard to make this carnival happen for someone to be sabotaging things. I waved off the notion, thinking I was just looking for mischief given the recent chaos I'd been through. But all of that was behind me now. It was time I started looking for peace and tranquility.

Pulling out my favorite deck of tarot cards, I used fanning powder to keep the cards from sticking together. It was time consuming to individually cover each card with powder and then wipe them off, but it was well worth the effort. The powder made the cards feel wonderful in your hands. When I was finished, I rubbed essential oil on my hands to help invoke the senses of the person I was doing the reading for, and I set out a bowl of chocolates to share.

Now I just needed my first querent to arrive.

"Yoo-hoo. Are you open yet, darling?" a voice said from behind me only moments later.

I spun around in surprise, relieved to finally have my first bona fide customer. She had to be around Granny Gert's age, but that was where the similarity stopped.

Granny had snow white hair that had been bleached at the age of sixteen from scarlet fever, false teeth, snappy brown eyes, and homemade aprons made from flour sacks. Having lived through the Depression, my granny was a firm believer in waste not, want not and reused everything, even though she had more money than she knew what to do with.

This woman had neatly styled strawberry blond hair, faded blue eyes, and all her own teeth by the look of it, not to mention expensive clothing. She was sharply dressed in tan slacks, a light blue blouse, with a cream-colored cardigan sweater draped loosely over her boney shoulders. Even though the forecast predicted eighty degrees today, mornings were still chilly in New York during the month of June.

She kind of reminded me of what my mother might look like at that age, only this woman seemed a lot more pleasant already. I loved my mother, but she didn't make life easy.

I pasted a smile on my face and unhooked the rope, wondering who this woman was. I hadn't seen her around town before. "I'm absolutely open. Step right up, Miss . . . ?"

"Atwater." She nodded once, all proud-like. "Fiona Atwater in the flesh."

"Well, I hope so." I winked, liking her already. "We wouldn't want to scare anyone away by you standing here without your flesh, now would we?"

She hooted with laughter and waved her

16

hand at me. "Oh, go on with you. You're Sunny, I take it?" She pointed to my sign.

"Sunshine Meadows in the flesh, but yes, please call me Sunny."

"Wonderful! The name suits you. With your spiky blond hair and pale green eyes, you look like a big ball of sunshine, no makeup necessary. Aren't you a lucky one?"

"Flattery will get you everywhere." I laughed. "Come on in and have a seat, Fiona, and we'll get started." My smile remained, and for the second time that morning, I felt like things were looking up.

She followed me and sat on the other side of the table. "Oh, what a lovely cat." She reached out to pet Morty, but he hissed at her, and she snatched her hand back. Then he leapt off the railing to prance over to the other side, refusing to look at either of us.

"I'm so sorry," I said, then gave Morty a stern look that scolded, *Naughty boy.* Though I had to admit, my curiosity was piqued. Morty was finicky and didn't warm up to many people easily, but I couldn't imagine what he found so distasteful about Fiona.

"No worries." She waved her hand. "I'm more of a dog lover. Maybe he can sense that."

"I haven't seen you around before. What

brings you to Divinity?" I asked, trying to get to know her better and help her relax. I handed her a piece of chocolate.

"Oh, my. Thank you. I adore chocolate." She ate the dark square before responding. "Actually, I'm here with my knitting group. We call ourselves the Knitting Nanas. We're from the city, but we like to get out and explore the small towns within driving distance every summer. This year we chose Divinity, and I have to say it's just darling."

"Thank you. We like to think so." It felt good saying *we*, like I finally belonged here.

I'd moved to Divinity from the big city to start over nearly six months ago last January. In my book that was long enough to call myself a local, even though some people would like to forget I existed since two murders had happened after my arrival. But all was good now, at least I hoped so. Divinity certainly didn't need any more drama.

Frankly, neither did I.

"You picked the perfect weekend since today is the opening day of our Summer Solstice Carnival," I added, focusing on more positive things.

"Well, then, it's my lucky day. The girls are at the craft tent, of course, but I couldn't resist your gazebo. I've always wanted to have my tarot cards read, but Phillip would

18

never allow anything like that." Her face looked pinched when she spoke of him. "Now that he's gone, I do what I want."

"I'm so sorry for your loss."

"Trust me, darling, it was no loss. He's too ornery to die and leave me, so I left him with half his money. I —"

I held up my hand. "Wait. Don't tell me any more, or there won't be anything left for the reading," I interjected, sensing this woman could talk for hours.

"Oh, my. You're so right. My mouth runs away from me sometimes." She pretended to lock her lips and throw away the key, but then she spoke again anyway, as though it killed her to do anything less. "What do we do first?"

"First we center ourselves by breathing deeply and calming our minds and bodies." I showed her how, and she followed along with me. "Then we ground ourselves by seeing ourselves connected to the earth and pulling the earth's energy into our core." She did as I did, and I asked the universe to guide me and help me hear and see my vision clearly. "Can I have your permission to connect with your Higher Self?"

She blinked. "I guess . . . yes. Yes, you may." She nodded once, sharply, with renewed conviction.

"Good. Place your hands in front of me with your palms up, please."

She did so without hesitation this time. I slid my hands over hers with my palms down until they lightly touched. I closed my eyes and focused on Fiona, allowing my Higher Self to talk to hers. "I ask for guidance during this reading and that the connection between us remain intact until the reading is complete." Then I removed my hands from hers.

I opened my eyes and focused on her. "Now, I would like you to ask a question you are seeking the answers to."

"Oh, this is so exciting." She stared off in deep concentration, then said, "I've got one. I would like to know if I am going to have an exciting vacation this week."

"Let's see what the cards have to say. There are several spreads in tarot reading and many ways to interpret the cards. I am going to use a three-card spread for this reading." I shuffled the cards three times, and then I placed them facedown one at a time on the silk scarf between us. "This first card represents your past. The middle card represents the present. And this last card represents your future."

Fiona clapped her hands together. "Turn them over, please. I can't wait anymore. The suspense is killing me."

I stifled a chuckle and flipped the first card over. XIII Death stared back at me. "It's the Death card," I said calmly, already lost in concentration as I considered what it could mean for her in regard to her question.

Fiona gasped loudly and clutched at her heart with both hands, nearly falling off the bench. "Oh, Lordy, I'm not ready to meet my maker."

I glanced at her in surprise. "I'm sorry. I didn't mean to startle you," I rushed to say as I reached out and patted her arm. "The Death card rarely means you will physically die. It simply means you have experienced a transformation or new beginning."

"Honey, startled doesn't begin to describe how I just felt." She fanned her pale face. "At my age my heart can't take a scare like that."

"There's nothing to be afraid of. The card represents the end of something people fear. Based on its position and on what you told me, I suspect this card is referring to the end of your marriage." I squeezed her hand.

She blinked hard as though I'd touched a nerve, but she was too proud to admit it. "You're good," she said. "I thought I was doing a better job of covering my emotions."

"It's okay to be a little sad that your marriage has ended, and it's okay to be afraid of starting over at this stage in your life. Change isn't always a bad thing."

She sniffed sharply and pursed her lips before saying, "Things could have been so different if a certain someone hadn't ruined my life." Her face hardened. "But the past is the past," she muttered more to herself. "I'm ready to move on. Show me the next card please."

"Good for you." I turned over the middle card and X The Wheel of Fortune stared back at me. Change might not always be a bad thing, but it wasn't always a good thing, either. I frowned.

"Why are you frowning? What's wrong now?"

"I'm not sure. Maybe nothing. This is the Wheel of Fortune card."

Fiona squealed in delight. "Now, that's more like it. Nothing wrong with that card. I love to gamble. Love not knowing how things are going to turn out."

"Then you're going to love this card. The Wheel of Fortune means that random change is at hand. Only, wheels don't always just turn on their own. Sometimes they are spun. When that happens, no one knows where it might stop. This card basically

22

means your wheel is about to be spun, and things may be up in the air for a while."

"I'm okay with that. I need for my world to be turned upside down a bit. I need some excitement." She leaned forward and gave me a devilish look. "I need an adventure."

"By the look of these cards, I think you're about to have one. Let's see what the last card has in store for you." I turned over the last card, and XI Justice stared back at me. "Wow, this has been quite the reading."

"How so?" she asked.

"All three of your cards have been part of the Major Arcana."

"What's that?"

"Major Arcana cards represent the big secrets or mysteries of your life. Whereas the Minor Arcana and court cards represent the smaller secrets and mysteries of your life. I'd say this reading is quite significant."

"Good. Like I said, I'm ready for a big change. You said the last card represents the future. What card did you draw for that?"

"Well, with all this change you're about to experience, you will be forced to act. The Justice card represents the consequences of your actions. This card is not random at all, so think carefully about what you say and do this week. I know you want change, but Karma is a powerful beast. . . ."

Everything around me suddenly blurred, and I fell into the same tunnel vision I always did when my psychic abilities took over. I could see into the future. I was in a woman's body, but I couldn't see who she was. I stood across from Fiona, holding a plate of cookies as she held a lemon meringue pie. She was staring down at the pie, looking sad. An overwhelming sense of loss radiated off her. A certain clarity hit me that lemon meringue had been her ex-husband Phillip's favorite pie, and that he was the one who had left her, not the other way around.

The woman whose body I occupied started speaking, yanking Fiona from her memories, and suddenly we were in a heated argument. I couldn't hear what words we were shouting at each other, but the feeling of animosity and anger toward Fiona was strong. And Fiona didn't look any happier to be near the woman. Suddenly, Fiona threw the pie in my face, and a whispered vow coursed through my veins to get even with her at any cost. . . .

"What is wrong with you? Did you see something?" Fiona asked, pulling me from my vision.

I blinked to wash away the darkness and resume my full sight, and then I cleared my throat. "I saw lemon meringue pie."

I waited to see if she understood the significance and wanted to talk about it, but she stiffened her spine. I could see in her eyes that she knew I knew the truth. But that's not what she came here for, so I let it go.

"You were arguing with someone you really didn't like," I went on.

"Oh, is that all?" She waved me away and sat back in relief as though arguing were as natural to her as breathing. "You had me worried for a minute. Who doesn't have some enemies?"

I stared deeply into her eyes to make my point more important and hoped she heeded my warning about Karma. "Either you already have an enemy in your Knitting Nanas, or you will make one in town."

"She already made one sixty-one years ago," a familiar voice said from behind me.

I whirled around and said, "Granny Gert?" at the same moment that a red-faced Fiona surged to her feet and sputtered, "Gertie Nichols, what on earth are you doing here?"

"I live here, you nincompoop." Granny ignored me as she untied her plastic rain cap and glared at the other woman. It didn't matter that the weather was bright and

25

sunny; Granny never rode in any car without her rain cap. "Fiona Atwater, get your frilly fanny out of my town!"

I gasped. That was as close to cussing as I'd ever heard my granny get. Now Morty's hissing made perfect sense. No one messed with his GG — aka Great Granny. My gaze shifted back and forth between the two, and the woman holding the cookies in my vision suddenly became crystal clear.

Granny Gert was Fiona's enemy.

"How do you two know each other?" I asked, thoroughly confused.

"Just so you know, I'm not going any-where, and *you're* the nincompoop," Fiona snapped back at Granny and then faced me. "You want to know how we know each other?" Fiona asked, then jabbed a finger in Granny's direction as she said with pure bitterness, "Say hello to the woman who ruined my life."

2

Later Friday night when the carnival had closed, I pulled into my driveway at the end of Shadow Lane and cut the engine to my old VW bug. She might have some rust spots in her white paint with the orange, yellow, and pink flowers on the side, but she had character. Unlike the monstrosity she sat next to: Granny's brand-new sparkling white Cadillac.

Granny had finally gotten her license a couple of months ago. Everyone in town knew that when she was behind the wheel, it was best to duck and run for cover.

I shook my head on a chuckle and made my way inside of the fully furnished ancient Victorian house I'd bought for a steal six months ago because the townsfolk thought she was haunted. I'd nicknamed her Vicky and had pretty much suspected the mysterious cat I'd found inside was the one doing the haunting. I couldn't prove it, but with his jet black eyes and nearly glowing thick white fur, as well as his appearing and disappearing at lightning speeds and making mysterious things happen, I was convinced he was immortal.

Exactly *what* he was remained a mystery, but he was mine . . . or I was his, since he'd sort of adopted me and had decided I could stay. Same with Granny. He'd allowed her to stay as well, and most of the time I was happy about that, but today my sweet little granny had acted like someone I didn't even recognize.

After the incident with Fiona, Granny had stormed off without another word to join her Sewing Sisters. Fiona had done the same, leaving me with more questions than anything else. After that drama, I'd been packed with clients for the rest of the day. Most of them simply wanted the "scoop" rather than a reading of their own, which had resulted in one whopper of a headache for me.

Gotta love small-town living.

Heading into the main part of my kitchen, which servants once ate in years ago, for a cup of cocoa, I stopped short in the doorway. Granny stuck to a strict schedule: Monday cleaning, Tuesday laundry, Wednesday ironing, Thursday baking, and Friday hair washed and set at the salon. Saturdays and Sundays were left for her bridge group, her sewing circle, and the occasional cooking class.

Today was Friday, not Thursday, so why was Granny elbow-deep in cookie dough?

"Granny, what's going on? You're acting so different today. First at the carnival and now here. Does it have anything to do with Fiona Atwater and her Knitting Nanas?" I headed to the medicine cupboard and pulled out some painkillers.

"Fiona Shmona and her Knitting Ninnies is more like it." Granny tsked, adding chocolate chips to her cookie mixture and stirring furiously with her wooden spoon. The normally neat, long, wooden harvest table was covered with every cookie ingredient she'd ever used, and her homemade apron was stained with chocolate.

That alone had me worried.

I was about to question her further, when she made a beeline past the fireplace in the corner and through the scullery where dishes and vegetables were once washed. Then she took the stairs to the root cellar.

I put the teakettle on top of the gas stove that had replaced the original coal-burning stove from days gone by. Sleepy-time mint tea sounded better than cocoa, since at the moment, all I wanted to do was crawl into bed and forget my frustrating day.

Granny emerged with more ingredients and an obvious grudge. Who in the world was this Fiona Atwater? If there was ever going to be peace in this house again, I needed to find out. Besides, I wanted my chipper Granny back.

"Granny, what did Fiona mean when she said you were the woman who ruined her life?"

"I ruined *her* life? Ha!" Granny waved her spoon around wildly as she ranted, with bits of cookie dough flying about. "That's a fine fiddledeedee. We used to be best friends, until Frank Nichols came to town our senior year of high school. She liked him first, but he took a shine to me. After that, she turned into my nemesis, competing with me on virtually everything: grades, sewing, cooking, *everything*!"

"She liked Grandpa Frank?"

"Obsessed over him is more like it." Granny rolled out another batch of dough and then attacked it with cookie cutters. "She married Phillip just because he and Frank were friends, and then she went and had three children and six grandchildren, knowing I was only blessed with one child and one grandchild. And then after Frank

30

died, she up and left Phillip, proving me right. She never loved him; she was just out for revenge."

"Granny, I know you don't want to hear this, but I saw good in her, too, during her reading. And in the end, she really did come to love Phillip, but it was too late. He resented her. He was the one who left her."

Granny blinked, looking surprised, but then she shrugged off her hesitation and continued attacking the cookie dough.

"She really did come here to get away and start over," I went on. "She wants to have an adventure."

"You must be mistaken, dearie. There's no way she's in Divinity with her Knitting Ninnies by coincidence. I find it hard to believe she didn't know I had moved here. Mark my words, she has her ways. She came here just to make my life miserable. I bet she even knew my Sewing Sisters and I were putting on the carnival. Your mother probably told her since they run in the same hoity-toity circle of society."

"So that's why you're baking," I mused aloud. "You think Fiona has come to outdo you in the bakeoff, and you're trying to outdo yourself with some new cookie recipe that will win for sure."

"That's right." Granny pointed her spoon

31

at me. "This is my town, not hers. *My* bake-off."

"Granny, I don't think —"

"I saw Mimi Pots this morning down at Pump up the Volume salon. I didn't even recognize her," Granny said, clearly ending the subject.

Too tired to argue with her, I let it go for the time being. "I'd heard that Abigail Brook's cousin gave Mimi a makeover. I haven't seen Mimi since she got back from Atlantic City for Abby and Chuck Webb's wedding."

Abby used to be smitten with Detective Stone, until his ex-girlfriend Isabel ran her out of town. She'd returned from her cousin's, looking like a new woman, and had finally moved on to a new man — Divinity Hotel owner and ultimate bachelor Chuck Webb. A recovered alcoholic, he'd nearly lost everything and didn't even have his own place anymore. Instead, he stayed in one of his hotel rooms, living the simple life with less to worry about losing if he slipped up again. But then Abby came along and saved him, whisking him away to *her* castle — a small trailer on the outskirts of town — while Chuck vowed to stay clean and build her a real castle someday.

Mimi was Abby's neighbor, like a mother

to her, and fiercely protective of her. She lived in her own old trailer on the outskirts of town, right next door, and didn't mix well with the folks in town.

The last time Mitch and I had shown up on her doorstep, she'd greeted us in her housecoat with a shotgun, no teeth, and a mouthful of chewing tobacco. I was glad to see she was finally starting to come around. Seeing folks happy will do that to you. I'd give anything for that same happiness right about now.

"Speaking of weddings, when's Detective Stone due home?" Granny asked as though reading my mind.

"Any day now. I'm just waiting for him to call. And don't jump the gun, Granny. We only agreed to start dating, not do anything crazy like get married. Not that I'm against getting married, but I know Mitch. I'll be lucky just to get him to take me out."

"You never know what can happen, dear, you just have to be open to it." She placed the last tray of cookies in the oven and set the timer. "He's such a good man."

"I agree. I can't wait to see him again. Two months has been a long time."

After Mitch broke his leg in a car accident, he was assigned to desk duty until he recovered. A week of that was all he could take. He went stir-crazy. So when an old NYPD buddy of his called, asking for his help on a cold case, he'd jumped at the opportunity and had spent the past two months in New York City. But his cast was off now, and he was cleared to resume his full activities back in Divinity.

Hopefully, those activities included dating me.

We'd never been on an "official" date, but we'd both agreed to give *us* a shot. I had hoped he'd come to believe in my abilities, but after nearly dying, I'd come to realize there were worse things. I knew he cared about me, and that he wanted a romantic relationship with me. After his sister's death, it had been hard for him to open up. The fact that he was letting me into his life at all would have to be enough . . . for now.

Except, two months had gone by, and all we'd done is talk on the phone. I missed him — really missed him — which gave me high hopes for our relationship to progress to the next level. If only I could keep the drama at bay.

"He'll be home soon, dear," Granny said, as she finished cleaning up the kitchen. "I'm happy for you. You deserve this, you know. And if you're lucky, you'll have what Grandpa Frank and I had. Maybe then you'll settle down."

"Maybe then *everything* will settle down," I added hopefully.

"Maybe when Fiona leaves town," Granny firmly stated. "And I've got just the boot to help her on her way. That woman has me so worked up and stressed out, my leg cramps are back. Now I'm going to have to sleep with a bar of soap at the bottom of my bed between the sheets near my feet. She'd better pray it works," she muttered, glancing around to make sure she hadn't missed a crumb, then hung up her apron and called for Morty. He appeared, wearing his usual nightcap and dressing gown, and they huffed off to bed.

Granny was into all the latest fads she read about every Friday when she was having her hair washed and set down at Pump up the Volume hair salon. It didn't matter how bizarre or crazy the fad might sound. You'd swear those magazines were the gospel.

Maybe everything would settle down? I thought. "Maybe not," I mumbled to myself.

I sure hoped the soap worked, too. Something told me that settling down was the last thing that was about to happen with one stirred-up Granny Gert.

Look out Fiona Atwater . . . Karma really

was an angry beast.

"With that Ace of Cups, you will be faced with an unexpected opportunity for an emotional experience filled with great promise. Since your question was about romance, I'd say be on the lookout. These opportunities don't last long, so act quickly," I said to Sean O'Malley as we sat inside the gazebo on Saturday afternoon.

Nothing major had happened on the drama front, just some minor occurrences like someone knocking the craft tent over. Of course the Sewing Sisters had blamed the Knitting Nanas and vice versa, but a few more minor oddities had occurred that made me wonder if someone really was up to a bit of mischief. I didn't know who or why, but I was determined to get to the bottom of it. I hadn't seen Granny at all yet today, but Sean had shown up to support me.

The blond-haired, blue-eyed Irish hottie was one of my best friends and so much fun to be around. He worked as a bartender for my other best friend, Joanne Burnham, a buxom redhead who owned Smokey Jo's tavern. When Sean wasn't at Jo's, he was a physical trainer for Wally down at Wally's

World gym and the biggest ladies' man in town.

The weather was perfect. Bright blue skies and a balmy breeze. Sean rested his weight on his elbows, his biceps flexing beneath his tight, dry-fit, light blue T-shirt as he flashed his killer dimples.

"A romance opportunity you say? Well, then, let's go, lass. When are you going to give up on the detective and go out with me?"

Morty chose that moment to make an appearance and rub up against his legs, purring loudly. Morty loved Sean — the detective, not so much. Sean reached down and scratched Morty between the ears.

"See, even Morty agrees with me."

"Not a chance, Romeo. Besides, you'd get bored." I laughed. "But seriously. You're not getting any younger. Don't you think it's time you settled down?"

"Not a chance," he threw my words back at me and winked. "And you're right. I probably would get bored." I smacked him playfully. "You want me to be serious? I can seriously say it will take one special woman to ever make me want to settle down for good. I love women. *All* women."

"I know, and that's the problem. But I am curious. Why did you ask that question?"

"I just wanted to know if I would have a date for this weekend." He grinned.

"You are such a devil." I shook my head and glanced to the side, then did a double take. "Wow, is that Mimi Pots?"

Sean squinted and looked in the same direction. "Sure is. Shocker, right? That makeover might have made her pretty on the outside, but she's still just as sour on the inside."

Now she sported a full set of gleaming white dentures, her hair neatly styled, and summer slacks and a blouse that took ten years off her appearance. She'd warmed up to me okay, but she hadn't liked Mitch one bit. Hadn't liked anyone in town, actually.

"I don't know. Everyone has some good in them," I said. "It looks like she even made a friend. Isn't that Bernadette Baldwin of BB's Baked Goods?"

"Doesn't surprise me that those two became friends." Sean scoffed. "Bernadette isn't very well liked, either."

"Be nice. They're coming our way." I smiled wide when Mimi and Bernadette stopped by the gazebo. I'd heard of Bernadette, but I didn't really know her. But having been judged my whole life, I was always willing to give everyone the benefit of the doubt.

Bernadette was sharply dressed and well put together with neatly trimmed, short dark hair. She had to be in her fifties or sixties, but she wore her age well. My lips flattened when she didn't even attempt to smile back. Just like Mimi, I guess she didn't feel the need to wear her "pretty" on the inside.

"Where's your granny? Home baking?" Bernadette said smugly. "She should rest those old bones. She doesn't have what it takes to beat me in the bakeoff. Isn't that right, Mimi?"

Mimi gave me a slight wince, but then shrugged. "I predict a huge victory, Bernadette," she said, glancing at my tarot cards.

"You tell your granny to leave my booth alone. Playing dirty won't increase her chances of winning. Besides, I'm meaner, and that only means I fight dirtier."

"Hey, isn't that Sam?" Mimi pointed off in the distance.

Bernadette whirled around. "Why, that little cheater. He's bringing pastries to the crew putting together the bakeoff booth. Come on." She hustled off after him with Mimi hot on her heels.

I was suddenly reminded of Parks and Rec manager Quincy kicking Ozzie's Animal Angels' sign over by his booth, Trixie accusing the Knitting Nanas of tampering with

the Sewing Sisters' booth, and now Bernadette said someone had messed with her
booth. Could it have been Sam since Sam's
Bakery was in direct competition with BB's
Baked Goods? Either they'd all gone crazy,
or someone was trying to sabotage the
entire carnival.

All of this mischief was making me dizzy.
I shook my head, filing away the clues and
list of possible suspects when my cell phone
rang. I glanced at the caller ID. What on
earth was Gretta Frey doing calling me at
this time when I knew for a fact that she
was working at her mini-mart? "Gretta, is
anything wrong?" I asked as I answered.

"Yes, something's wrong." She sounded
annoyed and out of breath. "There's been a
scuffle."

"Why are you calling me instead of the
police?"

"Because Granny is one of the people
scuffling."

"Excuse me?" I squeaked.

"I know it sounds crazy, but she and that
Fiona Atwater woman are in a tussle over
the last bag of flour on my shelves. I told
them I have a truck coming in this afternoon, but neither one would listen. They're
fighting over that puppy like it was part of
the crown jewels. I've never seen anything

like it. You'd better get down here now before they do any more damage to my store."

"I'm on my way." I hung up and looked at Sean. "Can you hold down the fort? I have to go stop Granny before she lands herself in jail."

"Granny? You're kidding."

"I wish I were."

"Don't worry. I can't read tarot cards, but I know a thing or two about the human palm and what to do with it."

"Behave." I pointed my finger at him. "And for goodness' sake, don't do a reading of any kind for anyone. Just watch my stuff, and let anyone who stops by know that I'll be back soon." I glanced at Morty. "I'm counting on you to keep him out of trouble."

Morty yawned, looking bored.

"Relax, I'm always good," Sean said. "And, hey, I hope everything is okay with your grandmother. She's so sweet."

"She's something," I mumbled and grabbed my purse as I jogged to my car.

Five minutes later, I pulled into the parking lot of Gretta's Mini-Mart. When I walked through the doors, I couldn't believe the sight playing out before my eyes.

A lot of Divinity's businesses chose to go

with a theme when decorating. Many chose historical themes from Italy, Greece, and even the West. Gretta, however, had chosen flower power as her theme.

Her floor was green with yellow walls and flowers stenciled everywhere to the point of making one's head spin. I blinked to focus but didn't like what I saw one bit. A crowd had gathered in a circle around the scuffling women, filled with Knitting Nanas and Sewing Sisters front and center.

"Fiona has just as much of a right to that flour as Gertie does," a Nana said.

"Oh, no, she doesn't! This is our town. And besides, *Granny* was here first," a Sister replied. "No one calls her Gertie."

"Well, *Gertie* can come back later," another Nana said. "We have plans."

"Who says we don't?" another Sister responded. "We certainly don't sit around on our bums."

"I don't know. You're looking a little heavy on the bottom to me," someone else chimed in.

Meanwhile, Granny and Fiona kept tugging the bag of flour back and forth between them, knocking over display cases and various items off the shelves. Gretta scrambled after them, attempting to pick up the mess and hollering at them to cease and desist at once or she would call the cops.

"Ladies, stop this at once." I tried to step between them. "This isn't doing anyone any good. You're acting like children. The bake-off isn't until Sunday, for Pete's sake."

The bag of flour ripped in half, with a shower of white flying up in the air like a snow globe at Christmastime. The women stumbled backward, leaving me standing alone in the middle with no umbrella. I thought to hold my breath, thank goodness, until all the flour settled. The room quieted as I blinked to clear my eyes. There wasn't a speck on me that wasn't snow white.

That was the exact moment Mitch Stone walked back into my life.

He strode through the doors, stopped, and stared. More like gaped. His usual scowl was gone, and the corners of his full lips tipped up ever so slightly as he arched a thick black brow and let his gaze run over every inch of me. His ink black hair was tousled from the summer breeze, and his whiskered face was in need of a shave.

The long jagged scar on his square jaw pulsed in his obvious attempt to stifle a laugh, but it was his dark eyes that held me captive. I hadn't seen him in two months. He looked amazing, standing there with his hands on his hips in a tight gray T-shirt and jeans, while I looked like a big ole pastry puff mess.

Not the way I had wanted to greet him for the first time. I had wanted to look hot . . . not like a hot-crossed bun.

"Why am I not surprised to see you involved in this ruckus, Tink?"

"Funny, Grumpy Pants," I said with a smirk.

He'd nicknamed me Tink — short for Tinker Bell — when we first met, while I'd nicknamed him Grumpy Pants because of his permanent scowl and cranky disposition. Though I had to admit, he'd grown on me. The nicknames had somehow stuck but were uttered with much more endearment these days.

"I, uh, stopped by your fortune-teller booth at the carnival. You know, to see you first," he said, looking awkward at having to reveal even that much affection, especially in front of a captive audience. "Sean was there, looking pretty comfortable." Mitch frowned, his scowl slightly back. "Anyway," he shrugged, "Sean sent me here." Mitch surveyed the scene around him. "What on earth is going on?"

"Anyone care to tell *Detective* Stone what's going on, ladies?" I crossed my arms and stared down the crowd.

"Whoops, look at the time. The flour's all yours, Gertie," Fiona said, and with that, she and her Nanas scooted out of the store as quickly as their little old legs could carry them.

"Darn right it is," Granny Gert hollered after her. "And don't bother coming back because I'm buying all the bags off the delivery truck, just see if I don't."

"Who's going to pay for this mess and damaged goods?" Gretta asked.

"Don't you worry, Ms. Frey. I'll take care of the damages. I've got plenty of dough of the monetary kind in my shoe boxes and freezer bags back at the house. It will be worth every penny if Fiona gives up and leaves town for good. In the meantime, send me the bill, dear," Granny said to Gretta. "I've got more cookies to bake." She left the store without another word.

"Welcome home, Detective." I gave him a sheepish grin.

"I'm not so sure I want to be back after all this." He grunted. "Will someone please tell me what's going on?"

"He's all yours," Gretta said to me. "It's going to take me all day to clean up this mess."

"Speaking of messes. I'd like to clean up a little myself. Rain check?" I asked Mitch, hoping he would understand.

His gaze softened. "Sure," he said in a gentle tone. "I just got in anyway. I need to unpack and check in with the captain. I'll call you later."

"That sounds good."

He looked like he wanted to hug me, but then he must have thought better of it. "See you later." He turned to leave but stopped just short of the door and looked over his shoulder, a bit uncertain and a whole lot uncomfortable. Then he cleared his throat and said in that deep smooth voice I'd missed so much, "It's good to see you again, Sunny."

My smile came slow and sweet, and my heart fluttered as I melted inside. "You too, Mitch. Really good."

He nodded once and then walked out the door.

3

The rest of the day went by in a blur. After showering and changing at home, I went back to the carnival and sent Sean home. I kept my eyes open, but there were so many outsiders in town because of the carnival, it was hard to see anything suspicious. Nothing eventful happened to top the mini-mart incident, so I went home that evening to wait for Mitch to call.

He didn't.

It was only his first night back and he had a lot to do, but still. What about me? Us? Didn't he miss me like I did him? He hadn't dated in a very long time. Maybe he'd forgotten how. Who was I kidding? Maybe this was all one big mistake.

Morty appeared at that moment and gave me a look that confirmed my doubts, his plaid bow tie firmly in place. It was hard to take him seriously when he looked like that. He wore a knowing expression, then stuck his nose in the air and pranced out of the room with his arrogance swirling cosmically around him. He'd warmed up a smidgen toward Mitch, but not enough to allow him into our lives on a more permanent basis.

The question was, could I?

Only one way to find out.

Wearing my shorty pajamas and fuzzy slippers, I wandered into the room I'd set aside for my readings. My sanctuary. Parting the strands of crystal beads, I entered and immediately felt at peace in the small cozy room. I took in the soft blue walls and inhaled the scent of my aromatherapy oils, feeling their calming effect.

I bypassed the plants and tropical fish tank in one corner and headed for the other corner that housed a small fireplace and my supply shelves. I pulled my tarot cards down and spread out a silk scarf on the old-fashioned tea table in the center of the room.

Sitting at the table, I shuffled my cards three times and thought about exactly what I wanted to know as I stared up at the constellations on my ceiling. I didn't need to know what would happen in the past; I was more concerned with the future. Was I supposed to be with Mitch, and did our relationship stand a chance?

I chose a three-card spread with no positional order. I drew three cards and laid them all down at once, faceup, then studied the spread as a whole. I had drawn the Major Arcana cards of VIII Strength and XIX The Sun and the Minor Arcana card the Two of Cups. Given the question that I'd asked, relief washed over me.

The strength card represented a calm controlling force that soothes a situation. It featured a woman with her hand on the head of a lion. The woman was necessary to the beast, calming and soothing his thoughts and guiding them in a healthy direction. Mitch needed me. I knew that much for sure.

The sun card represented a straightforward clarity that brings joy. Like my name and bright sunshine, it is positive, happy, and joyful. I could see beneath Mitch's darkness and was pleased with what I'd uncovered. Being with him would make all things right in the world, and everything exactly as it should be.

But what I was most excited about was the Two of Cups. This card represented a deep emotional connection or attraction, making me believe our relationship really did stand a chance. The two indicated the relationship was new, and it verified there was a strong attraction between us, and that was a start. It didn't predict the attraction would remain or last a long time, but it was enough for me to feel confident in pursuing what was between us.

If only it came with an instruction manual for him.

I wouldn't get mad that he hadn't called when he said he would. It wasn't his fault I'd fantasized for two months about what his homecoming would be like. I would simply remain patient and calm and guide him through the dating process. Because one thing was for certain . . . the man didn't have a clue.

"It's getting really hard to remain calm and patient," I said on Monday morning to my best friend Jo in Warm Beginnings & Cozy Endings Café.

We'd just entered and passed by Ozzie, who looked a bit agitated. I didn't know him, but I recognized him from the carnival when he'd been arguing with Quincy. Not two minutes later, we were nearly run over by two very large men in their haste to exit the café. They were two of the outsiders I'd seen hanging out at Animal Angels yesterday. Maybe Ozzie had an issue with allowing them to adopt one of his rescued dogs.

Maybe they were the ones sabotaging the carnival because of it. Maybe it was time I started doing some digging.

"Earth to Sunny, I said maybe Mitch needs some help in the field of dating. It's been a while, you know," Jo said, leading me to a small, round wrought-iron table by the window, with a view of the library across the street. The waitress appeared and we placed our order for breakfast.

"Mitch doesn't need an instruction manual for dating; he needs a knock upside the head." I played with the handle on the ceramic mug sitting before me. Minutes later the waitress brought us our breakfast. I dug in immediately, regretting bringing up Mitch in the first place.

Jo studied me with her smoky gray eyes. As the owner of a bar, she was a student of human nature and had a knack for sizing up people just from looking at them. And since she'd started dating the local carpenter, Cole West, she'd become wise in the ways of love. "Knock him upside the head, then." She wagged her winged auburn brows. "And then make his boo-boo all better."

I laughed. "I would if I ever saw the man. He's been home for two days, and I've only seen him once. Saturday he spent all day

51

sorting his belongings back in order and settling in. I get that. I mean, he's been gone for two whole months."

I traced the rim of the mug with my fingertip. "But then Sunday he called me from his office saying he'd have to reschedule our date for Monday because it was going to take him all night to get caught up at work. What the heck is up with that? If you were gone that long, wouldn't you want to see the person you supposedly cared about?"

"Look on the bright side." She took a bite of toast and looked off as though considering her words. "Today is Monday, so you should get to see him tonight, right?"

"*Should* is the operative word." I sipped my raspberry cocoa, almost afraid to utter the words running through my mind out loud. "With my luck, that won't happen, either."

"What happened to my optimistic Sunny?" Jo chugged her espresso.

"The pessimistic clouds have rolled in and rained on my parade."

"This is a busy week for everyone, sweetie. You really can't complain too much because your days are consumed with the carnival. Don't you have lunch and dinner breaks?"

"Yes, but so far none of our breaks have

been at the same time. It feels like he's not even home. I have been looking forward to him coming home for so long now, but I think I talked to him more when he was away. That's depressing."

"It will get better. You just have to get through this week."

"Easier said than done. Something suspicious is going on at the carnival. Quincy and Ozzie are butting heads for some reason. Sam and Bernadette are trying to outdo each other in the bakery department. Strangers in town are acting suspicious. And the Sewing Sisters and Knitting Nanas are at each other constantly. Granny says Fiona has always tried to outdo her, and she's at it again. It's not just the two of them, either. Both groups are more competitive than high school athletic teams. You'd think they were teenagers with the amount of energy they suddenly have. I'm exhausted just watching them. I don't think they'll stop until someone gets hurt. Meanwhile, I'm spending all my energy trying to make sure the carnival doesn't get ruined, and no one seems to care."

"Listen to you. You sound like a mother hen."

"I can't help it. If one more thing happens, I'm putting them all in a time-out and calling it quits."

"Come on. I'll drop you off at the carnival before you're late. When did Big Don say your car would be ready?"

Big Don was a giant of a man at six-foot-six. He ran the local auto body and had finally opened his eyes to Lulubelle — a jovial woman who was the head of the Bunco Babes, had more gossip than anyone in town, and had a heart as big as her triple chins. Seemed everyone was in a relationship these days except me.

I tried not to let my social life get me down. "Tonight. He's just giving her a tune-up for me," I answered as I followed Jo outside and climbed into her big Suburban.

Cole's skullcap hung from her rearview mirror. Jo liked her cars big and her men bigger. Cole was about as big as they came with a buzz cut, tattoos, and muscles galore. His wife had died on the motorcycle he'd been driving, and Jo had helped him learn how to love again. If anyone deserved happiness, it was them.

"Speaking of relationships, how is everything going between you and Cole?" They'd started dating just over two months ago and seemed really happy. I couldn't help but be a teensy bit jealous. I could be where they were right now if Mitch hadn't left town. "Things seem to be moving right along for you guys."

Jo chewed her bottom lip, looking hesitant.

"What is it? Is something wrong?" I asked.

"Not exactly. In fact, everything is perfect. I had planned on telling you at breakfast, but then you were so frustrated and upset over your situation with Mitch, that I didn't think the timing was right."

"Timing for what?"

"To tell you that Cole and I are engaged." She glanced at me quickly and then stared back at the road.

"That's fantastic," I said with enthusiasm and meant it. "I'm sorry for being such a downer." I touched her arm. "I really am happy for you both. With all he's been through, and you too, I am just thrilled. Truly."

She smiled in relief. "Thanks. We just figured we know we love each other, and life can be so short. Why wait?"

"Have you decided where you'll live?" I asked. Jo rented an apartment above her bar, and Cole owned a small house. But it was the house he and his first wife had shared.

"He's going to put his house up for sale, and we're going to start hunting for a place of our own. I'd love something on the outskirts of town with lots of land for kids and maybe a dog."

"That sounds great, Jo. I'm sure you'll find the perfect spot. Rosemary's Realty does a fantastic job. When's the big date?"

"Well, I don't know diddly about planning a wedding and neither do my sisters, but the nice thing about coming from a big family is that we have tons of relatives. Also, I don't have time to plan a wedding since summer is my busiest time of year. My cousin is going to come into town to help me. She's a party planner, so she can pretty much work from anywhere. I really want a fall wedding. It's such a pretty season."

I did a double take. "Wow, that's quick. Will that give you enough time to plan a wedding?"

"I don't know, and I don't care." Jo radiated happiness. "I just want to be married, already. I don't need anything big or fancy. Besides, Zoe pulls off miracles all the time."

I couldn't help getting caught up in her excitement. "I'm sure it will be perfect."

"It will be . . . if you agree to be my maid of honor." She glanced at me with misty eyes. "You really have become my best friend."

My eyes welled up as well. "Awww, that is

so sweet. And you're my best friend, too. I can honestly say I've never had a friend like you before moving to Divinity. I would be honored to be your maid of honor. Just tell me what you need, and I'm on it."

"I'll leave that to Zoe. Like I said, I have no clue what needs to be done when it comes to weddings, and I only plan to do this once. Sean's the best man since he and Cole have gotten pretty close. I'll hook you both up with Zoe when she gets here. She's a little quiet but really sweet."

"Sounds good," I said as we pulled into the parking lot of Mini Central Park and stopped and stared, "but *that* certainly doesn't look good. What on earth is going on now?"

"I don't know, but I have some time to kill before I have to open Smokey Jo's to the lunch crowd. Let's go find out."

Granny Gert and Fiona Atwater were in yet another heated argument at the auction tent. Both were dressed in slacks and blouses, making them look sophisticated and proper in their own ways, but their actions suggested otherwise. As Jo and I drew near, their shouts grew louder.

"Great jumping juniper, Hazel. What in blue blazes were you thinking?" Granny asked, rosy cheeked and all aflutter.

Hazel Kissinger was in her sixties and part of Granny's sewing circle. A quiet woman with brown curly hair and small glasses perched on the end of her upturned nose, she was the chair of the auction and in charge of what items were to be included in the raffle.

"I'm so sorry, Granny, but a few more mishaps have happened. And now several auction items have gone missing. There was a hole in the back of the tent like someone had cut right through it." I made a mental note to look into that as well. Hazel wrung her hands as she continued. "I just figured the more the merrier. After all, isn't the point to raise as much money as we can to help the Animal Angels?"

"Well yes, but not by accepting something they spent all day making while we were in church," Granny countered. "Especially when the Sewing Sisters already donated this beautiful quilt for the auction."

Granny was never judgmental. Fiona showing up in town had her acting like a completely different person than the one I had grown up with.

It turned out the Knitting Nanas had made hundreds of granny squares and put them together to make an afghan for the raffle on Saturday. Granny and Fiona

58

started arguing about whose merchandise was of better quality. They picked on everything from the color choices to the stitch patterns used to the amount of time it took to create.

"A quilt and an afghan are not the same thing. I think they both will fetch nice prices. Can't we just all get along?" Hazel pleaded, pushing her glasses up her nose.

"I agree," Ophelia Edwards said. She was a Knitting Nana, also appearing to be in her sixties with long, bright, hippy-style, orange-red hair and clothes to match. She'd made it clear to everyone in town that she didn't much care for Fiona, and she thought this whole competition was ridiculous. "This is certainly *not* the vacation I signed up for."

"Oh, hush up, you. Gertie and I aren't through with each other yet," Fiona snapped.

"Ladies, ladies, what's all this fuss I've been hearing about lately?" Captain Grady Walker joined the growing circle. He was a tall, impressive-looking man in his late sixties with a bald head and neatly trimmed goatee. Granny had taken a shine to him the moment she set eyes on him, even though she was a decade older.

"Why, Captain Walker, it's lovely to see

you." Granny fluttered her eyelids. "How's that cookie jar of yours these days? Are you in need of a fresh supply?" She leaned forward and whispered, "You know there's a cookie for darn near everything."

"Why, that's good to know, and I do believe I am in need of more cookies if it's not too much work. Thank you, Granny." His smile reached his eyes.

"Oh, fiddlesticks, it's no work at all." She waved her hands about. "Anytime."

Fiona looked from Granny to the captain and back to Granny, and the biggest brightest smile I'd ever seen her don spread wide across her rosy cheeks. Granny's smile dimmed, and her brown eyes narrowed to a devilish dark chocolate.

Oh, Lord, that couldn't be good.

Fiona stepped between them and held out her hand. "Captain Walker. I've heard a lot about you. I don't believe we've formally met. My name is Fiona Atwater."

The captain smiled kindly and shook her hand. "Much obliged, Ms. Atwater. I have to say I've heard lots about you as well."

"All good I hope." She twittered, smoothing her strawberry blond hair behind her ear.

"Mostly." He chuckled.

"Well, it's no fun being *all* good, now is

it?" she snickered.

"Depends on just how bad you plan to be," he said gently. "The sewing circle has put a lot of work into this carnival. I would hate for anything negative to put a damper on that. You think you can be somewhat good?"

"You have no idea just how good I can be." She poked him in the arm.

"Glad to hear it." He tipped his hat and then turned to Granny. "And, Granny, you think you can make an exception and let both items be auctioned off for the sake of Animal Angels?"

"I suppose so." She scowled at Fiona and then turned her own bright smile on the captain as she finished with, "Since you asked so nicely." Her eyelashes fluttered about, faster than a hummingbird's wings. I was afraid she would go cross-eyed if she didn't stop.

"Though I'd wager my cookie jar the Sewing Sisters' quilt will fetch a better price than the Knitting Ninnies' afghan," she just had to add.

Ignoring her jab at Fiona, he said, "Wonderful. Now that we have that settled, I'm off to BB's Baked Goods' tent. Bernadette Baldwin makes the best apple turnovers in the county. Darn sweet tooth is going to be the downfall of me yet."

"I make a scrumptious cake," Hazel interjected, but the captain didn't seem to notice she was alive.

"Bernadette, you say?" Fiona muttered, her eyes already scheming up God knew what. "I'll walk with you," she said louder, rushing to catch up to the captain. "I heard you were judging the bakeoff, and I'm just dying to tell you all about my lemon meringue pie." She hooked his arm with hers and shot a parting evil grin in Granny's direction.

Quincy Turner rushed after the captain, making me wonder what that was all about. I looked twice when Ozzie Zuckerman followed closely on his heels. Something was definitely up.

"All right, folks, show's over," I said to the crowd, who finally decided to disperse.

Jo let out a long whistle. "You weren't kidding about the drama," she said to me. "I feel like I'm back in high school."

"More like geriatric school." I scoffed.

She squeezed my shoulder. As she turned to walk back to her car, she called back, "Good luck with that."

Something told me it was going to take a lot more than luck to put an end to the drama. I'd take high school over geriatric school any day.

"That woman is a menace to society, I tell you." Granny paced in front of me. "The nerve of her. I told you she was set on outdoing me. I make a quilt, so she makes an afghan. I offer to make the captain cookies, and you watch her bring him a pie."

"Granny, calm down. Your blood pressure."

"I'm not going to calm down. I'm going to — to —" Her face brightened like a full moon in a cloudless sky. "I'm going to beat her at her own game. And then I'm going to win." She marched away with a determined purpose to her gait.

Oh, brother. There was no telling what that meant.

4

Monday night and Tuesday had been a bust as far as seeing Mitch went. So I'd snooped around behind the auction tent, and I'd found a pocketknife on the ground nearby. I was keeping a close eye on who might want to sabotage the carnival. Quincy and Ozzy obviously didn't like each other, while Bernadette and Sam were in definite competition, not to mention the Knitting Nanas and Sewing Sisters were at each other constantly. I could see them tampering with each other's booths, but I couldn't see them wanting to ruin the carnival completely. None of them would benefit from that. The question was: who would?

Granny was in a tizzy because Bernadette had started a petition to have the proceeds from the carnival auction and bakeoff go to Quincy and his Parks and Rec Program instead of Ozzie and his Animal Angels charity. I was surprised because Bernadette was the one who had given Granny the idea to choose the Animal Angels Organization in the first place. Granny said Bernadette was even more ornery than usual and acting just plain odd. I couldn't help but wonder what had changed her mind.

Not to mention all the Fiona stuff going on had convinced Granny to give herself a makeover. To get a little more hip as she put it. I told her not to worry about trying to look like Fiona, which had sent her over the edge. She made it clear she didn't plan to look like Fiona, she planned to look better.

Her schedule was off to say the least.

We had no food, no clean clothes, no new bow ties for Morty, and the house was a mess. Because she was frazzled, Morty was frazzled, and that pretty much made it impossible for Mitch and I to have some quality alone time. We'd rescheduled yet again. This time shooting for Saturday night after the carnival auction, out in public for dinner on a *real* date.

No exceptions, no excuses, no more cancelations.

Then Sunday would be the bakeoff, the carnival would end — if I could keep someone from destroying it first — Fiona and the Knitting Nanas would leave, and we could all get back to our regular lives. So much for the Summer Solstice Carnival kicking off the summer with a bang. This week had been sheer torture so far.

And Granny Gert had lost her mind!

She'd tried every fad out there on her quest for self-improvement. I suspected Fiona flirting with Captain Walker had something to do with it. First it was the soap in the bottom of her bed for the leg cramps, which she swore worked like a charm, but I think the result was all mental.

Then for her insomnia she used some qigong — pronounced chee-gung — method of relieving stress and anxiety that first originated from Tao priests in China. She'd said she read about it in a magazine down at Pump up the Volume salon, so it *must* be true.

She would sit on the bed with the heel of one foot resting on the opposite knee and rub the entire bottom of her foot one hundred times with the palm of her hand. Then she would switch sides and repeat. She said the rubbing stimulated energy meridians associated with sleep while the repetition shifted her awareness away from her head so she could empty her mind. Her mind was empty, all right.

She was acting crazier than an upside-down deck of cards these days.

I could actually buy into the qigong method, but I drew the line when it came to the Shake Weight. First off, it just looked wrong. Second, I couldn't imagine shaking some silly weight back and forth would actually be effective in toning her arms. All it had given her was a bad case of tennis elbow.

And the neckline slimmer she'd resorted to next was absolutely ridiculous. It consisted of this bizarre contraption that rested on her chest with a protruding extension that sat under her chin. Then she would proceed to smile as she opened and closed her mouth repeatedly like a ventriloquist's dummy. She swore the resistance of the spring would tone the flab under her chin. All it had done so far was give her lockjaw and a permanently smiling face that made her look like the Joker.

By Wednesday morning I couldn't take any more, so I'd brought her to the gym with me. She packed a bag of workout clothes and was changing in the locker room while I went out to talk to Sean.

"Did you check into that matter for me?" I asked.

He glanced around, making sure no one was listening. "I sure did. The pocketknife you found behind the auction booth belonged to Quincy. He bought it at Eddy's Gun Emporium last fall."

"But the carnival is held in his park. Why on earth would he be trying to sabotage the whole thing? Even though his Parks and Rec Program isn't getting the money, he still has a booth here. It's a great advertisement for him. It doesn't make any sense that he wouldn't want that. Not to mention he now seems to have Bernadette in his corner."

"That's what I thought, so I asked him about it. I pretended I found it and since it had his initials on it, I assumed it was his. He said that someone had stolen it from his office, but he hadn't had time to report it missing yet."

"Do you think he's telling the truth?"

"I'm not sure. He's definitely hiding something."

"I'll find a way to talk to him soon. In the meantime, are you ready for Friday night?"

We were supposed to meet Jo's cousin Zoe on my dinner break from the carnival Friday night at Smokey Jo's. I just loved weddings and was hoping all the romantic juju would rub off on Mitch.

"Actually, I —"

"Oh, no," I said as I stared out into the main section of the gym.

"Oh, what?" Sean asked, following my gaze. "Oh, boy."

Fiona Atwater was dressed to the nines in the latest yoga athletic wear, headband and all, looking picture-perfect in every way. She was walking on a treadmill that sat right beside the one Captain Walker was on.

They were chatting and smiling, and she kept throwing her head back, making her earrings twinkle like the constellations in my sanctuary, and patting her chest repeatedly. If I had a figure like hers at that age, I'd probably draw attention to it, too, I had to admit. I shook off my thoughts as I remembered the issue at hand.

"Oh, brother. This is not good." I was about to turn around to intercept Granny from the locker room, but I was too late.

She'd already slipped out, and I could tell by her expression that she had just spotted the twittering twosome. I'd never seen her pump her arms that fast as she hoisted her head high and marched over to hop onto the treadmill on the other side of the captain, wearing . . .

"Good Lord, where did she get that outfit?" I sputtered.

Apparently she'd found more of Vicky's old curtains and had made herself her own version of yoga pants, but they looked more like floral bell bottoms from the seventies, with a matching bandanna instead of her standard plastic rain cap. She was moving like she had dance fever, all right, or ants in her pants. If she didn't stop all that gyrating, she was going to need more than a pair of Depends.

"She's a cheeky lass, I'll give her that. Now I know where you get your spunk from." Sean chuckled, crossing his arms and cocking his head as though settling in to enjoy the show.

The captain's smile slipped a bit and a wary expression took its place as he looked from one woman to the next and then up to Sean and I. His eyes were wide like he was caught in the middle of a horror flick with a skip in the DVD as the terrifying scene playing out before him repeated itself over and over and over.

Granny now chattered as much as Fiona, both obviously trying to outdo one another. And the speed of the treadmills kept increasing until both women were holding on tight to the rails and now running with everything on them jiggling in the breeze.

"Sean, do something before one of them breaks a hip," I said, then added half under my breath, "or scares everyone into therapy."

70

"Looks like Wally already beat me to it."

Wally was the owner of Wally's World gym and a massive man. Six feet eight inches of creamy milk chocolate and not a speck of hair on his big beautiful body. His wide smile and blazing white teeth were in full effect as he hoisted Granny under one arm and Fiona under the other as if they were as light as a couple of lumpy pillows. They quieted instantly, staring up in awe at his exotic features.

Wally's smile actually broadened.

Stopping in front of Sean and I, he gently set the women on their feet. "Why don't you try something more your speed, ladies? Wouldn't want such precious cargo getting hurt on one of my machines. Yoga room's that way." He patted both of them on their bottoms.

Fiona let out a kitty-cat meow, and Granny fluttered her lashes, which looked longer than they had this morning, like she'd slapped on a pair of falsies. When her feather-duster eyelashes stopped fluttering, one was suspiciously crooked.

Good Lord.

"I think we're done, Granny," I said. "Let's go."

"I think you're right," Granny responded, fanning herself. "Land sakes, that was quite

71

the workout. We've got to get to the carnival. There's so much to do before the bakeoff."

"You're not going to win. You heard how much the captain likes Bernadette's apple turnovers," Fiona pointed out smugly. "And she wins *every* year."

"Bernadette's turnovers don't hold a candle to my cookies. Ask her yourself. She's been trying to get my secret ingredient out of me since the day I arrived, yet she never shares her recipe with anyone. Not even her staff."

"Well, you've never tasted my lemon meringue pie."

"Thank my lucky stars for that small miracle." Granny grabbed her heart as though she was about to faint, then added, "And buttering the judge's muffin isn't going to score you any points, either."

"At least I still know how to butter a muffin," Fiona shot back. "Why, I ought to —"

"I think I just saw one of your nanas walk by," Sean said, pointing out the window. "She looked distressed. You might want to go see if anything's wrong."

"Oh, dear me. Duty calls," Fiona said and dashed off out the door.

"Duty smuty." Granny harrumphed and rubbed her eyes until one set of her eye lashes was dangling off the corner of her eye and bouncing off her cheek as she talked. "Fiona left because she knew she was losing the argument. Let's go, Sunny. We've got our own duty calling our names. Besides, I could use my heating pad right about now. It's painful to be beautiful." Granny hobbled off to the locker room.

"Thanks, Sean." I blew out a breath and smiled at him.

"Anytime, love. See you on Friday."

If I made it until then, it would be a miracle.

Friday night I pushed open the heavy door to Smokey Jo's tavern and headed into the bar. I slid on a stool, slipped my fringed knapsack over the back, and then folded my arms on top of the rich mahogany surface.

"You're early. Bet I can guess what you want," Jo said from behind the bar, expertly sliding an ice-cold beer across the surface until it stopped directly before me.

"You read my mind." I took a sip, glancing around at the amber lighting and listening to the soothing sounds of the seventies folk music as it oozed softly out of the speakers. "It's been a heck of a week."

"Careful, lass, it's not over yet." Sean gave my shoulders a squeeze and then slid onto the stool next to me. "A lot can still happen."

I groaned. "Don't remind me."

"Don't remind you of what?" Cole asked as he wandered out of the kitchen behind the bar and slipped his arms around Jo. He was a Sasquatch of a man, intimidating most with his deep voice, five-o'clock shadow, and chain-link tattoo around his neck. But he was so unbelievably gentle with her, I got teary-eyed watching them.

Jo leaned her head back against his chest and looked up at him with pure love shining in her smoky gray eyes. She was a voluptuous redhead, but he made her look like a Disney Princess. That was one of the things she loved about him. He made her feel petite, and beautiful, and loved.

"I haven't congratulated you yet," I amended, popping some bar nuts into my mouth. "I really am so happy for you both."

He winked at me. "I heard your detective was back in town. Haven't seen him around much."

"He's not my anything, yet. Turns out we have something in common, Cole, because I haven't seen him around, either."

"Like I said, when are you going to dump him and take me up on that offer of romance, lass?" Sean wagged his eyebrows at me and flashed his famous dimples.

"When Fiona and Granny stop fighting."

"Basically never, then?" Sean pretended to be wounded by slapping his hand over his heart. "Guess I'll have to set my sights on some other lucky lady."

"Trust me, you don't want to be involved in my life these days. I wouldn't wish that on anyone. Another lucky lady sounds perfect for you."

The bells over the door chimed, and we turned around to see a petite woman walk inside.

"Aye, like that lovely lass right there." Sean started to stand.

"Easy, Romeo, have a seat," Jo said. "That, my friends, is my cousin Zoe."

Sean lowered himself slowly to the bar-stool, looking transfixed.

Zoe glanced around the bar, spotted Jo, waved, and made her way through the crowd toward us. She looked like Jo, but she was petite and short — in fact I don't think she was any taller than five feet — and she had silky straight red hair instead of a mass of curls.

She also had gray eyes, but a lighter shade than Jo's, and there was a dusting of freckles sprinkled across the bridge of her nose. She wasn't the most beautiful woman I'd ever seen, but there was something sprite-like and innocent and utterly captivating about her.

"Hi, guys, I'm Zoe," she said in a soft lyrical voice when she reached us. "And you must be Sunny and Sean."

"So nice to meet you," I said, shaking her hand.

"Pleasure's all mine, lass," Sean said and tried to kiss her hand, but she discreetly pulled away before his lips could touch her flesh. He paused, but then his lips quirked into a lopsided grin. "Hard to get. I like that."

"Exactly. The church you wanted is fully booked and incredibly hard to get, Jo," Zoe said, oblivious to Sean. "And there's nothing to like about that. But I've got some other ideas." She pulled Jo over to a booth, already deep in conversation, with Sean completely forgotten.

"Huh. Imagine that. A woman who *isn't* susceptible to your charms." I grinned at Sean.

"Please. Give her time. She'll come around," he said, then hopped over the bar, but the crease between his baby blues was unmistakable.

"Isn't that your Granny?" Cole said, squinting as he looked across the bar and out through the window.

I whipped my head to the side and stared in disbelief. Great. Here comes trouble. All I'd wanted was one night of peace and quiet from the Granny and Fiona Show. I winced as she swerved to miss a mailbox, jumped the curb, and nicked the light post out front before she came to a jarring stop. She shut off her car, leaving the keys in the ignition as usual, then grabbed her cookies and marched toward the front door in all her finery — rain cap, apron, and all.

She actually wore a dress obviously made from yet another set of my curtains. Good thing my house had a lot of windows and enough extra fabric to keep her in curtain supplies for years to come. She must have forgotten to take her apron off when she left, though.

She spotted me and stopped by the bar. "Hi, dearie."

"Hi, Granny. Um, did you forget something?" I asked in a low voice, pointing down.

"Oh, fiddlesticks." She handed me the cookies and pulled off her rain cap. Then she untied her apron, slipped it off, and traded me her belongings for the cookies.

I wadded them up and shoved the bundle in my knapsack. "You look nice." My gaze roamed over her body, stopping on her legs. "I haven't seen you in a dress in ages." I wrinkled my brow. "Since when did your legs get so tan? And what's wrong with your toes? They almost look blue compared to the rest of your feet."

"Sandal-foot nylons," she whispered. "Not sandal toe, those are different, you see, for open-toed shoes. These are made for actual sandals. The trick is the toes are literally cut out, and the nylon hooks over your big toe to keep the material in place. Aren't they just the bee's knees? With my sandals on, you can't even tell I'm wearing nylons, even if they do pinch a snippet."

"They're something, all right." I smiled, thinking she should have chosen a lighter shade. These made her look like her circulation had literally stopped at the balls of her feet with her toes all but dead.

"At least I won't get skin cancer like Phony Bologna Fiona with all the tanning she must do." Granny tsked.

"What are you doing here, anyway?"

"I'm on a mission of sorts. Have you seen Captain Walker? Someone said he eats here on Friday nights."

"Granny, what are you up to with that plate of cookies?" I asked in dread.

"Well," she looked left and right as though

she were about to reveal a clever secret, "I thought I'd give Grady a little sample to wet his whistle for Sunday's bakeoff. I just found out Bernadette wins every year, but I'm about to dethrone her. I just have to figure out which type of cookie the captain likes best. So I baked all of my favorites. Want one?"

Since when had he become *Grady* instead of Captain Walker? "No, thanks," I answered. "It's pretty crowded in here, but he usually sits in the corner over there by . . . oh . . . my . . . God!"

"What? What's wrong?" Granny followed my gaze and gasped. "Why that little floozy. She stole my idea!" Granny shrieked and then pushed her way through the crowd with me hot on her heels to make sure no more *scuffling* occurred.

"Gertie, fancy seeing you here," Fiona purred, wearing a designer dress, with naturally tanned legs and normal-looking toes. A towering lemon meringue pie perched on the table in front of her. She sat on one side of the captain, and Granny plopped down on the other side of the captain. I nabbed the last seat across from him and between the two women.

His full-sized pan pizza had been devoured. *Wow, he sure has an appetite,* was all I could think as I stared at the size of the pizza. His gaze met mine with a pleading, helpless look, distracting me. I gave him a look back that said, *Welcome to my world.*

"Fancy that, indeed," Granny responded to Fiona. "You always carry around a pie with you?"

"Well, you obviously carry around cookies with you."

"My daughter's best friend owns this place. I was bringing her a plate of cookies in celebration of her engagement." Granny shot me a look that said mum's the word on bringing the cookies for the captain.

"Speaking of grandchildren," Fiona said, then leaned in closer, "all six of mine are married and successful and live in big beautiful houses." Her eyes cut to mine in a sheepish but determined look that said, *All's fair in the battle of the bakeoff.*

No words were necessary.

She was basically pointing out the obvious: I, Granny's only grandchild, was single, didn't hold a "real" job, and lived in an ancient, run-down, haunted monstrosity. But I was okay with that. I loved my life.

Except for this past week, anyway.

Bernadette chose that moment to walk out of the ladies' room and head back to the captain's table . . . *her* table. She stopped

80

short when she saw all of us. "Wow, what a nice leaning tower of Fiona. Interesting meringue there, Ms. Atwater."

"Why, I —"

"And Granny, I see you brought your cookies as usual. Not that they're boring, or anything. Sometimes less is more."

"Of all the —"

"Yes, well, if you're ready, Grady. I don't much care for the atmosphere here. Let's go back to my place for some real dessert."

The captain took one look at Fiona, another at Granny, and then gave me an apologetic smile as he bolted to the door, taking Bernadette by the arm and leading her outside toward his car.

"Look what you did, you nincompoop," Granny snapped. "Scared him right into the competition's arms. She's a shoo-in for sure now."

"Me?" Fiona shrieked. "You were the one who scared him half to death with your horrible driving in that hearsemobile."

"I was in a rush to give Jo her cookies, that's all."

"Right," Fiona said.

"That's right. Everyone loves my cookies," Granny added. "And Frank loved them the most."

"Yeah, well, Phillip loved my lemon meringue pie more than anyone."

"Then I have nothing to worry about," Granny leaned across the table, "considering he left you."

Oh, no, you didn't, Granny, I thought as Fiona gasped, gave me an accusing look, and then proceeded to throw her pie at Granny. Of course Fiona's aim was off, and it landed in my face before she stormed out of Smokey Jo's.

Why was it every time these two got together, I wound up a mess? I licked my lips and couldn't deny the pie was really good. With a shrug, I winced at Granny as I said, "If I were you, I'd start worrying."

"Ooooh, that horrible bakezilla! I'll beat her if it's the last thing I ever do," Granny said, grabbing her belongings from my knapsack and huffing back to her car, limping all the way. She slapped the rain cap on her head, roared the engine of her Cadillac, and peeled away from the curb, the plastic ties of her rain cap flapping in the evening breeze in time with her annoyance.

I wasn't the only one a mess; my life was a mess, and I'd had about as much as I could take. I was trying to save the carnival, but no one seemed to care, and my love life was nonexistent. Maybe it was time I did something about it. Forget everyone else; I was going to start thinking of me.

5

Saturday night was finally here. The auction had gone great, raising lots of money for Animal Angels. Granny wasn't happy because the Knitting Nanas' afghan pulled in a slightly bigger price than the Sewing Sisters' quilt. Now all she had left was the bakeoff, and she'd be darned if she'd let either the Ninnies or Bernadette Baldwin win.

Needless to say, I'd never looked forward to a date more than I did that night, for many reasons.

"I passed Mimi Pots today in town. Looks like she traded in that old rusted truck of hers for a new car," Mitch said.

"That's not the only thing that's new. You should see her. She's had quite the makeover. She's even made a friend in Bernadette."

"Really? How did all of this come about?"

"Abigail and Chuck's wedding."

"Ah," Mitch said, but at the mention of the word *wedding,* his face had paled dramatically. "You, uh, you look good," he said in a deep voice, his intensely fierce dark gaze roaming over every inch of me and lingering on my features.

If I didn't know him as well as I did, it would be intimidating. To me it was endearing because, like the cards had shown, he needed me to soften him up. To tame the beast. This was all new to him. He hadn't dated in a very long time, and expressing his feelings didn't come easily for him.

That's why I was looking forward to this carnival week ending soon. Some time alone with no distractions or drama was exactly what we needed if we were going to give *us* a fighting chance.

"I like what you've done with your hair," he added.

"Thanks." I smiled warmly, pleased he'd noticed.

I'd let Jo talk me into darker blond lowlights, and I'd left my hair soft and natural instead of my gelled spiky style. She'd also convinced me to wear dangling, pale green stone earrings that matched my eyes, as well as a matching gauzy green cocktail dress. While it wasn't my usual style, I had to admit I felt like a princess.

"It's the truth." He hoisted a shoulder and looked away uncomfortably.

"You look very handsome tonight," I responded in kind.

I let my eyes drink in the sight of him. He'd semi-tamed his thick, black tresses and had even shaved his face, but the shadow on his cheeks was still somewhat there. And he'd replaced his usual jeans, dress shirt, and sport coat with black dress slacks and a burgundy-colored, silk shirt that caressed his impressive shoulders and chest, much in the way I was longing to do.

He gave me one sharp nod in thanks and then picked up his menu, saying casually, "Maybe we can go back to my place for a nightcap."

"I'd like that," I said softly. Morty had been in a mood when Mitch had picked me up. A nightcap at his place sounded perfect.

We'd chosen to eat at Papas Greek restaurant. The first case we'd worked together, we'd spent a fair amount of time there. And since the last guy I'd dated had taken me to Nikko's Italian restaurant, that place was out of the question. Neither one of us wanted any negative memories intruding on our very first official date.

Like most of the businesses in Divinity, Papas had a theme. They'd chosen ancient

Athens. I just loved the marble statues of godlike men and women, and the food was incredible. The night couldn't be more perfect.

"Ready to order?" our waiter asked.

I was about to say something when Mitch's phone rang. He glanced at the caller ID and then frowned. "It's Captain Walker. He wouldn't call me unless it was important. I'd better take this."

"Go ahead," I said, and the waiter discreetly stepped away from our table to give us privacy.

"I hope this is important, Grady," Mitch said into the phone. He and Captain Grady Walker were not just coworkers, they were friends. He was like a father to Mitch.

Mitch's face changed from one of irritation to concern. His gaze met mine, and a feeling of doom swept through me. "Be right there," he finished and then hung up.

So much for the night being perfect.

I sighed. "What is it? Let me guess. This has to do with Granny and Fiona, doesn't it?"

He nodded slowly.

"That's it. I have had it with the two of them. They are both going to be in serious trouble when I get a hold of them."

"They already are."

The tone in his voice made me pause. "What do you mean? What on earth have they done this time?"

"Granny Gert and Fiona Atwater have been arrested for the murder of Bernadette Baldwin," he said gravely.

"Whaaat?" I shrieked, drawing stares from everyone around us. Karma was an angry beast, all right, but I hadn't thought it was downright ruthless or that it would sink its ugly teeth into my granny.

Granny and Fiona had done a lot of naughty things this past week, including wanting to throttle each other, but murder? Neither one of them was capable of murder. There had to be a mistake, but I was afraid this was one mess even I couldn't fix. My mother always said, family was family, for better or worse . . . ruined dates and all.

"There has to be a mistake, Captain," I said. Mitch and I sat across from Captain Walker in his office with his desk between us at the precinct.

He steepled his fingers with a grim look on his face, reminding me of the King of Swords. "I have to admit it doesn't look good for either of them. Granny hasn't acted like her normal sweet self since Fiona came to town. According to Fiona's friends, she's been out of sorts since she found out Granny lived in Divinity. The whole town can see how they've been determined to outdo each other at any cost. I've had more calls of complaints against those two this week than I've had for anyone else all month."

"I'll admit they both have been behaving very badly all week long, but that hardly makes them capable of murder," I said, wringing my hands. "There has to be something more."

"There is. It all started at the auction earlier. Fiona's afghan took in more money than Granny's quilt, but Bernadette's lace doilies, placemats, and tablecloths earned the most," he said.

"Even I heard those two weren't happy about that," Mitch stated. "But disappointment doesn't equal murder."

"It went beyond not being happy," the captain added. "Everyone there heard both Granny and Fiona arguing with Bernadette, telling her they'd make sure she didn't win the bakeoff. The baked goods were supposed to be delivered tonight to Trixie, who is not only the head of the sewing circle but is also in charge of the bakeoff. Only, the goods never made it."

"What exactly happened?" Mitch asked,

taking notes as always. He hadn't complained at all when our date ended prematurely. Instead, he'd driven me here without a single word and sat strong and supportive beside me. I knew if anyone could help free Granny and get to the bottom of this, it would be Mitch.

"Well, Trixie said a bunch of the Sewing Sisters and Knitting Nanas showed up at the same time to deliver their baked goods for safekeeping and cataloguing. With all the commotion, Fiona's and Granny's pie and cookies wound up missing. Of course they accused each other of trying to sabotage the other person, but when a search of the premises didn't produce their merchandise, they wondered if Bernadette had anything to do with it since she was nowhere in sight."

"I can't believe they actually agreed on something," I muttered, still in shock over all that had happened.

"So much so that it appears they conspired to commit murder. Trixie said they went off in search of Bernadette and their merchandise. Meanwhile, I got an anonymous phone call at the office saying Granny and Fiona were seen getting into Granny's car together and driving off. Not long after, we received a 911 call that Bernadette

Baldwin had been hit by a big white Cadillac. I drove there myself only to find Bernadette beneath Granny's car with Fiona and Granny fighting over her BB's Baked Goods box of turnovers."

"That just doesn't make any sense," I said.

"That's what I thought, so I asked them about it. I do have to say they both seemed surprised and a bit horrified when they discovered Bernadette was beneath the car. They both say they went outside, but Granny's car was missing. When they walked down the hill a ways, they spotted it on the curb in the distance."

"Why didn't they call the police then?" Mitch asked.

"They had planned on it, but once they reached it, they found Granny's cookies and purse as well as Fiona's pie and handbag on the front seat. They got distracted with Bernadette's turnovers about ten feet away. With more questions than answers, they were fighting over who was going to return the box of turnovers and speculating over what might have happened to her."

"I'm sure they are telling the truth," I said. "Someone else must be trying to set them up. Someone has been trying to sabotage the carnival from the beginning. That same person could have killed Bernadette, knowing the carnival would be cancelled for sure that way."

"I understand this is upsetting for you, Sunny, and I promise we will look into every lead, but between the threats they were heard giving Bernadette earlier after the auction, the anonymous phone call saying they were seen together in the car, and me finding them at the scene of the crime, things don't look good for either of them. Not to mention the note from Bernadette addressed to me personally that was found beneath the turnovers in the bottom of the box."

"N-Note?" I swallowed hard.

"It said, 'I hope you like these turnovers the best. I deserve to win. Granny Gert and Fiona Atwater are plum crazy. In fact, I think they want to kill me.' " The captain met my eyes with sympathy as he added, "Bernadette's death has been ruled a murder. Granny and Fiona are pleading innocent, but with all the evidence against them, they've both been arrested."

"This is insane," I said.

"Divinity doesn't need another scandal. Chief Spencer wants this case wrapped up immediately. That doesn't mean we're not investigating every angle. It just means we don't have much time. It also means since you're so close to this case, we won't be using your help this time."

I gasped. "But Mayor Cromwell —"

"Is out of town on political business," Mitch chimed in.

"And Chief Spencer has never liked me," I finished glumly.

"I'm assigning Mitch to the case," Captain Walker said. "You just worry about taking care of your grandmother and keeping your nose out of trouble."

"Finally, someone is talking sense," Mitch said to the captain.

"Excuse me?" I asked, my jaw falling open.

"Don't get me wrong," Mitch quickly clarified. "I think you're great, just not a great detective. I'm back and better than ever."

"Oh, you're back, all right, but hardly better than ever. And to think I almost wasted a whole evening to find that out."

"Sunny, come on. Don't be like that." He reached out to touch my hand, but I moved away.

"Don't you *Sunny* me. I've never tried to be a detective or to do your job. But I have helped this department in many ways. I *am* a good consultant, whether you believe in my gifts or not."

"All right, you two. Arguing isn't going to

help Granny Gert one bit." Captain Walker shot Mitch a look that said, *You really don't have a clue when it comes to women, buddy.*

Then he turned to me and said in a soft tone, "Unlike Detective Stone, I am fully aware of how much your abilities have helped this department, Sunny. However, in this case, I agree with him. You're too close to your grandmother to be impartial. It was the same way with Mitch when Isabel died. He was more of a hindrance than a help. You have to trust Mitch to do his job, okay?"

I nodded, still too angry to speak. I trusted Mitch to do his job, but that didn't mean I couldn't help as well. I would simply do it unofficially. The person who was sabotaging the carnival was somehow connected to the death of Bernadette, and I wouldn't rest until I found out who that person was. I would *not* let my granny take the fall for something she didn't do.

"Can I see her?" I asked.

"Not until the morning," the captain said with no nonsense in his voice. "While I don't believe either of them is capable of murder, I can't prove it. Besides, they do need to be taught a lesson. A night in jail will be like a big time-out for both of them. Let's hope they reflect on the consequences of their actions. I'll talk to the judge about bail in the morning. Come back then."

There was no avoiding it. Granny Gert needed help, all right, and that started with a good lawyer. Like it or not, we all knew who was the best. I groaned just thinking about what I had to do, and my empty stomach turned sour.

It was time to call my mother.

"Well, it wasn't easy, but I think I've worked it all out," Vivian Meadows said after walking through my front door and air-kissing my cheek, with my father Donald hot on her heels.

They'd hopped on the first flight from New York City to Divinity the second I called them. As much as we might butt heads, they were always there for me when I needed them. Same for Granny.

My mother's golden blond, chicly styled hair and size-two frame fooled many people, but she was actually a ruthless lawyer and queen of high society. If anyone was able to get Granny Gert off, it would be her. Meanwhile, my father Donald Meadows, the world-renowned cardiologist and king of his domain, had come along for moral support and most likely to gloat. Not to mention he had to be a part of everything, *control* everything.

I couldn't believe they were here again. After Easter, we had agreed not to see each other until Thanksgiving. They'd grudgingly left Granny Gert here against their better judgment, and now their smug *I told you so* expressions said it all. They might be here for me, but that didn't mean they wouldn't relish telling me exactly what they thought.

My mother looked around warily. "Where's the rat?" A door slammed, and a gust of wind whipped through the house. "You should close your windows when it's that windy out." She patted her hair.

"There aren't any open," I said, trying not to smile as I glanced outside at the still trees. "Morty's a cat, Mother, and I'm sure he's around here somewhere."

"Just so long as he doesn't come near me," Dad thundered, turning in a full circle. Yet his gray-streaked, perfectly coiffed, brown Ken-doll hair didn't move an inch. "I don't trust the look in his devil eyes. He's just plain creepy."

"What exactly did you work out, Mom?" I asked, weary already though we'd barely seen each other.

"Well, darling, your father paid Granny's bail. I had hoped that would mean she would be set free. But because of the seriousness of the crime she is accused of,

96

the judge ordered her under house arrest."

"I guess that's not so bad. At least she'll be able to come home and stay out of jail." I shuddered just picturing my sweet little granny in a cell with real criminals.

"Ah, if only it were that easy," Dad added. "You've got to love small-town judges. They always have conditions."

"Such as?" I asked.

"Well, for starters, Fiona Atwater is from out of town." Mom smoothed down the front of her expensive peach suit coat.

"What does that even mean?"

"Basically, that Fiona can't leave town until the case is closed," she finished.

"The problem is," Dad added, "Fiona doesn't have any family here. Since Granny and Fiona got themselves into this mess together, the judge feels they should stay together as a sort of punishment to work out their differences. He was quite angry that the carnival was cancelled early for the first time ever. Said those two women were a menace to society." Dad threw up his hands. "What can I say? Fair's fair, I guess. We're just lucky to have a retired judge staying at the inn where we are."

"Wait a minute. What retired judge?"

Mom shot Dad an odd look and then said, "Harold something or other. We met him when we checked in," Mom said.

"Hey, I know him. I met Harry when he helped me hang my shingle the first day of the carnival. Very nice guy. I haven't seen him since, though."

"That's because he's staying at Divine Inspiration, fishing Inspiration Lake. Or trying to." Mom chuckled. "I don't think he's caught a thing, but he seems like a nice enough fellow. Just not coping well with retirement, much like I imagine your father will be when the time comes."

Dad started to protest, but Mom shushed him and kept speaking. "Anyway, I've never heard of Harry, but Judge Eustace Navarra has, and that's all that matters. Without Harry's intervention, Granny and Fiona would probably still be in jail instead of staying with you."

The words *staying with you* finally registered. "They're staying here?" I sputtered. "At my house?" I choked. "Together?"

"Precisely." Dad smiled a big gloating smile.

A big boom sounded and the house shook as though it had just thundered outside.

Mom frowned, looking out at the sunny sky. "The Weather Channel didn't say it was supposed to storm today."

"Don't change the subject, Mother. You

98

did this on purpose, didn't you? Is this your idea of paying me back for making you leave right after Easter?"

"Don't be ridiculous, Sylvia. It's not like I would ever willingly move here. Besides, I *do* know how to be professional. Some things just can't be helped. At least your grandmother is out from behind bars."

I didn't bother to correct my parents anymore. I had changed my name to Sunshine years ago, but they'd refused to call me anything other than Sylvia. "And who exactly is supposed to be in charge of them?" I asked.

My parents didn't say a word. They didn't have to. The looks on their faces told me everything I needed to know.

"Oh, no. You have no idea how these two have behaved all week all while I was trying to stop whoever was trying to sabotage the carnival. Bernadette's murder might have been prevented if they had let me do my job. There is no way I am going to get stuck babysitting them. They'll wind up killing each other, and then you'll have an even bigger mess to clean up."

"No worries, darling, that's why I insisted on these." My mother held out a picture of a pair of thick, heavy iron contraptions that sort of looked like bracelets.

"Interesting choice of accessories. What are those?"

"Those, my dear, are ankle bracelets." Dad smiled again, even bigger this time. "They try to flee the coop, the bracelets go off, and they are in even bigger trouble. Game over."

"You're really enjoying this, aren't you?" I shook my head at him.

He shrugged. "Maybe now you and your grandmother will realize you don't know everything. You two living together was never a good idea, but no one listens to me."

"Look. None of us has the time to watch over your grandmother or Fiona," my mother pointed out. "I'm actually representing them both, which your grandmother nearly had a coronary over."

"Probably because they hate each other," I said.

"I've never quite understood why they don't like each other. They used to be friends, you know. In fact, they still have mutual friends. Fiona could afford to pay her own bail. But since they can't be trusted not to escape and get into even more trouble, it's imperative we know they will stay put when you're not around."

"Agreed." I huffed out a breath. "So I guess you'll be staying put for a while as well, then?"

"What a silly thing to say, Sylvia," Dad boomed. "Of course we're staying put. Someone has to take care of you, too. Your mother and I aren't going anywhere until we clean up this mess. Seems we've had to do that quite a bit since you moved out. Maybe we need to find a man to take care of you permanently."

"Oh, no, you don't. You are not to get involved in my love life again. Besides, Detective Stone and I are going to start dating." I was angry with Mitch for his comment about me not being capable at investigating, but that didn't mean I was ready to give up on a relationship with him. I just intended to make him sweat a bit.

"Ah, yes, the good detective. I suppose he's better than your last choice. He'll have to do," Dad said, rubbing his jaw. "Maybe I should have a talk with him."

"Um, yeah, maybe not."

The wind and rumbling stopped, and everything stilled to an eerie quiet. Morty suddenly appeared at my mother's feet, and she hopped about as if a cockroach had crawled across her toe. The unmistakable sound of Morty's hissing laughter could be heard as he hoisted his head and walked regally to the couch, leaping gracefully onto the cushion and settling in as if he owned the place.

Let's face it, he did.

"We don't have time for this nonsense," Mom squeaked. "If you need us, we'll be someplace dignified like Divine Inspiration. Come along, Donald. We've got work to do." Mom marched past me and through the door with Dad right behind her.

"Wait," I hollered after them. "What about Granny and Fiona?"

"They are just waiting on you, dear, to pick them up," Mom hollered back. "If I were you, I'd get going. No telling what other trouble they will manage to stir up before you get them home."

Great. Just what I needed to hear. I didn't want my granny locked up, but setting her free with her arch nemesis was the worst possible mistake anyone could make. And how in God's name had I ended up in charge of them?

6

"Are we there yet?" Fiona asked from the backseat.

"What are you, five?" Granny chimed in from the front seat beside me, adjusting the ties to her plastic rain cap.

"At least I don't look like I have a diaper on my head. You look like you're potty training out the wrong end."

"My words are the only thing that's going to leak out. And I have a few choice ones in mind."

My bug was not big enough for the three of us. I'd separated them, but even that hadn't done any good. "Would you two stop arguing?" I grumbled. "Because I seriously can't take much more. When we get home, I'm going to put you both in a time-out."

"Are these god-awful bracelet thingies really necessary? I mean, they don't match a single thing I'm wearing," Fiona complained.

"You're the god-awful one. Who cares about accessorizing, you jailbird. I'm not going to be able to walk if it keeps rubbing up against my phlebitis," Granny wailed.

"I'd rather be a jailbird than be a part of jailbait. You're nearly old enough to be the captain's mother. And no need to worry about walking. We won't get far in these things without setting off an alarm."

"Now that's the pot calling the kettle, since you're my age. You've been all over the captain since first laying eyes on him. Besides, we're not *that* much older than him." Granny's stark white eyebrows drew together, and she spoke as though thinking aloud. "I wonder who will show up if an alarm *does* go off?"

They were both suddenly quiet, and I could see Granny pondering that thought. I glanced in the rearview mirror and saw Fiona doing the same.

"Oh, no. If either one of you even so much as thinks about setting the ankle bracelet alarm off on purpose, I'll haul you back to jail myself and throw away the key. Prison uniforms are so bland. Try accessorizing *that,* ladies!"

They didn't speak for the rest of the way home.

"We're here," I said, pulling into my

empty driveway.

Granny's car had been impounded as evidence, not to mention the front grill needed some major bodywork after smashing into a streetlamp. The captain had said there were no skid marks. It was as though the person driving had never even attempted to touch the brakes. Just one more reason why the case hadn't been ruled an accident.

"Oh, joy," Fiona said as she climbed out of Buggy. "Lead the way to my cell, Sunny. I've got nothing against you, but being cooped up with Gertie is going to be a prison sentence."

"Having you stay under the same roof is no picnic for me, either, but you heard the judge. We don't have a choice," Granny said, climbing out as well and untying her rain cap along the way. "Just wait until Morty gets a load of you."

I opened the front door and headed straight for the medicine cabinet in my kitchen. After taking something for my whopping headache, I asked, "Would you care to call your children, Fiona?"

She looked horrified. "Absolutely not. Let them think I'm on some grand adventure. I don't want them to worry or be embarrassed."

"Your idea of a grand adventure has given

us plenty to worry about," Granny butted in, donning her apron and already looking more relaxed from that simple motion. "If it wasn't for you —"

"Me? Oh, that's rich. It wasn't my beast of a car that ran over Bernadette. I'd say we're in this mess because of you." Fiona stood with her hands on her hips, tapping her foot rapidly. "If you hadn't —"

From out of nowhere, Morty leapt on top of the kitchen table and hissed at both of them.

Fiona yelped, stumbling back a few steps and clutching at her heart. While Granny fluttered her hands and grabbed onto the nearest chair for support, her face paler than her hair for once.

"It appears Morty has had enough of your squabbling as well," I said, smiling at Morty and giving him a grateful look.

Granny patted her hair and headed upstairs without another word. Her door clicked closed louder than normal. Fiona gave Morty a wary look and then pursed her lips, looking helpless.

"Your room is at the top of the stairs to the right, Fiona. Your Knitting Nanas dropped your suitcase off earlier, and there's a bathroom in the hallway two doors down from your room. The linen closet is inside the bathroom, with everything you might need."

"Thank you," she said and marched up the stairs, firmly shutting her own door.

I sighed. So much for finishing out the week with no more drama. Guess Mitch and I wouldn't be getting back to normal anytime soon. Speaking of Mitch, there was something I had to do.

I gave Morty a rub behind his ears and said, "Keep an eye on them, boy." I winked.

He just blinked at me, yawned, and then leapt off the table to disappear as quickly as he'd arrived. Whether he would watch them or not was anyone's guess, but I couldn't worry about that now. I needed answers, and no matter how frustrated I was with Mitch, he was right about one thing. He was a great detective.

And I needed a plan.

It was late afternoon on Sunday, and the days were getting longer. The temperature had reached eighty-one today, and the warm balmy breeze felt relaxing against my skin. I took a moment to enjoy the sounds of summer as I stood outside of Mitch's apartment building.

Somewhere off in the distance, a dog barked and children squealed in delight.

Someone was mowing a lawn, and the smell of barbecue drifted past my nose. This was my favorite time of year, and I couldn't even enjoy it because of all that had happened.

Slowly climbing the cast-iron stairs of Mitch's redbrick apartment building, I reached the top, took a breath, and knocked. A minute later, he opened the door. His eyes widened in surprise and then filled with wariness.

He looked mouthwatering, as usual. His thick black hair was still damp and curling up slightly at the ends as if he'd just gotten out of the shower. He'd thrown on a pair of silky basketball shorts and a muscle shirt as though he'd been in a hurry to answer the door.

"Can I come in?" I asked, smoothing down the front of my own T-shirt and shorts.

He stepped back and opened the door wide. I headed inside and sat in his living room on a big black leather sofa. Scanning the walls, I took in the white painted bookshelves, fabulous paintings of New York City, and marble sculptures atop tile and glass end tables. I'd missed his modern, elegant, and classy sense of style these past two months.

I'd missed him.

He shut the door and followed me over to

the couch to sit down beside me.

"Mitch, I —"

"Sunny, I —"

We both started speaking at the same time.

"Normally, I'd say ladies first, but I need to get this out," he said, taking my hand and threading his fingers between mine. His gaze finally lifted to my eyes and stayed there. "Sunny, I'm sorry. I never meant to hurt your feelings. It's not that I think you're not an asset to the department. I just don't like you helping, period."

I gave him a frustrated look. "Why?"

"Ah, hell, you know I'm no good with words." He ran his thumb over the back of my hand as his fingers tightened around mine. "If anything happened to you, I'd never get over it, okay?"

I melted inside. "Okay," I said softly and squeezed his hand back.

He blinked. "So, you're not still mad at me?"

"I didn't say that." I lightly punched him on the arm. "But we've been through too much together to let something like a difference of opinion keep us apart."

"Does that mean you're still willing to go out with me?" he asked, sounding hopeful.

"If the drama would ever quit and we get a moment of peace and quiet alone, then yes. I still want to go out with you. Do you know how long it's been since I've been on a real date?"

"Longer than the two months I've been gone I hope," he said.

I reached out my hand and cupped his cheek. "Did you miss me, Detective?"

"You have no idea," he said in husky voice and then pulled me onto his lap.

His gaze searched mine as he cradled me in his strong arms, and then he lowered his head. He pressed his wide firm lips to mine, and a feeling of warmth spread throughout every cell of my body. I slipped my arms around his neck and plunged my hands into his hair. He groaned and then deepened the kiss, laying me back on the sofa and stretching out beside me all in one movement with our lips still locked.

I wanted him more than I'd ever wanted anyone, but I wanted *us* to be about more than this. I wanted us to be different and special and meaningful. I wanted to see if we stood a real shot at being a couple.

I wanted to be courted.

I tore my lips away from his, though it killed me to do so, and said, "I think it's time."

"Yeah?" he asked, his eyelids lowering slightly.

"Yeah," I said and slid out from beneath him. "It's time to we put our heads together to solve this case."

"You're killing me," he said with a groan and scrubbed his hands over his face as he sat up.

"Whatever do you mean?" I asked with a devilish grin on my face. "What did you think I meant? Dessert?"

"Something like that."

"Silly man, don't you know anything? Dessert comes after dinner, which we still haven't had."

"Point taken. When are you available?"

"Just as soon as we solve this case."

"Sunny, you know what the captain said. There *is* no we on this one."

"No, he said I couldn't investigate with you. That doesn't mean I can't brainstorm with you. You know the saying, two heads are always better than one. Besides, the quicker we solve this case, the quicker we can move on with our date . . . and dessert."

He sighed. "Fine, no dessert until the case is solved," he grumbled, sounding like the grump-butt I adored. "I need a shower."

"I thought you just took one," I said to his retreating back.

"Not a cold one. Help yourself to the

111

fridge, and when I get back, do me a favor, Tink."

"What's that?"

"Keep your cute little fanny far away from me, or I can't be held accountable for my actions."

"Deal," I said and then pressed my lips together to keep from changing my mind.

I'd never been much of a dessert person. Dessert was rich and fulfilling and satisfying, but it wasn't the healthiest thing for you. And I wanted our relationship to be long lasting and healthy. Not to mention, Mitch needed a clear head with no distractions. My granny's future depended on it. Nope, I really wasn't much of a dessert person, but suddenly I wanted nothing more.

Yes, indeedy, this was going to be one very long summer.

Monday morning I decided to take matters into my own hands. I had promised Mitch that I wouldn't interfere with his investigation. Now that I knew he didn't want me involved because he was worried about me, I found it sweet and endearing. I had no intention of getting in his way, but that didn't mean I couldn't ask around town and see if I could find anything out.

Mitch hadn't been much help yet, because the police didn't have a lot to go on. Bernadette had a strong personality, but she had been closemouthed when it came to her personal life. The captain *had* been out on a date with her that night at Smokey Jo's, but that was it, and he had assured everyone it wouldn't have affected his judging the bakeoff. He was, after all, an honorable man. He just couldn't resist Bernadette's turnovers. We knew Sam's and Bernadette's stores competed with each other, but that didn't mean they were enemies. She rubbed half the town the wrong way, but we weren't sure who her actual enemies might be, other than Granny Gert and Fiona.

I still believed that someone was trying to set them up, and I was convinced it was the same person who was sabotaging the carnival, so I decided to look into the people who knew them best. The Knitting Nanas and Sewing Sisters. I didn't really know the Nanas, so I started with the head of the Sewing Sisters, Trixie Irving.

Trixie was a retired schoolteacher but still worked as the local seamstress. When someone needed a pair of pants hemmed or a zipper on a coat fixed, they went to Trixie. That's why she'd been the perfect choice as president of the sewing circle. In fact, she held the meetings at her house every Saturday.

I didn't want to wait until Saturday to talk to her and meet the other sisters. Besides, I thought it best to meet with her one-on-one the first time and see if I could learn any inside scoop. Not to mention her house was where all the trouble had started the night the candidates had dropped off their baked goods for the bakeoff.

I'd cancelled my readings for the day and left the house under the pretense of picking up more cleaning supplies, since today was Monday, after all. That way I was covered in case Mitch called. And I really would pick up more cleaning supplies, but I would also make a slight pit stop along the way.

It felt strange passing the crime scene at the bottom of the hill. The streetlight was still bent in half, but the captain was right — no skid marks. Whoever had been behind the wheel hadn't even attempted to stop at all. Other than the bent light post, nothing looked out of the ordinary. There hadn't even been any blood spilled. Bernadette had died almost immediately of internal injuries.

I kept driving up the hill and came to a stop outside of Trixie's house. Pulling up to the curb, I put my car in park and then decided to put on the parking brake for good measure. She only had a one-lane driveway with her car already parked in it, and she lived on quite a steep hill.

I stepped out of the car, and the hairs on the back of my neck stood up. I turned around in a full circle but didn't see anyone. If I didn't know any better, I'd swear someone was watching me. Locking my bug, I hurried to Trixie's door and knocked.

Trixie was a thin, short woman with black hair streaked with gray she kept in a low bun at the base of her neck. She slipped on her glasses and squinted up at me. "Sunny Meadows, what a pleasant surprise. Please, come in."

She stepped back, and I entered her small but cozy house. Handmade pillows, blankets, afghans, doilies, and curtains in all sorts of styles and fabrics displayed her work throughout her house.

"I've just started some tea. Would you care for some?" she asked.

"Tea sounds wonderful," I said, sitting at her kitchen table and setting my knapsack in front of me.

"To what do I owe this lovely surprise this fine morning?" she asked.

"Well, I have a skirt with a tattered hem I need to have repaired." I pulled my long skirt out of my knapsack. I'd ripped it

115

intentionally this morning so I'd have a reason to stop by Trixie's.

A puckered frown crossed Trixie's face. "Your grandmother is a better cook than she is a seamstress, but this is a simple hem job. Why on earth would you pay someone to fix that for you when you have her at your disposal?"

"I'm sure you've heard by now that both Granny and Fiona are under house arrest and staying with me."

"Yes. I'm afraid news does travel fast in small towns." Trixie poured our tea into lovely quilt-patterned china cups and sat down across from me.

"I admit I brought my skirt to you so I could escape the madness of my house at the moment and to avoid World War Three. If I left the skirt for Granny, Fiona would find a way to try to outdo her, and who knows what I'd end up with. Probably a miniskirt by the time they were both done *fixing* each other's work."

Trixie snickered. "You're probably right, dear. No problem. Just leave it with me, and I'll have it repaired by the end of the week."

"Thank you so much, for the tea and the escape." I sipped from my cup.

"How are you holding up?" she asked, just as I'd hoped she would.

"I'm okay. Anyone who knows Granny has to know she's not capable of murdering anyone, except maybe Fiona." I rubbed my temples. "But seriously, I can't see either one of them murdering anyone. The only thing I can think of is either Bernadette had enemies, or someone was trying to frame Granny and Fiona. But I have no idea who it could be or where to start looking."

"Well, I'm not one to gossip, but I can tell you one thing. That Ophelia Edwards woman — you know, she's the Knitting Nana who didn't like Fiona very much — seemed pretty suspicious to me. She complained the entire week about Fiona being so bossy and always getting to choose where they went on vacation. Let's just say she was *not* having fun."

"I thought that myself every time I was around her. She had a permanent sour puss on her face."

"I also overheard her saying that it wasn't fair that Fiona beat her out for the president position of their group. That sounds like someone who has motive to want to frame Fiona to me. I mean, that's what one might think if they were into gossip, and all. Which I'm not, mind you."

"Of course," I agreed. "I never would have thought you were. It's a shame the bakeoff was cancelled. Everyone put so much work into that. I heard you had quite a turnout."

"You see my house." Trixie gestured around her. "It's not that big. I had so many people here, dropping off their baked goods, there was no way to keep everything straight. Granny and Fiona both swear they put their cookies and pie on the table when they first arrived, but when I checked, their baked goods were missing."

"Anyone could have taken them," I mused aloud.

"Exactly." She tsked. "Between you and me, I've never seen such a competitive group as the Sisters and the Nanas, which is silly if you ask me. The real winner is the charitable group we chose. All the proceeds go to them. Now all they will receive is the money from the auction." Trixie looked pensive and sad. "Such a shame indeed."

I sipped my tea, thinking maybe it was time I paid Ophelia Edwards a visit and got to know her a bit. "Thank you so much for the tea. Guess I'd better get back to check on Granny and Fiona. Lord knows what those two will get into next."

Trixie stood and led the way to her door. "You take care, dear. And let me know if I can help in any way. It's just such a tragedy that Granny has to stay with that horrible

Fiona woman. Everyone in town knows those Nanas are nothing but trouble."

"Thank you, Trixie. I'll tell Granny you send her your best."

"You do that, dear, and I'll give you a call when your skirt is done."

I waved good-bye and headed out the door on a mission.

7

Ten minutes later, I pulled into the parking lot of the Divinity Hotel. The hotel was small but quaint and showcased the Art Deco style of the 1930s, inspired by the artists of Paris. I entered the lobby, filled with lacquered wood furniture combined with brushed steel and lined with zebra-skin upholstery.

Colorful starburst motifs covered the floors and walls in exotic oranges and greens with black and gold designs arranged in geometric shapes. And the fireplace was spectacular. It was the focal point of the lobby.

The mantel was made out of mahogany, walnut, and oak wood, because those kinds of woods were easy to carve and had such contrasting grains, which made for a more creative design. Beading, flowers, and leaves were carved into the frieze, and a beveled mirror was built right into the center with hand-painted tiles surrounding the outside.

"Let me guess. You think I'm a suspect in Bernadette Baldwin's murder, too?" Chuck Webb asked from behind the front desk. He was an average-sized man, around fifty, with a muscular frame and military brown hair. He rubbed his red nose, left over from his alcohol-laden days.

"What's she doing here?" Abigail Brook-Webb asked, stepping out of the office in the back to stand beside her new husband. Abby used to be pear-shaped, with mousy brown hair and no makeup, and completely obsessed with Mitch. But after her cousin gave her a makeover, she'd transformed into a confident attractive woman with full-bodied hair and short, sassy bangs.

"Of course you're not a suspect, Mr. Webb. I just happened to be in the neighborhood, and I thought I'd stop by and say congratulations to you both. I heard you got married in Atlantic City."

Abby eyed me warily and then mumbled, "Thanks. We're very happy."

The bell behind us chimed and in walked Mimi Pots. Mimi was an introvert who lived alone in a trailer on the outskirts of town, since her husband had abandoned her years ago. He was an ornery man, tight with his money, and kept a fierce grip on things that were his. It was rumored that even though he'd walked away, he still considered Mimi his and kept tabs on her.

People talked, and the story goes that he'd ventured into some shady dealings, yet he never sent her any money even though they were never officially divorced. Needless to say, she didn't like men too much. Although, she was very close to Abby and appeared glad to see her happy.

"Wow, Mimi, I still can't get over how amazing you look," I said, thinking back to the first day of the carnival, when I saw her with Bernadette. I was hoping her sourness that day had mostly been Bernadette rubbing off on her. I really was rooting for Mimi to come out of her shell and be a part of our town.

She flushed, but I could tell she was pleased. But then just as quickly, she frowned as she scanned the room, looking nervous. "Your feller ain't lurking about, is he?"

"No, ma'am. Detective Stone is working." She really didn't like men. "I just stopped by to wish Abby and Chuck congratulations."

"Abby's a good girl. She deserves to be happy, even if that means getting hitched to the enemy." Mimi scowled at Chuck and stepped closer to Abby.

Chuck rolled his eyes but didn't say anything, since Abby obviously adored Mimi. That was proof right there of how much Chuck must adore Abby.

"You deserve to be happy, too," Abby said, looping her arm through Mimi's. "Didn't my cousin do a fabulous job?" She beamed proudly. "Mimi looked wonderful when she gave me away." Abby and Mimi walked into the office, chatting away, not waiting for a response from me.

Chuck sighed, throwing up his hands in defeat, and returned to balancing his books. I was trying to think of a way to meet Ophelia Edwards when she walked through the lobby. I followed her outside and into the parking lot.

"Ophelia, hi." I stuck out my hand. "I don't think we had a chance to officially meet yet."

She narrowed her eyes at me, refusing to shake my hand. "I know who you are. You're Gertie's granddaughter. The fortune-teller."

I lowered my hand. "That's right. My name is Sunny."

"I don't care what your name is. I already answered all that detective's questions this morning. Same as I told him, I might not like Fiona, but I sure wouldn't resort to murder just to set her up. I don't want to be president that badly."

Wow, so Mitch had known who he was going to talk to first, yet he had played dumb just to keep me from getting involved. Fine. Two could play at this game. If he wasn't going to share with me, then I wouldn't share with him. Stubborn man. We could accomplish much more if we worked together.

"I'm not sure I know what you're talking about," I hedged, focusing back on Ophelia so I wouldn't miss any clues.

"I'm not stupid, Miss Meadows. You'd do anything to take the suspicion off your grandmother. I get that. And it's no secret I don't much care for Fiona, but I got no beef with your grandmother. If you really want to look at someone who has a reason to set those two up, then you might want to talk to that Sewing Sister."

"What Sewing Sister?"

"Hazel Kissinger. The one in charge of the auction who your granny and Fiona yelled at. It's so obvious Hazel has the hots for Captain Walker. And heck, she's more his age than either Granny or Fiona, but he doesn't give Hazel the time of day. He talks more to Fiona and Granny, and shoot, he even talked to Bernadette herself, but not a word to Hazel. Maybe she got rid of her competition in one fell swoop. Kill Bernadette and frame Fiona and Granny. Makes sense to me."

"You might have a point."

Her face hardened. "Tell that to the police. No one will listen to me, and now I'm stuck here. All the other Nanas got to leave, but not me. I can't help it I'm no good at baking. I didn't go to Trixie's the night of the bakeoff. I stayed in my hotel room and watched movies, but no one saw me. Just because I don't have an alibi, I have to stay in town. That just don't seem right."

"I'm sorry," I said to Ophelia's retreating back.

"Tell it to the judge. I'm through with all of you." She kept marching toward her rental car, with her long red hair flying rebelliously in the afternoon breeze.

Well, that was a waste of time. I should have known the Sisters would blame the Nanas, and the Nanas would blame the Sisters. Looks like I was back to square one.

I pulled into my driveway and cut the engine, staring at Mitch's squad car with dread. What was he doing here? Had he discovered what I was up to? I guess there was only one way to find out.

125

I took a deep breath and carried in my grocery bag of cleaning supplies with a smile on my face as I entered Vicky. I hung my keys on the hook of the heavy mirrored hat stand in the foyer.

I loved the romance of the Victorian era, inspired by Queen Victoria herself. Dark wood with ornate carvings, end tables with marble tops, and various knickknacks were scattered about extravagantly. Not to mention the Grecian busts and statues that were strategically placed beneath large, dark, heavy-gilded frames that graced most of the walls. I'd never been more thankful that Vicky had come fully furnished, or more grateful that Granny was here to help keep her clean.

"Mitch, how nice to see you. What are you doing here?" I asked as he walked by several large vases filled with huge floral arrangements and plant stands with potted palms to join me.

He narrowed his eyes. "The question is what *aren't* you doing here?"

"Just because I agreed not to interfere with your investigation this time doesn't mean I have to stay home twenty-four-seven." I bumped him with my hip. "I have a life, you know."

"What about Granny and Fiona?" He took

one of the grocery bags from me, and a whiff of his aftershave drifted to my nose.

God, he smelled good, I thought, but ignored that fact and responded with, "They are the ones on house arrest, not me. Someone has to get the food and other supplies now that Granny can't. Besides, they are wearing ankle bracelets, if you haven't noticed."

"Oh, I've noticed, all right. They haven't stopped complaining about it since the moment I arrived."

"Welcome to my world." I walked across the Oriental rug–covered hardwood floors to enter the kitchen and set my supplies on the counter. "Speaking of the Dynamic Duo, where are they?"

"Who knows, but don't speak too loudly. They might —"

"Too late," I interrupted. "I hear them."

Seconds later, they scurried around the corner, arguing as usual.

"You are ridiculous. Morty doesn't want one of your cookies any more than I do. That's why he dropped the dog biscuit at your feet. To tell you they are dog-nasty, not to have you make him dog biscuit cookies out of cat food," Fiona snapped.

"Well, he certainly doesn't want you to make him a cat-sized ankle bracelet like ours. He dropped that puppy collar at your feet to let you know how much he loves me and the stuffed puppy I bought him."

"That's even sillier. Who buys stuffed animals for a cat, especially a stuffed dog? You've done gone and lost your marbles, Gertie."

"Better my marbles than your common sense," Granny said, tying her apron over her sensible, navy blue cotton slacks and pale pink, short-sleeved cotton shirt. "The butler didn't kill Bernadette. There *is* no butler, you buffoon. In fact, I'm beginning to think there is no brain inside that head of yours." She snatched the wooden spoon from the pocket of her apron and thrust it in Fiona's direction.

"How do you know Trixie doesn't have a butler?" Fiona shot back, swiping the spoon away from her face and then smoothing her hands down the front of her non-sensible, powder blue, summer silk jumpsuit.

"Have you seen her house? Not everyone has money like you." Granny gave Fiona the once-over with a distasteful expression on her face.

"You should talk." Fiona sputtered. "Just because you refuse to keep your money in the bank where it belongs doesn't mean you don't have lots of it in those silly shoe boxes and freezer bags. And the gardener in the garage with a pair of hedge clippers and a hearty appetite isn't any more reasonable than my suggestion."

"Says who? Tending a lawn burns a lot of calories. He might have worked up an appetite and taken our pie and cookies."

"My pie I could see, but I doubt he had any interest in your cookies." Fiona turned up her nose in a snooty way, and Granny made a sound like she'd given her the raspberries, or her Metamucil was kicking in. It was hard to tell these days. "Besides, how does that relate back to Bernadette's death?"

"Don't you listen to anything? Like I said, hard work leads to a hearty appetite. You heard the captain. He said Bernadette's turnovers were to die for."

"Oh, for the love of —"

"Ladies, this isn't a game of clue," Mitch interjected, rubbing a hand over his whiskered face and rolling his head on his neck as though trying to stop an impending headache. Too bad it did nothing to stop mine.

"No, it's the Granny and Fiona Show," I corrected him, making a mental note to buy more pain medicine.

"About that, I think the Fiona and Gertie

Show has a better ring," Fiona said, making me change my mind about the pain medicine. It had to be five o'clock somewhere, and I needed a drink.

"Fiona and Gertie? Hardly," Granny said. "I think . . ."

"You see?" I raised my brows at Mitch, pulling him into the living room as they continued on their new rant.

We sat on the heavily upholstered overstuffed sofa, sporting a uniquely shaped and curved back. I took a moment to breathe deeply and try to relax. Sunlight streamed through stained-glass windows draped in heavy fabrics of deep reds, greens, gold, and rich browns. They blended perfectly and were lined with lace and pulled back with heavy cording and tassels. I pulled a needlepoint pillow onto my lap and played with the fringe and cording as I listened to Mitch talk.

"Yeah. While you were gone, they gave me a twenty-minute lecture on how it was taking me way too long to do my job. And that, without your help, it was going to take me forever to solve this case."

"Maybe they have a point."

"Sunny, we've been over this."

"No, you've been over it. I still think there's a way for me to help if you'd just listen to me."

He ignored that comment and continued, "I tried to point out that today was only the first day, but according to them, they have a truce. They've decided to work together and solve this murder themselves."

"This is their idea of a truce?" I sputtered.

"Apparently." He sighed, looking tired, but I was too frustrated with him to even attempt to comfort him. He tried to take my hand, but I picked up the pillow once more.

"So, any leads?"

"Nothing substantial." He rubbed the back of his neck with his hand. "I'm just following up with the people closest to Granny and Fiona and even Bernadette."

"So, no new information or persons of interest?" I dug a little deeper, wondering if he was going to reveal anything like he'd promised.

He studied me carefully before finally speaking. "No. Why? Did you find something out?"

"Don't be silly." I busied myself with straightening a few knickknacks on the table in front of us, not quite meeting his eyes. "How could I find out anything? I'm not supposed to be working this case, remember?"

"I do." He stilled my hand with his own until my gaze met his, and then he raised a thick black brow. "Do you?"

"Do you also remember you're supposed to be keeping me in the loop?" I pulled my hand out from under his and folded them in my lap. "You promised to keep me informed. That's all I asked."

"And I will just as soon as I discover anything."

"Then why do you look like you're hiding something?" I thrust my chin up and watched him closely as he answered.

"Why do you?" He leaned into me, nearly touching my nose with his.

Morty let out a loud meow at our feet, and we jumped apart.

"He's the one who's hiding something." Mitch eyed him warily.

"Oh, please, you big scaredy cat." I pulled the carnival flyer from Morty's mouth and dusted his flour paw print off of the Animal Angels logo. Granny must be baking again. "He gets into things like any other cat. Speaking of pets, did the Animal Angels get their check from the auction?"

"That's still being worked out," Mitch said, taking the flyer from my hands with a pondering look. "Before Bernadette died, she gathered quite a few signatures on her petition to have the carnival proceeds go to the original charity: Quincy's Parks and Rec Program."

"I really thought Quincy was the one sabotaging the carnival, but it doesn't make sense for him to ruin it if there was even a chance the money from the auction could go to him instead of Animal Angels."

"Agreed, but someone definitely wanted the carnival to end early. The question is who would benefit?"

"I don't know." I shrugged, intending to find out but not about to tell him so. Instead, I responded, "I do, however, know that the Parks and Rec buildings are in need of renovation, but they aren't about to fall down, and the swans will survive another year without their pond spruced up. I feel bad, but I do think the carnival board made a smart decision. Everyone knows those rescued animals are in need of so much more. Animal Angels is truly a blessing."

Morty let out what sounded like a groan, bumped up against Mitch's leg, and Mitch dropped the flyer. Morty hissed at him, snatched the paper in his mouth, and pranced out of the room as though he were a king and we were lowly peons.

"For the record, that cat freaks me out. If I ever do have dessert again, it sure as hell won't be in your kitchen."

"Probably a good idea," I said, thinking that at the rate we were going, dessert was a long way off.

Late Monday afternoon, I pulled into the parking lot of the Divinity Police Department. Looking around, I didn't see Mitch's car, which only made me wonder what he was up to. Earlier, he had given Morty a funny look, and then he said there was something he had to do. The next thing I knew, he was gone, leaving me alone with Granny and Fiona still arguing over whose suspect was the more logical choice as they baked and stitched their buns off in the kitchen.

One good thing came out of their bakeathon: Granny gave me a box of cookies for Captain Walker, and of course, Fiona baked him a pie, which set off a whole new argument. More than happy to run their errands for them, if only to escape the insanity, I'd headed into town.

Carrying my basket of goodies, I wandered down the hall, hoping to avoid a certain someone. I hurried around the corner and had almost reached my destination.

"Miss Meadows, why am I not surprised to see you here?" Chief Spencer asked.

I stopped, closed my eyes for a moment, then took a deep breath and turned around with a smile on my face. "Chief Spencer, so nice to see you."

"Is it?" He stood tall with his shoulders squared to precision. He had a full head of salt-and-pepper hair parted on the side and precisely trimmed. His glare and frown put Detective Grumpy Pants's to shame.

"Of course it is." I had never understood what I'd done for him to dislike me. "Granny asked me to bring Captain Walker some cookies, and Fiona baked him a pie."

"Really, now? Did you check them for anything lethal?" His eyes narrowed. "You know . . . accidents happen."

I stiffened my spine but kept my brilliant smile in place. "Granny's a careful cook. I'm sure nothing like that would ever happen to her food."

"I don't know. She's getting old, and her eyesight isn't the best. I've heard stories about other things accidentally winding up in her food not that long ago. I'd hate to see anything else *illegal* happen."

"So would I." I opened the basket, pulled out a cookie, and took a big bite. "Delicious. Want one?"

He just grunted and walked back into his office.

8

A door down the hall opened. "I thought that was you," Captain Walker said after poking his head out. "Something smells good. Those are for me, I hope?" He pushed his door open wider.

"Absolutely," I said and gladly followed him inside. I set the basket down on his desk and then plopped into the nearest chair.

"Rough day?" A sympathetic expression crossed his face.

"Rough week." I rubbed my temples. "Is Mitch around?"

"No." Captain Walker studied me carefully the same way Mitch had. It must be a cop thing. "Why?"

"No reason. Just curious."

"You know what they say about curiosity."

"No worries, Captain. I'm behaving," I said a little more tersely than I had planned.

The captain's face softened as he wiped a

crumb from his goatee. "Sunny, I know it's hard for you, but you have to stay out of this one. Trust Detective Stone. He'll find something."

"I know, and I am, but a certain someone wants this solved yesterday." I glanced toward the door. "I don't know why he hates me."

"Chief Spencer doesn't hate you. He's just protective of Mitch. He knows what Mitch went through with Isabel, and you didn't hear this from me, but Spencer's been burned by a woman as well. He doesn't have any family, so Mitch is like a younger brother to him. Trouble does tend to follow you around." The captain winked.

"Wow, that explains a lot." I thought about what he said, and I could understand the chief's desire to want to protect Mitch's heart. It was kind of sweet, actually. "Thanks, Captain. I'll behave. You can count on me."

"That's what I like to hear. Now, if you don't mind, I think it's time for a coffee break." He reached for the basket of cookies and the pie, practically drooling as he did so.

I just smiled and slipped out of his office, leaving him alone with his beloved sweet tooth. I pondered his words and thought, he could count on me, all right. Count on me to behave like an undercover agent, aka Sunny the Super Spy.

I knew I wasn't a real detective, but this was my granny we were talking about. I'd be darned if I'd sit around like a boxed-up deck of tarot cards and do nothing. I exited the police station and ran smack-dab into Hazel Kissinger in the parking lot.

It was a sign.

"Sunny, hi. I'm so sorry to hear about your grandmother," Hazel said, carrying a cake box and wearing a pretty yellow sundress. "I just don't know what those two were thinking, arguing over what should or shouldn't be allowed in an auction." Her face hardened for a moment as though she just couldn't let that go. "I mean, isn't the point of the auction to raise money for charity?"

"Well, yes, but —"

"And, my goodness, what on earth was Bernadette thinking with starting that petition?" Hazel tsked, her brown curls jiggling as she shook her head. "Animal Angels was her idea to begin with. She had to know that trying to change the charity to the Parks and Rec Program mid-carnival was going to stir up trouble. Although, I can understand why Quincy Turner was so upset. The carnival board promised him last year that his Parks and Rec Program would receive the proceeds this year."

"I understand, but —"

"You know how bad the economy is these days. With his state funding cut so drastically, he'll be lucky to stay open. Have you seen the gazebo and swan pond? They are in dire need of repairs. In fact the whole place could use a face-lift if you ask me, but no one seems to notice." She stared off as if in deep thought. "People should pay more attention to things."

"But I thought —" I started, but she snapped out of her dreamy state and cut me off again.

"Me, too," she said, not having a clue what I was about to say. "I know Animal Angels is new, and all, and rescuing animals is a great cause, but you know Granny is very persuasive. She wanted you to read tarot cards at the carnival. We all knew if the proceeds went to Animal Angels, then you would say yes on account of your love for animals. I mean, you did let that crazy cat stay at your house."

More like he let *me* stick around, I thought, and if you asked me, this woman was the crazy one. "I never —"

She held up her hand. "I know, I know,

but what's fair is fair. Just saying. Still, Granny made some enemies by lobbying for Animal Angels instead of the Parks and Rec Program, and Bernadette knew it."

And I couldn't help but wonder if Hazel was one of them. In fact, I wouldn't be surprised if she was the one to sabotage the carnival just to get back at Granny and Fiona.

"Well, nice chatting with you. I've got to run. Captain Walker is expecting me." She beamed.

"Really?" I could bet she had her chocolate cake in that box. The same cake she had chosen for the bakeoff, no doubt.

Her jaw bulged like she was grinding her teeth. "Don't look so surprised. I can cook, you know." She huffed off into the station, but I heard her mumble, "It's about time he noticed me."

And what if he hadn't? It made me wonder just how far Hazel might have gone to make him.

Monday night, I stood in the back of the room at Pearl's Funeral Parlor for Bernadette Baldwin's calling hours. Since Bernadette was a local business owner, most of the town was there. Bernadette was aggressive and loved to be the center of attention, but she wasn't that well liked. She was respected as a businesswoman, but not so much as a person.

"There you are, child," Lulubelle said, giving me a big squeeze. She was a large woman with even larger hair, but her spirit was her biggest part of all. She let out a bawdy, raucous laugh, not giving a hoot that people were frowning at her. "How've you been, Sunshine?"

I smiled warmly. The woman was infectious. "I've been better."

Her eyes softened sympathetically. "You poor baby. I heard about those crazy rumors that your sweet granny killed Bernadette. Now, that Fiona, I wouldn't put it past. But Granny? No way."

"Thanks, Belle."

"No problem, sugar. Would you look at all these people? Bernadette would be tickled pink. I'm surprised to see Sam. His bakeshop is right next door to BB's Baked Goods, and they knew each other quite well. They used to get along, but for a few months now they have been at odds and competing over every bake job out there. I was out front of their stores before Bernadette died and overheard them arguing over who was going to make the cake for your friend Jo's wedding. And I even saw some of Bernadette's employees asking him for a job."

"I'm surprised to see Chuck Webb here," I said. "Although, now that he's married to Abby, she's keeping him on the respectable path. Looks like they brought Mimi Pots. Unlike some, she looks upset," I observed, figuring Belle would know why. She always had the latest scoop. "I guess she and Bernadette were closer than I realized."

"Bernadette didn't have many friends, and once Mimi had her makeover, she started coming to town more often. I think Bernadette was the first friend Mimi's had in a long time, other than Abby."

"Poor Mimi. I was hoping her makeover would finally help her come out of her shell. She looks like she's doing well."

"She's getting involved more, even selling some of her canned fruits and vegetables in town, but she's still an odd duck. Now that her only friend has died and Abby's a newlywed, I'm afraid we won't be seeing a lot of Mimi around town much longer. Although she has been talking to the widow Ida Ray. Ida has been a regular at BB's Baked Goods for more years than I can count."

"That's good. I hope they become friends." I knew exactly what if felt like to feel alone. Not to feel like you fit in. "Or maybe Mimi just needs to find a man of her own."

"That's true. Love can sure make the world a better place." Belle stared at Don across the room and glowed with adoration.

"How's Sissy?" Sissy was Don's daughter and had just had a baby two months ago.

"She's doing great now that the baby is over his colic. In fact, she's back to work at the garage, so things are back to normal. Maybe Don and I can finally have some free time together."

"That's wonderful, Belle. I'm so happy for you." The longing in my voice couldn't be hidden.

"Don't you worry, honey. Things will get better now that those Knitting Nanas are gone. They were something else, I'll tell you," Belle went on. "Can you believe that Ophelia saying she was in her room all night?" Belle snorted. "Yeah, right. Detective Fuller's wife subbed at Bunco this week, and she let it slip that Ophelia's prints were all over Fiona's lemon meringue pie that was in Granny's car when it ran over Bernadette."

"Really, that's interesting," I said nonchalantly, squashing my anger. I felt like smacking Mitch. So much for keeping me in the loop.

"And get this. Ophelia's not the only thing full of hot air. That pie was full of laxatives. Can you imagine if poor Captain Walker had eaten it? He'd have the runs for a week. But you probably already knew that, being that your handsome detective is back in town, and all."

"Right," I said with a stiff smile.

"You okay, honey? You look a little constipated. Maybe you should have eaten some of that pie yourself. It's not good to keep it all bottled up inside, you know."

"Don't you worry. I plan to let it all out just as soon as I get home," I muttered as I ground my teeth.

"Would you lookie there? I never thought I'd see those two here. Maybe Quincy, since Bernadette started that petition to change the charity in his favor. But that Ozzie feller was dead set against it and angry as a stirred-up hornets' nest, so why on earth did he come to her funeral? To gloat?"

"I have no idea." I was about to excuse myself and walk over to introduce myself, when someone tapped on my shoulder. I turned around and blinked in surprise then smiled. "Harry, nice to see you again."

"Likewise." He smiled back.

"How's the fishing?"

"Not so good. I gave up. Started spending more time in town, although, there's not much to do now that the carnival is shut down."

"Speaking of that, thanks so much for talking to Judge Navarra."

"You're very welcome. I'm glad to help. Your parents are very persuasive people."

"Don't even get me started." I laughed, and then had a brilliant idea. "Since you're here, I'd like to introduce you to someone."

"Sure. Lead the way."

I brought him to the front of the room and stopped by the picture board of Bernadette, surrounded by a wall full of floral bouquets. "Mimi, I'd like to introduce you to my new friend, Harry . . ." I suddenly realized I'd never gotten his last name.

"Dingleburg," he finished for me.

My eyebrows shot up. Well, that was different. "Harry Dingleburg," I repeated.

Mimi turned around with red-rimmed misty eyes and glanced at Harry then looked at me in confusion. "Why?"

She might look better on the outside, but she still had a lot of work to do on the inside. And she was still jumpy around men. "Well, I thought since you were retired, and Harry is new here, that maybe you could

145

show him around town."

Mimi's face puckered like a pickle.

"Oh, I —" Harry started to say.

"He's with me," Hazel said louder than normal as she miraculously appeared by his side and looped her arm through his. She kept glancing over at Captain Walker, who, as usual, paid no attention to her.

"Whoopdidoo." Mimi twirled her finger through the air, gave me a look as though I'd lost my mind, and then wandered over to the open casket muttering, "Crazy dang fool," beneath her breath.

"Sorry," Harry said. "I met Hazel in town at the coffee shop today and offered to escort her here tonight. She looked like she could use a friendly ear."

"No problem. That's all I was trying to give Mimi, but I guess she's not ready for that. Maybe another time."

"If he's not busy," Hazel jumped in again. "Come along, Harry. I have someone I want to introduce you to, as well." She tugged him away and made a beeline for the far side of the room.

Straight in Captain Walker's direction.

"She broke the washer," Granny uttered indignantly. "Today is Tuesday. How am I supposed to do laundry?"

146

"You and your stupid schedule." Fiona rolled her eyes. The lights flickered, and her eyes grew wary as she said more to the room than to Granny, "It's not my fault your apron was all tangled up in there. Now I have nothing to wear because of you."

"After you shrunk the rest of my aprons, I can't blame this sucker for holding on tight and fighting for its life." Granny huffed out a breath, trying to tug an apron down that looked more like a bib. "What a waste of good material."

"What happened to your truce?" I asked, exhausted.

"She doesn't know how to bite her tongue *or* how to solve a case." Granny gave up on the apron, crossing her arms over her chest and refusing to look at Fiona.

"Me? First Einstein here comes up with the idea of the gardener and his hearty appetite stealing our baked goods. And now she thinks the car salesman purposely sold her a lemon just to get her into trouble. I tried to break it to her that her car is not the lemon. *She* is. She can't drive worth a hoot."

"I can drive just fine. My car has to be a lemon. Why, it hasn't worked right since the day I got it. And my idea is for darn sure better than yours. First you pick the butler,

147

when Trixie has no need for a butler of any sort. And now you say Gremlins did it. Just because you watched the movie with your grandkids doesn't mean it's true. Your brain is a lemon."

"I'll call someone to fix the washer," I said. "In the meantime try not to kill each other until Mom gets here. She needs to go over a few things regarding your case. I have a dress fitting with Jo."

Both their faces brightened into wistful smiles, as they chattered on about weddings and young love. I walked out the door, deciding they both had gone as cuckoo as the clock in my sanctuary.

Five minutes later, I pulled into the parking lot of Ursula's Boutique, a quaint little dress store in the shopping district. This was the type of place my mother shopped at. I, on the other hand, adored unique artsy and retro shops. Unfortunately, Jo was more like my mother in this regard, and it was her wedding, after all.

I took a deep, calming breath and pasted a smile on my face as I walked through the front door. The aroma of jasmine with a slight hint of starch and a smidgen of someone's perfume welcomed me.

Jo turned around and clapped her hands, looking like a teenager going to her first dance. "You made it," she squealed, hopping up and down and then giving me a bear hug. Her mass of curls was piled high on her head, and her face glowed with happiness.

"Barely. I love my house, but lately, I can't stand being home. My readings are on hold. There is no concentrating with the Dynamic Duo in residence."

"You poor thing," Zoe said, handing me a glass of iced tea with lemon. Her sleek strands of auburn hair were pulled back into a low bun, the freckles on her face standing out as she looked at me with sympathy.

"Well snap out of it. We have work to do." Jo grabbed a couple of dresses and stepped into the fitting room.

"Speaking of work, what's Sean up to?" I asked Zoe.

"I have no idea," she said nonchalantly while looking through the dress racks for bridesmaids' dresses. "Why ask me?"

"You really don't know?"

"Know what?" She looked at me curiously.

"Wow, I would have thought he would have succeeded by now. It never takes him this long."

"Succeeded at what?" Zoe looked completely baffled.

Jo stuck her head out from the fitting room. "In convincing you to go out with him."

Zoe blinked. "Me? Why on earth would he want to go out with me? I am definitely not his type, nor is he mine."

"Double wow," I muttered. "I've never met anyone who didn't fall under Sean's charm, myself included."

"Yes, he's charming. And yes, he's more handsome than a man has a right to be," Zoe said, and Jo and I eyed each other knowingly. "I'm just a one-man type of woman and not in the market for a playboy."

"Maybe you're just the woman to tame him," Jo said dreamily. "Love can be pretty miraculous. I never thought I'd speak to Cole again, let alone marry him, yet here I am shopping for a wedding dress."

"Touché." I laughed, raising my glass of tea to them both. "Cheers to believing that there's hope for us all." Even though I wanted to smack Mitch at the moment for not leveling with me.

We all clinked glasses and drank, then Jo disappeared back into the fitting room. I glanced outside the window and caught sight of Ophelia as she headed across the street toward Eddy's Gun Emporium.

"Pick me out a winner, Zoe," I said, head-

150

ing toward the door.

"Where on earth are you going?" she asked in a low voice, running after me. "Jo will kill us both if she comes out of that fitting room and finds you gone. You have no idea the kind of bridezilla women turn into after getting engaged."

"This is Jo we're talking about."

"Exactly," Zoe said. "Fiery, redheaded, hot-tempered Jo. Do you really want to mess with that?"

"Just cover for me." I glanced at the fitting room door. "I'll be back in a jiffy, I promise. I need to do something that can't wait." I bolted out the door and hurried across the street before Zoe could argue further.

"Ms. Edwards," I said, catching Ophelia before she could enter the gun shop. Lord knew what she would come out with.

"I collect throwing knives," she said as though reading my mind. "Since I'm stuck here, I thought I'd get in a little target practice." Her eyes narrowed on my face.

"Oh. That's interesting." I swallowed hard and tried to erase the image of my face as her target. "Do you mind if I ask you a couple more questions?"

"Yeah, I do mind." She leaned back and looked me over with indecision. "I heard you weren't helping the police with this case."

"That's true. I'm not helping . . . officially." I glanced up and down both sides of the street, but the coast was still clear. "Look, Ophelia. It's my granny we're talking about. I'm just trying to get to the bottom of what happened. That's all."

She studied me closely and then seemed to make up her mind about something. "Like I said before. I got no beef with your granny. It's Fiona I have a problem with. I'm not a killer. I might not have an alibi, but it doesn't matter. The police aren't going to find anything on me."

"Actually, they found your prints on Fiona's pie plate. The one that was in Granny's car when it ran over Bernadette."

Ophelia flinched. "They did?" She sat down heavily on a bench by a streetlamp. "I didn't think I'd get caught."

That's what they all say, I thought. I sat beside her and gave her a minute to absorb everything I'd just said before asking, "What exactly did you get caught at?"

"Like I said, I don't much care for Fiona. I can't stand her being so bossy and running everything. She ruined our vacation. That's why I was trying to ruin the carnival. I figured if it ended, then we could leave

152

and salvage what was left of our vacation."

"Quincy's knife?" I asked, floored. I hadn't seen that one coming.

She nodded guiltily. "There was no way I wanted her to win the bakeoff, too." Ophelia lifted her troubled eyes to mine. "I snuck into her hotel room before she left for Trixie's and sabotaged her pie."

"I heard about the laxatives. How on earth did you get them in there?"

"I'm a diabetic. I used one of my insulin syringes and filled it with liquid laxatives. Then I injected her pie. And that's all I did. I just wanted her to lose. I swear to you I never left the hotel that night, and I saw Fiona carry that pie herself. The rest of the Knitting Nanas can verify that."

"I believe you, but you don't exactly have proof that you didn't leave the hotel. The police might think you snuck into Trixie's while everyone was distracted, stole Granny's cookies and Fiona's pie, put them in the Grannymobile, and then ran over Bernadette."

"They might, or you might?" The distrust was back in her eyes.

"I'm just trying to cover all possible scenarios." I felt for Ophelia because I really did think she was innocent, but I wasn't about to let my granny take the fall.

Ophelia raised her chin defiantly, any fear she might have had completely erased. "Anyone at that party could have stolen the cookies and pie, stolen Granny's car, and run over Bernadette. They all wanted to win. I just wanted to get my vacation back. And while you're checking all angles, you might want to talk to the BB's Baked Goods staff."

"Why? I know people didn't like her much as a person, but I thought that people respected her as a businesswoman. And she'd just done so well at the auction."

"If she was such a great businesswoman, then why did she call a meeting the morning that she died and fire her entire staff?"

"How do you know that?"

"I was going in to buy some turnovers like I've done every day since I've been in town, but the doors were locked. Some sort of meeting was going on, so I went next door to Sam's. When the meeting was done, a staff member rushed out in tears and came into Sam's, looking for a job. When a second employee stormed into Sam's, almost knocking me down, I'd had enough. I demanded to know what was going on. That's when they told me."

Why indeed, I thought, my mind already spinning with my next move.

"Sunshine Eleanor Meadows, get your scrawny behind back in here this instant," Joanne bellowed from across the street.

I spun around and gave her a sheepish grin, but the expression on her face said she was way beyond forgiveness. She was in full-blown bridezilla mode, and I was so getting the most hideous bridesmaid's gown of all.

9

"She likes you, you know," I said to Sean Tuesday evening as we parked on the street in front of BB's Baked Goods.

Storm clouds had rolled in, promising the threat of rain. The washing machine was fixed, and my parents had the Dynamic Duo in hand . . . which meant a free evening for me. I hadn't heard a word from Mitch, but after all I'd found out, that didn't surprise me.

He was up to something.

Jo was working, and Sean had the night off. Not that I would have asked Jo to go with me to question Bernadette's staff. Jo hadn't quite come out of bridezilla mode, and I wasn't taking any chances. The dress she'd picked for me? So not pretty. I had decided to wait until she was in a better mood, and then beg her to have pity on me.

"Who likes me?" Sean perked up and stared at me with the most serious, intense gaze he'd ever given me.

"Wow." I laughed, having almost forgotten what I'd said. "You've got it bad."

He lowered his eyelids defensively over his baby blues, his dimples disappearing from sight. "What are you talking about?" He shoved a hand through his blond hair.

"I'm just in shock. I can't believe a woman has finally gotten to you."

"I still don't know who you are talking about." He stepped out of my bug and closed the door behind him, pacing in front of its rounded hood and headlight eyes.

I hurried after him and locked the car behind me. "Yeah right. You are so smitten with Zoe Burnham, you don't have a clue what to do with yourself. I just never thought I'd see the day, that's all."

He turned around to face me, with hands on hips, and shook his blond head with a half smile. Even when Sean was frustrated, he was still adorable. "You're crazy, lass."

"Remember my reading?" I wagged my brows, shaking my own blond spiky hair. "I think not."

"Doesn't matter." His face fell, and his shoulders drooped a bit. "When she looks at me at all, she looks as though I'm about as appealing as gum on the bottom of her shoe."

"That's because you're going about it all wrong." I grabbed his hand and squeezed. "Don't try to feed her the same pick-up lines you feed all the bimbos you meet."

He straightened, and his shoulders stiffened. "Zoe is hardly a bimbo."

"That's my point." I dropped my hand. "Look, you help me tonight, and I will help you in return."

"I'm listening." He looked skeptical.

"By the end of summer, I will get Zoe to agree to be your date to Jo's wedding. All you have to do is help me solve Bernadette Baldwin's murder. Deal?"

"Deal." And just like that, his dimples were back.

"Let's go, Romeo. I have a craving for turnovers."

"I thought you'd never ask." He followed right behind me, but we both stopped short.

"BB's is closed," I said. There was no police tape since this wasn't the scene of the crime. Just a closed sign taped inside the front door with the lights turned off.

"Huh. Maybe it's closed because of Bernadette's death," Sean reasoned.

"Or maybe because she fired all her staff, and there's no one left to run it."

"Wait, what?" He looked as stunned as I'd felt when I heard it. "Why in the world would she do that?"

"That's the million-dollar question. She made it seem like she was doing well, but Ophelia Edwards said that when she went for her morning pastry, the doors were locked and some sort of meeting was going on inside. She said she went next door to Sam's instead, and when the meeting ended, some of Bernadette's staff came into Sam's, looking for a job. Belle said she saw the same thing."

"Maybe we should talk to Sam then," Sean said.

"It couldn't hurt, I suppose." We headed next door into Sam's Bakery. The place was packed. The widow Ida and Mimi were there, as well as Quincy, Harry, Hazel, and even Ophelia.

"Evening, folks. What can I do for you?" Sam asked when it was finally our turn at the counter.

"Actually, I was wondering, could I have a word with your employee, Zach Ewing?" I asked, smiling at Zach, who suddenly looked very uncomfortable at the sound of his name.

Sam looked at me, and then Sean, and then back to me. "Sure." He turned and faced Zach. "I've got it. Take your break now. Be back in ten."

Zach didn't look pleased, but he nodded his consent, peeled off his apron, and then joined us out front. We led the way outside to one of the patio chairs where it was less crowded.

"Hi, Zach. I'm Sunny M—"

"I know who you are. What do you want with me?" He ran his wrinkled hand over his gleaming bald head and eyed me warily.

"Well, I was wondering if you could help explain what happened at BB's Baked Goods?" I asked. "Why is it closed down, and why on earth did she fire all of her staff?"

"Don't know." He shrugged. "For a while there, we all thought she was hurting for money. But then business started to pick up, and everything was great. Then, whammy, out of the blue she ups and fires us all. It don't make a lick of sense. I just thank my lucky stars that Sam gave me a job. Others got a job at the café, but not everyone came out so lucky."

"And you have no idea what happened to make Bernadette suddenly have a money crisis?" Sean asked.

"Not a clue. Like I said, I could see if the business was doing poorly, but it wasn't. Business had picked up, and Bernadette seemed to have money to spare. I don't know what the heck happened. All I can say is she made a lot of people very angry."

"Angry enough to kill her?" I asked.

"Anything's possible." He suddenly seemed to realize how his words sounded, and he held up his hands. "I was home all night, complaining to my wife. Just ask her."

"We will," Sean said firmly, tossing me a wink, which I took to mean he was the bad cop. "And while you're sharing information, care to share a list of all her employees?"

"Wait a minute," Zach said and narrowed his eyes. "Didn't I hear that you weren't supposed to be working on this case?"

Darn small town!

"And what's up with him?" Zach jerked his head at Sean. "He doesn't have anything to do with the police at all, so why's he here with you asking me questions he has no right to?"

"Never mind. I'm sure we can find it," I said in full good-cop mode. "I think your ten minutes are up, but thanks for your help. Shouldn't you be getting back to work?"

He gave me a dirty look and walked off, mumbling, "Damn waste of a break."

"Now what?" Sean asked.

"Now, we wait."

"For what?"

"For everyone to leave so we can snoop around BB's. There has to be a reason she fired everyone, and I'm not going home until I find it."

Sean blew out a breath. "Zoe better be worth all this. That's all I can say."

"Oh, please." I shoved him. "You'd help me either way just for the sheer adventure of it."

"Probably," he admitted, lightly shoving me back.

We climbed into my bug to drive around back and down the street to wait for night-fall. I'd learned my lesson about hiding my car. It did tend to stick out, and the last thing I needed was one ornery detective figuring out what I was up to.

A while later, once it was fully dark outside, we crept out of my car and snuck around the back of BB's Baked Goods.

"It's time," I said.

"For what? A little B and E?" Sean rubbed his hands together, looking a little too excited about the prospect.

"No. I don't want to get into any more trouble than I have to this time around." I gave him a devilish grin. "I have something else in mind."

He looked at me with dread. "Like what?"

"Dumpster diving."

"Are you serious?" The shocked and disgusted look on his face was priceless.

"As serious as Father Moody in church on Sunday." I bit back a laugh as Sean made the sign of the cross. "Don't be such a wimp."

"If there are any rats in there, you're gonna pay, lass." He leaned forward and added, "Dearly."

"Yeah, yeah." I patted his chest. "We're wasting time, Romeo." I crept forward and peeked over the side of the full, smelly Dumpster. Wrinkling my nose, I batted my lashes at Sean and said, "After you, my hero."

"Oh, no. Me poor mother would skin me hide if I wasn't a gentleman." He purposely laid on a thick Irish accent as he stepped aside and gallantly swept his hand in front of him. "Ladies first."

"I was afraid you'd say that." I pulled a pair of latex gloves from my purse and set it on the ground just as a boom of thunder rumbled overhead.

Sean raised a blond brow at me.

"What can I say, my dad's a doctor. I grew up around these things. I've suddenly found a great use for them. They come in handy on certain undercover assignments."

I slipped on the gloves and huffed out a breath as I climbed to the top of the Dumpster, rethinking my decision for a second, but then raising my chin in determination. "This one's for you, Granny," I muttered and then plugged my nose as I jumped in feet first. Thank goodness I'd thought to wear sneakers instead of sandals.

"You're crazy, love." Sean started laughing from the top of the Dumpster. "I can't believe you actually did it."

"Ewwww, it's so nasty in here." I tried to pull my sneakers free of the muck with no success. "It was in the eighties today. Do you *know* what that does to garbage?" I gagged and tried not to breathe through my nose.

"I work in a restaurant, darlin'. My mama might have raised a gentleman, but she didn't raise no fool. That's why I'm up here, and you're down there."

"What does that mean?" I narrowed my eyes. "You're supposed to be helping me."

"I am. I'm your lookout." He winked. "Besides, someone has to watch your purse."

My jaw fell open as I gave an outraged gasp.

"Better close your mouth, love. Wouldn't want any bugs flying in." He overexaggerated his shudder.

"You look inside my purse, you're a dead man." I pointed my finger at him, praying I didn't have anything embarrassing in there.

He held a hand over his heart. "You wound me. I would never think of doing such a thing."

"Next thing we do, you're going first. End of discussion. Period. Amen."

He had the nerve to laugh again. "Deal."

"Gee, where did I hear that before?" I grumbled.

"What was it you said? Oh, yeah. We're wasting time. Better hurry, there, Sunshine. It's about to downpour. I'll whistle if anyone is coming." He disappeared before I could argue further.

Having no choice and already ankle deep in garbage, I started wading my way through trash bags. Most bags were filled with baked goods and plates and utensils and napkins. Your average, everyday bakeshop paraphernalia. I was covered in all kinds of icky sticky debris and getting worried I wouldn't find anything useful.

I tripped over another pile of garbage and fell face-first onto a small trash bag. Thank God this one was only full of paper. I sat back and ripped the bag open. Tons of shredded documents. I sifted through the whole thing, and had just about given up, when I found a partially shredded note. I carefully pulled what was left of it out and read it.

I know what you're doing. You're a fraud. Do what I say, or I'll tell everybody and you will be ruined.

Holy cow. Someone had been blackmailing Bernadette. What was she doing? What did the blackmailer want from her? This could be a note from the killer. It was creepy. The letters were cut out glued onto plain white copy paper like a serial killer might do.

I carefully folded what was left of the note and slipped it into my shorts' pocket just in time. A flash of lightning lit up the black sky. Sean started whistling, and I scrambled to my feet the best I could, given that they were buried under mounds of muck.

"Evening, Sean." The unmistakable deep timber of Detective Stone's voice rang out loud and clear.

I froze. As carefully as I could, I leaned forward until I could peek out a crack in the corner of the Dumpster. Sean stood nonchalantly, wearing tan golf shorts, a polo shirt, and my fringed purse over his shoulder. While Mitch wore jeans with a T-shirt tucked in and a shoulder holster with his gun slung diagonally across his wide muscular chest.

On duty and working as always.

"Evening yourself, Detective. And a fine one it is, don't you think?" Sean pasted on an unnatural smile that looked way too bright. We'd have to work on his game face if he was going to be my partner in crime, so to speak.

"You wouldn't happen to know where Sunny is, would you? She hasn't answered her phone, and I was getting worried."

He had some nerve. He hadn't told me where he was going, and he hadn't bothered to check in all day. Not that we were an official item yet, and our one and only date had ended before it even got started, but still. We were supposed to be trying.

"Sorry, man." Sean shrugged. "I haven't seen her around."

"Really?" Mitch let his gaze run over Sean from head to toe before adding, "Then why are you holding her purse?"

"Oh, that." Sean laughed as though he'd forgotten he even had it slung over his shoulder. "Well, actually, I saw her earlier at Sam's. I was picking up bread for Smokey Jo's, and Sunny came along for the ride. Granny and Fiona are driving her a bit crazy. She needed a break."

Mitch's eyes narrowed slightly. "That still doesn't explain why you're holding her purse."

"She left it at Sam's. I was looking for her so I could return it."

"Out back of BB's Baked Goods?"

"She wasn't out front, so I decided to check all over. You know how funny Sunny is sometimes. No telling how that mind of hers works." Sean fidgeted with the fringe on my knapsack, looking ridiculous.

"Right," Mitch said, his gaze dropping to Sean's hands. "Where's the bread for Jo?"

"She called and said never mind," Sean said without missing a beat. He was getting better at improvising and had even stopped moving his hands. He stood a little straighter and shoved his hands in his pockets. "She found a bunch of bread in the back storage closet, but forgot. Women." He shook his head. "Must be wedding jitters has scrambled her brain."

"Hmmm. Must be." Mitch glanced around, his gaze settling on the Dumpster, and I held my breath. He finally looked back at Sean. "Where's your car?"

"Sunny drove."

Mitch's eyebrows disappeared into his hairline. "And she just left you here?"

"Like I said, she's a funny girl. Maybe

something came up with her granny. Who knows? All I know is I went to the bathroom, and when I came out, she was gone. Had to be something urgent for her to forget her purse."

"Must be." There was a silent pause between them, and then Mitch finally said, "Come on. I'll give you a ride home, and I can return Sunny's purse to her when I stop by her place. I was on my way there when I saw you standing out back of BB's as I drove by Sam's."

"Oh, that's okay. I can walk." Sean shifted his weight from side to side.

"You live clear across town. Don't be ridiculous. I insist."

"Well, if you insist, then I guess I have no choice," he said louder than necessary, and Mitch gave him a funny look. "Lead the way, Detective," Sean quickly added.

I wilted in relief at the sound of their retreating footsteps, followed by a groan of despair as I realized my keys were in my purse, which Mitch now had. Then another realization hit me hard.

I looked up. It was a heck of a lot easier to dive into a Dumpster than to try to climb back out. It would take a miracle for me to pull myself out. It would take an even bigger miracle for me to explain my way out of this one to Mitch.

With that thought, I bowed my head and prayed, promising to get to church more often. And the heavens chose that moment to open up and drench me good. It was either God blessing me or attempting to wash away my sins.

I was betting on the latter.

10

An hour later, after building a trash ladder as high as I could, I still couldn't climb out of the Dumpster. Everything on me was slimy, and the bags were wet. Even if I did manage to get out, my phone was in my purse. My keys were in my purse. My purse was with Detective Grumpy Pants.

My nerves were shot.

The rain started coming down harder now. I sat back and pressed my lips together tightly, trying not to cry. I had nothing left in me. What a stupid idea this had been.

"You had enough yet, Tink?" said a deep, rumbly voice from somewhere outside the Dumpster walls.

I blinked. Was I hallucinating? His voice was music to my ears. As much as I knew he'd be angry with me, I couldn't stop from wilting in relief. "Mitch?" I called out in a shaky, exhausted voice.

Within moments, his big dark head appeared over the edge of the Dumpster. An inky black eyebrow crept up ever so slightly. "Do I even want to know the story?"

"Probably not." I looked at him sheepishly. "I should have known nothing gets by you."

"You should be grateful it doesn't."

"I am, but why did you wait an hour?"

"To give you time to think about your actions." He reached out his large hands. "You ready to go home?"

I nodded past the lump in my throat and reached out to grab his wrists as he locked onto mine. He hoisted me up without much effort and lifted me over the edge. When my feet hit the ground, he stood there for a minute, just holding me.

"I'm sorry. Now you're a mess, too." I couldn't stop tears of exhaustion and relief from slipping out and rolling down my cheeks as I wrapped my arms tighter around his thick neck.

He shrugged, his own eyes softening a bit as he tightened his hold on me. "Life's messy, Tink. I'll live. But now we both need a shower."

Our eyes met and held. Was he thinking what I was thinking? After all that had happened, I was almost ready to cave. Almost ready to break the rules and forget having dinner first. Almost ready to throw the love diet in the Dumpster with the rest of the crap.

"Don't worry. Dessert's the last thing on my mind. You stink."

I laughed. "Is my face really that readable?"

"Pretty much." His lips quirked, and he carried me as we headed toward his car.

"I can walk, you know."

"I know." He continued to carry me until we reached the road. "Your car's at my place along with your purse. You can shower there if you want."

"Wait. How did you find my car?"

"It's my job, Sunny. I knew something wasn't right. Sean only gave me your purse, but he wouldn't say a word about you. I circled back and found your car. One of my officers met me and followed me home, and then I came back for you."

"How'd you know I was in here?"

"Call it a hunch."

"Oh, well, thanks." I lowered my head as he set me on my feet. "I thought you'd be furious with me."

"Who says I'm not?" My eyes snapped up to see his face turn serious. "We'll get to that soon enough. I just figured you needed a bit of a break first."

173

"Oh." I didn't know what to say, and I was admittedly nervous about exactly what *we'll get to that soon enough* meant, but also irritated because I had some things I wanted to *get to* as well. Like why he hadn't kept me in the loop like he'd promised. "Thanks . . . I think."

He unlocked the car, reached inside, and then handed me a towel. He walked around the car, grabbed his own towel, and then climbed in the driver's side without another word. I slid into the other side, and neither one of us spoke again until we reached his apartment.

A half hour later, I was squeaky clean and wearing a pair of his cotton shorts and one of his soft-spun T-shirts. I'd had to roll the elastic waistband on his shorts several times and tie a knot in the bottom of his T-shirt to make them semi-fit. But I had to admit I felt comfy and cozy and safe wearing his clothes. They felt right. *We* felt right.

Even though I still wanted to smack him most of the time.

When I walked out of his bathroom, his gaze locked on me. It took him a minute before he could speak, then he cleared his throat and said, "You look cute. Now, *I* need a shower, and a cold one at that, dammit. Help yourself to anything."

He disappeared before I could say a word, but that didn't stop me from grinning like a fool. Served him right for all he was putting me through lately by not trusting me to help in my granny's case. I suddenly realized he was in the shower, and he'd invited me into his apartment.

Where he kept his notes on the case.

No breaking and entering needed. I didn't want to snoop, and I would *never* pry into his personal business, but the case was a different matter. He still wasn't sharing information, and Granny was still in jeopardy. I would do whatever I had to in order to help clear her name.

I hurried to the little table by the front door. His gun, badge, and notebook were there by his keys. I quickly flipped through the pages. He had notes on the Parks and Rec Program and the Animal Angels Organization, but nothing I didn't already know.

The water shut off in the bathroom, so I knew he was almost finished. I darted into his bedroom. He had a small desk in there with all sorts of papers scattered about. I carefully rifled through them, looking for something . . . anything.

I saw a copy of the original note that Bernadette wrote to the captain that said she hoped he would choose her because she deserved to win, and that she thought Granny and Fiona wanted to kill her. Lying beneath it was a copy of a second note I didn't know anything about.

A handwritten one that someone must have given to her that said for her to back off from the captain or else. Was this note from the same blackmailer who had written the serial killer–type note I'd found in the Dumpster, or had someone else been threatening Bernadette as well?

I quickly fired up Mitch's printer/photocopier, praying he wouldn't hear me, and made a copy of all three notes: Bernadette's note to the captain, the blackmail note I'd found in the Dumpster, and the handwritten threatening note that Mitch had. I had just turned off the printer, folded up the notes, and stuffed them in my bag of dirty clothes by the front door when Mitch came out of the bathroom.

"What are you doing?" he asked from behind me, and I tried not to jump.

Swallowing hard and willing my heart to slow to a normal beat, I took a leap of faith and hoped he would do the same. I pulled out the blackmail note I'd found in the Dumpster — knowing full well I had a copy in my bag — with the rubber gloves I still had in there and turned around to face him.

"I'm coming clean with you." *Sort of.*

He gave me a skeptical look. "Really? I can't wait to hear this one."

I raised my chin a notch. "Well, if you must know, Sean and I went to the bakery to get bread for Jo."

"So he told me. Go on." Mitch crossed his muscular arms over his NYPD T-shirt and basketball shorts.

"Sean had to use the restroom, and Sam's was so busy, I decided to move my car. I didn't want to take up space out front for other customers. So I moved it around back, and that's when I heard the kitty."

"Excuse me?" He looked at me as though I'd lost my mind.

"I know I heard a poor little kitty in the Dumpster. So I took my spare rubber gloves out of my car, because I left my purse in Sam's, and I tried to find the poor kitty and I slipped and fell overboard, smack-dab into the Dumpster."

"Uh-huh. Then why didn't you speak up when Sean and I were outside talking?"

"Because I knew you wouldn't believe me, and you would think I was purposely interfering with this case, which I'm not." I crossed my fingers behind my back, and pointed out in an accusatory tone, "Even though you promised to share any information with me, which you haven't."

"Sunny, you of all people should know there are certain things I'm not at liberty to discuss while the investigation is ongoing."

"Oh, don't give me that." Anger surged through me. After all we'd been through together with past investigations. "We both know there are ways around that. This is my grandmother we're talking about."

"Exactly. And you are way too close to her to be objective about anything. I don't want you influencing what I think, either. Let me draw my own objective conclusions based on the facts." He leaned forward and stared me down. "Let me do my job, Tink."

"Fine, Grumpy Pants. You're all on your own." I gave him a pointed look. "In every way imaginable."

"Mind telling me what you have there?" He ignored my comment and pointed to my hands.

"By all means. I wouldn't want to interfere with justice being served or influence you in any way with my thoughts. I stumbled across this piece of evidence, and now I'm turning it over to the police. Do your job, Detective. I'm going home."

"Sunny, don't be like that. I —"

"Need to get to work. I get it." I grabbed my bag of dirty clothes and my purse and left without another word.

Five minutes later, I pulled into my driveway to find the fire department, the ambulance, and the police there. Just what I needed after the day I'd had. My anger vanished and worry set in.

I rushed over to Captain Walker. "Oh my gosh. What happened? Is everyone okay?"

The captain eyed my attire, but he didn't say a word about it. Instead, he said, "They are rescuing Fiona as we speak," and then he looked up in the tree.

I followed his gaze and couldn't believe my eyes. Fiona was suspended twenty feet in the air, clinging to a tree branch with her pink pedal-pusher pants glowing like a beacon in the spotlight. The fire department reached her with their ladder basket, and a big strapping firefighter reached out and grabbed her in his big strong arms. It probably made her night.

More like her decade.

She swooned against him in a dramatic fashion, while Granny tapped her ankle-bracelet-clad foot rapidly on the ground. I walked over to Granny, who also eyed my attire and opened her mouth, more than ready to question me about it.

In no mood to be distracted, I snapped, "I swear I can't leave you two alone for a minute. What the heck is she doing up there?"

"A minute? Ha! You've been gone all day."

At least she's forgotten about my clothes, I thought.

"Your mother only stayed for a while today before she couldn't take any more of that numbskull over yonder. I guess Fiona got bored. She said she saw Morty climb the tree, and she was afraid he would get stuck. I tried to tell her Morty can take care of himself, but she wouldn't listen."

"How on earth did she get up there so high? She could have fallen and broken a hip or worse."

"Silly fool used the ladder from the garage and climbed the tree, but then the ladder fell over. I think she kicked it. I offered to put it back up, but she said she was scared to death of breaking her neck. She said to call 911 before she fainted. That woman will do anything for attention. She knew you'd get mad if she set off her ankle bracelet. Guess she found a way around that."

Granny pouted as Fiona reached the ground, and the captain walked over to make sure she was okay and comfort her. I suspected Granny was more upset over not being the one to have thought of the crazy stunt. Then a determined look crossed her face and she limped over to join them, saying the ladder fell on her foot and her bracelet was chafing her ankle.

I, on the other hand, threw up my hands at the lot of them and wearily made my way inside. I had bigger things to worry about, like figuring out who sent the threatening note and who on earth had been blackmailing Bernadette.

"Awww, look at him. I just want to reach out and give him a big ole hug," Jo said as we leaned over a pen in the Animal Angels facility on Wednesday morning.

A one-year-old Great Dane stood shivering in the back of his pen, eyeing us with unmistakable terror in his eyes. He was enormous already but had obviously been mistreated. He had the short, smooth coat of a soft and creamy fawn, with black pointy high-set ears and a large black muzzle.

He kind of reminded me of Cole with his dark buzz cut and five o'clock shadow. They were both great in size, heart, and nobility, always dependable and even-tempered. The Apollo of dogs with his handsome outline and aristocratic bearing. He would make a great pet for them, as Great Danes made excellent watchdogs, with their large size and deep bark that would scare most people.

And they were good with children.

"Your heart can't help but go out to these animals," I responded, my heart melting. Morty would never allow a dog in the house, but Jo and Cole were looking to adopt one. I smiled, knowing Jo. It was her way of testing herself as a parent before she added a baby to the mix.

I had to hand it to Ozzie Zuckerman. He was new in town and had just started his animal rescue operation. He said he planned to take in all sorts of animals that had been abused and find loving homes for them. Glancing around, all I saw were dogs. He said they were the easiest to start with, but he hoped the charity money would help him grow his business.

Ozzie wasn't here at the moment. In fact, each time I had dropped by, he was never available. His assistant, Yvonne Lennox, pretty much handled the day-to-day operations. She walked over to us and smiled, her wide-set brown eyes full of kindness. She looked to be somewhere in her twenties.

Yvonne brushed her chestnut hair over her shoulders. "Hi again, Miss Meadows. Anything I can help you with today?"

"Actually, yes. I brought my friend Joanne Burnham with me. She and her fiancé are looking to adopt one of your dogs."

"That's wonderful," she said and shook Jo's hand.

"I really like this big guy right here. I'll have to bring my fiancé Cole back with me first before I decide for sure, but I have a few questions."

"Absolutely. Fire away."

"He looks pretty scared. I was wondering if we could talk to some of the other people who have adopted from you. I'd love to hear what works best in caring for these animals. If there's something we should be aware of right up front."

"Well, I just started working for Mr. Zuckerman. I'm going to college to be a veterinarian and am actually interning for Dr. Sherry Parker, but I couldn't resist volunteering my time here for such a good cause. We actually take the animals to see her first to be treated. That's how I found out about this place."

"I know Sherry quite well. She's given me lots of advice regarding Morty, even though he's never actually allowed her to examine him. She's even made house calls."

"Dr. Parker is fantastic. If I turn out to be half the vet she is, then I'll be a happy woman. Anyway, Mr. Zuckerman is very busy trying to find suitable homes for these animals, so he's not around much. I'm finding he's very picky about who he adopts them out to, probably because of the nature of their situations. He's turned down several people in town, which I think is a bit extreme, but he's had a couple people from out of town interested in adopting the dogs. I'll see if he can arrange for you to meet with one of those people. Maybe they've dealt with abused animals before."

"That would be perfect. And please, put in a good word for us. Being cautious is one thing, but isn't the point to find these poor animals good homes? I know plenty of people in town who are looking for pets and fit the criteria to be wonderful pet parents."

"I agree. And you have my word that I'll do everything I can to get him to say yes to you." Yvonne winked.

"Thanks, Yvonne." I waved good-bye as she walked away, then I said to Jo, "I have a couple questions I need to ask Sherry about Morty. Want to pick her brain about this big fellow here?"

"You read my mind. I mean, what's up with not adopting to people in town? That's just weird."

"Now you're reading *my* mind." I studied the Great Dane carefully. "Something's definitely up with that, and I aim to find out what."

■ ■ ■ ■

"I know Morty is finicky, but this feels different. Like something is really bothering him," I said to Dr. Parker. "He keeps dropping things at my feet, tearing up pages in the newspaper, and just plain acting ornery.

"I'd say bring him in, but we both know how that goes." She laughed, tucking her blond shoulder-length hair behind her ears and then shoving her hands into her lab coat. "He probably doesn't like his home in upheaval with both Granny and Fiona staying there and bickering constantly. I think everyone's schedules are probably off."

"You're right about that. And I admit even I have been in a foul mood lately." Between the Dynamic Duo and my squabbling with Mitch, but she didn't need to know that part.

"And as for you, Ms. Burnham, first of all congratulations are in order, I hear," Sherry said to Jo.

"That's right." Jo beamed, blushing slightly. "I've decided to let Cole make an honest woman out of me. And thank you."

"You're welcome. How can I help you?"

"Well, I am looking into adopting one of the dogs from Animal Angels. He's about

185

one year old and is a big, beautiful fawn-and-black Great Dane."

"I know exactly what dog you're talking about. And you're right, he is a beauty. He's big already, but just wait until his body catches up with the size of his paws. He's going to be massive."

"Jo likes her guys big," I said, and Jo just wagged her brows, not disagreeing with me in the least.

"What's his story?" Jo asked.

"Well, they found him neglected and chained outside. He was a bit malnourished, but otherwise, he looked pretty good. He didn't appear to have been physically abused, just mostly forgotten about. He's not used to people, but he's not mean. I do think he'll come around with the right family. Lots of love, time, and patience is all he needs, I suspect."

"Between Cole and myself, we fit the bill perfectly. Now if we could only pin down Ozzie Zuckerman and get him to say yes. Do you know he hasn't adopted any of his dogs to a single family in town?"

"That's what Yvonne said. Seems a bit odd to me. The other day he brought in some new dogs he'd rescued. One really mean one who'd been badly abused. I had to muzzle him just to treat him. I told Mr.

Zuckerman it would take a lot of rehabilitation to ever get that dog ready for someone to adopt."

"Wow, that's terrible," I said. "I can't imagine anyone who would treat an animal that way."

"Me either, but Zuckerman barely listened and didn't give off any warm and fuzzy vibes. Then he got a phone call and stepped outside, but that didn't stop me from hearing his raised voice. He'd definitely had some kind of argument and barely remembered to take the dogs when he left. He seemed worried and upset, but I didn't ask him about it. He didn't exactly seem in the mood to talk about it, and quite frankly, I was ready for him to leave."

"Thank you so much for the information, Dr. Parker," Jo said. "Yvonne is going to talk to him about me meeting up with one of his out-of-town adoptive parent prospects. I'll keep you posted. One way or another, Bigfoot will be mine."

"Oh, good Lord, she's already named him." I had to laugh. I had nicknamed Cole Sasquatch, and now she was naming her dog Bigfoot. What did that make her, Xena the Warrior Princess? I'd always known she was a voluptuous Amazon woman at heart. Their poor kids didn't stand a chance in the name department.

"Good luck to you," Sherry said.

"Oh, I don't need luck," Jo said with a look in her eye I knew all too well. "I just need a plan."

11

Wednesday nights were quiet at Smokey Jo's, so Sean covered the restaurant while Jo, Zoe, and I had a spa getaway at the Divinity Hotel. I'd suggested it because I knew how stressed Jo was about her wedding.

I also knew Ophelia was a spa addict.

I'd never had a massage, but I figured it was a good way to stay on the right side of Bridezilla since it was right up Jo's alley. Not to mention it might shed more light on Granny's case. Jo had agreed and scheduled dance lessons at the Song Bird when we were done.

In the past, she'd never set foot in the Song Bird because it was her competition. But she really just resented the fact that Cole chose to visit the karaoke bar instead of her place. He mostly did that because the locals hung out at Smokey Jo's and outsiders hung out at the Song Bird. After the accident and his wife's death, he hadn't been able to face the locals, but Jo had helped him through that. And now he was helping her to spread her wings and try new things.

Like dancing and karaoke.

Jo and Zoe were already in other spa rooms, and I requested the woman who'd worked on Ophelia the day after Bernadette's death. I sat on the massage table in nothing but a towel, waiting and feeling a bit vulnerable. A big, burly woman with a nametag that said BETSY finally entered.

"I'm Betsy." She shook my hand, and I tried not to wince at her extra-firm grip. "I heard you requested me. What can I do for you?"

"I was talking to a guest at the hotel named Ophelia Edwards. She said you worked on her not long ago, and she raved about your skills."

Betsy grunted. "I remember her, all right. That one and her friends, the Naughty Nanas, were something else. Biggest slobs I've ever seen."

"Really? How so?"

"My friend, Darla, had the displeasure of having to clean their rooms. Poor woman had to work overtime just to get them all done."

"Did she have any help?"

"Nope. It was just her the whole time they were here. I gave her a massage for free that week. You should have seen the knots in her back. Anyway, enough about that. Talking about those women gets me all fired up, and that's not the right mind-set to be in when giving a massage." She took a deep calming breath, and I swallowed hard. "What kind of massage would you like?"

"I'd like to purchase the same package Ophelia had," I said tentatively, testing the waters with just her name. I needed more information on her, but it didn't sound like I'd be getting any more from Betsy.

"You're sure?" She eyed me skeptically. "You're just a bitty thing."

"Absolutely." Ophelia was practically my grandmother's age, and a hippie flower child to boot. How bad could it be? And when I was done, I'd pay a little visit to Darla. Maids knew secrets people could only imagine. Hopefully, I'd learn more from her.

"Okay, then." Betsy cracked her knuckles. "Lie down on your stomach, and we'll get started."

I did as she suggested and was surprised at how comfortable the massage table was. She dimmed the lights and put on soft soothing classical music in the background

191

and even lit some aromatherapy candles. This wasn't so bad. It was actually kind of nice. I could see why people became hooked.

Betsy poured some warm scented oil on my back and began to rub me down. I moaned in pleasure . . . but it didn't take long before my moans turned to groans of agony.

I tried to lift my head to protest, but Betsy shoved me down and worked my muscles harder. "No talking," she snapped. "It messes with my mojo."

After an hour of agony, when I was positive I couldn't take any more, she rolled me over. I nearly cried out in relief, and I started to sit up.

"Oh, no, honey, this works better if you lie down."

"What works better?"

"The rest of your package."

"You mean there's more?" I squeaked.

She lifted a pot of steaming hot wax in response, and I nearly fainted with a whimper. I closed my eyes in dread. Lord only knew what I had gotten myself into.

"That was the best idea ever, Sunny," Jo said later that night as she sat next to Zoe at the bar in the Song Bird, waiting for our dance lessons to begin. We all wore pretty sundresses and sandals that showed off the pedicures we'd gotten.

The Song Bird was a Japanese karaoke bar on the edge of town. It was filled with eclectic out-of-town people with bizarre tastes in music, strange clothes, and *different* food. The stools were barely big enough to fit beneath our bottoms, but Cole loved it there. And Jo didn't want any of the locals seeing us learn to dance.

"Yeah. Great idea." I hobbled over, bow-legged, and gingerly took the stool on the other side of her. "You weren't the one who had to endure a deep-tissue massage. I'll be sore for a week. And who knew Ophelia was into Brazilian waxes. How am I supposed to dance when I walk like I've been riding a horse all day?"

"Why on earth would you say *I'll have what she had* when you had no idea what that was?" Jo snickered.

"Look at the bright side," Zoe said. "At least it's bathing suit season. You won't have to shave all summer." She and Jo couldn't stop giggling.

"Very funny. *Not!* Call me old-fashioned, but I'm thinking if we were meant to look like this, we would have been born this way. All I can say is *never* again. And to top it all off, I endured that torture for nothing." I groaned as I shifted uncomfortably.

"I ran into Darla the maid," I continued. "Turns out Ophelia has an alibi after all. Poor Darla was on the floor, cleaning up after the Nanas all night long the night Bernadette died. She said Ophelia only came out of her room long enough to get more snacks and drinks from the vending machines."

"What does that mean in regards to the case?" Jo asked after ordering us all beers in wavy multicolored draft glasses.

Normally, I wouldn't discuss a case with others not involved with the investigation. But since I wasn't officially on the case, and Mitch sure wasn't talking, I needed someone to run my thoughts by. Besides, I trusted these two completely.

"It means we have one less suspect." I took a sip and then sighed, in Heaven. Until my niggling doubts crept back in. "I hate to admit it, I'm starting to get worried."

"What does Mitch think?" Jo asked.

"I wouldn't know," I grumbled. "He won't share anything with me." I waved my hands in the air. "He says he doesn't want me to influence his objectivity."

"He does have a point," Zoe stated gently. "It *is* your grandmother who is being accused of murder, after all."

"I know, but come on. As much as I want to clear her name, I'm not going to accuse some innocent person just to set her free."

"What can we do to help?" Zoe asked.

"Exactly what you're doing right now. Listening."

"Do you have anyone else you're looking into?" Jo asked.

"The murder happened somewhere between seven and eight P.M. Most everyone had left Trixie's by seven, so a lot of people had opportunity. I've been trying to think of who might have had motive. Ophelia hated Fiona and wanted to be president of the Knitting Nanas, so at first I thought maybe she set her up."

"How so?" Jo asked.

"She was the one sabotaging the carnival, and then her prints were on Fiona's lemon meringue pie plate that was in Granny's car at the time of the accident. And she's a diabetic so she used one of her syringes to inject laxatives into the pie right before the Nanas left for Trixie's, hoping to ruin Fiona's chances of winning the bakeoff, but that's all. Now that the maid can confirm Ophelia never left the hotel, then that means she was telling the truth, and she's no longer a suspect."

"Do you have any other leads?" Zoe asked and then sipped her beer.

"Well, there is Hazel."

"The Sewing Sister who was in charge of the auction?" Jo asked, looking surprised.

"One and the same," I responded. "She wasn't happy when Granny got mad over her letting Fiona enter the Nanas' quilt. It's also so obvious that she's sweet on Captain Walker, but he never seems to notice she's alive. Maybe she killed Bernadette and framed Granny and Fiona so she could win the bakeoff with her cake, and then Captain Walker would be forced to notice her."

"I don't know," Jo speculated. "If she's so sweet on Captain Walker, then why is she constantly with that new guy, Harry, all the time these days?"

"Good point. But then if that's the case, I don't have much else to go on."

"What about Quincy Turner?" Jo asked. "He sure wasn't happy when Granny got the carnival committee to switch charities to the Animal Angels Organization instead of his Parks and Rec Program."

"I thought about that, but then Bernadette started that petition to switch charities to his instead. Why would he kill her when she was on his side? That made me think of Ozzie Zuckerman. He would have even more reason to kill Bernadette, to stop her from getting the petition passed. Something's not right about him."

"Agreed," Jo stated. "Even Dr. Parker said he didn't give her the warm fuzzies. And his whole charity seems off, with not adopting to people in town."

"Then there is the matter of the three notes. The first one Bernadette wrote about Granny and Fiona, and the captain found it in the bottom of her turnover box after she died," I went on.

"The second one was a note that Mitch had that was handwritten and warned Bernadette to stay away from the captain or else. I had it analyzed. The handwriting is left-handed. Fiona is right handed, but Granny is left. Just one more strike against her. Although, Granny can't spell to save her life, and her handwriting is nearly illegible. I found the third note in the Dumpster outside of BB's Baked Goods that was made up of cutout letters glued to paper, almost serial killer style."

"Oh my goodness," Zoe said. "That's creepy."

"That's what I thought. This note said, *I know what you're doing. You're a fraud. Do what I say, or I'll tell everybody and you will be ruined.*"

"Do you think that last one was from the same person who sent the handwritten one to Bernadette?" Jo asked.

"I'm not sure. I mean, they were two totally different styles of notes. One was a warning and the other was obviously blackmail. Who could have wanted Bernadette to stay away from the captain, and what exactly did Bernadette do that was blackmail-worthy?"

"I had no idea Bernadette was so mysterious," Jo said, chugging the rest of her beer and flagging the bartender for another round.

I knew what she was up to. She wanted a little liquid courage before she stepped foot on that dance floor, but it would take a lot more than liquid courage to cure what ailed me. I shifted again, still nowhere near comfortable.

"You never can tell what goes on behind closed doors in this town," Zoe speculated.

"Oh, and one other thing," I added. "Turns out Bernadette fired her entire staff the morning of her death."

Jo squinted in concentration. "But she'd just won the auction, and everything was going so well for her. That doesn't make sense at all."

"Exactly," I replied. "Not the actions of

someone whose business was supposedly booming."

"You actually still have a lot of leads, Sunny." Jo patted my arm.

"I know. It's just frustrating trying to figure out how to follow up on them all. At least I'm not working alone," I said, watching Zoe closely. "Sean has been such a help."

"Get out." Her face looked puzzled. "I would think he wouldn't help unless there was something in it for him. There has to be a catch, right?"

She had him pegged already. "Nope," I lied. "He's just that kind of guy." Sean was a great guy, that much was true. I hoped to plant the first seed that there might be more to him than she thought, even if she was right about him wanting something. She just had no clue that something was her.

"Speak of the devil. Our dance partners just walked in." Jo waved at Cole, Mitch, and Sean until they headed our way.

"But I thought Sean was running Smokey Jo's?" Zoe looked momentarily panicked, and I was beginning to think she liked him more than she let on. I just think he scared her.

"I told him to close early." Jo winked. "It's my wedding, and I want us all to look good on the dance floor." She hopped off her stool, downed the rest of her beer, and led the way to the dance floor.

Zoe reluctantly followed, stating, "I get Detective Stone. Sean is the best man and Sunny is the maid of honor. It only makes sense that they dance together."

"Great," I muttered as I got to my feet with a wince and took one wobbly, bow-legged step, then hobbled over to join them.

Mitch eyed me carefully and then raised one thick black brow in question.

"Don't ask," was all I said, not about to venture into *that*conversation.

The Fourth of July dawned sunny and warm on Thursday morning. It was going to be an early scorcher. I donned a flowy red, white, and blue sundress, ran a brush through my hair, fluffing the spiky strands, and then went outside in search of Morty.

I hadn't seen him last night or at all that morning. Dr. Parker was right. Granny and Fiona were getting to him as much as they were me. I searched around out back but only found a bunny rabbit munching on clover. Insects buzzed around flowers in full bloom, and birds flapped their wings, hopping from branch to branch in the trees that swayed in the warm summer breeze.

I made a note to mow my lawn as I

headed out front, checking both sides of the house along the way. There was no sign of him. Wandering down the road a ways, I paused when I heard the sound of distant sirens. Turning around, I nearly jumped out of my sundress.

Morty stood before me, not making a sound, just staring up at me intensely like he was frustrated I couldn't read his mind. His striped bow tie was askew and, good Lord in Heaven, Fiona had strapped a pair of knitted booties over his paws.

"There you are, boy," I said, bending down and picking him up, stroking his head and back. "I know you're having a hard time lately. I am, too. Hang in there with me. I promise we'll figure this whole thing out."

He purred and snuggled into me for a moment, but then seemed to realize what he was doing. He pulled back, shook off a bootie on a scowl, and then leapt out of my arms just as a fire truck went screeching by me. Where on earth was that truck going? There was nothing at the end of Shadow Lane except . . .

Vicky!

I broke into a run — more like a jog, given the amount of soreness I still felt from yesterday's lovely little adventure — and hurried back home as quickly as I could.

When I arrived, the firefighters were already inside, and Morty stood by the back of the truck. A flyer for the carnival with the Animal Angels charity listed on it was still taped to the red paint.

Hurrying inside, I stopped short at the sight of Granny and Fiona covered in black gooey soot.

"Is everything okay?" I asked with chest heaving as I was out of breath. Note to self: get back to the gym.

"It was all her fault," Granny said, jabbing a long, gnarly finger at Fiona, then wiping her hands on her red-and-blue-checkered apron.

"Not everything is my fault," Fiona countered, attempting to brush the soot from her blue-pleated skirt. "It was your idea to see if we could read her cards."

I gaped at them. "You went into my sanctuary? Are you crazy?" This went beyond putting them in a time-out. I was ready to lock them both in their rooms and throw away the key. "I thought I told you both my things were off limits."

"That's what I told her, but the crazy fool wouldn't listen," Granny said.

"I didn't *enter* your sanctuary," Fiona said with a twinkle in her eye. "I used an old fishing pole I found in the garage." She grinned like she was the most clever person alive. "Worked like a charm to snag your bag of cards off the table in there."

"Seriously?" I rubbed my temples, heaving a breath. "Why is the fire department here?"

"On account of the fire, silly," Fiona said, looking at Granny like I was the one with a screw loose.

Her words registered. "What fire?" I looked around, panicked. Vicky was so old and full of knickknacks, it wouldn't take much to turn her into a pile of ash.

"Calm down, dear. There was a teensy fire in the kitchen, but we put it out right away," Granny clarified, glaring at Fiona. "Mostly, we just set off the smoke alarms. Good thing you listened to me. Since they're hooked up to the emergency system, the fire department came immediately."

Knowing them, they set off the alarm on purpose, hoping Captain Walker would show up again. "How did this *teensy* fire happen?"

"Well, I've seen you do enough readings to know you use candles and incense and oils and all sorts of stuff," Granny explained, wringing her hands as though she dreaded telling me. She finally took a breath and blurted, "Fiona went overboard as usual, and the next thing we knew, the tablecloth was on fire."

"Don't you worry, Sunny." Fiona nodded, looking proud as a dirty heroic peacock. "We put it out straight away."

"She didn't put it out. The nitwit threw flour on it." Granny waved her wooden spoon about. "I tried to tell her flour is how you put out a grease fire. I saved the day, not her. I threw water over her flour, and well, everything was a charcoal doughy mess by the time all was said and done."

"Uh-huh." I shook my head, my entire skull throbbing now. "I'm with Morty. I need to escape."

"Just don't bother the captain," an older female firefighter said as she entered the kitchen, obviously hearing what I'd said. "He's had enough to deal with lately, especially regarding these two." She stood tall and firm as she gave me a no-nonsense, serious look and then exited my house promptly.

A thought hit me square in the gut. A warning to stay away from the captain. Gee, where had I heard that before?

12

Thursday afternoon I pulled into the fire department parking lot. I wanted to talk more with the firefighter who'd come to my house. Find out what her story was. Why, exactly, she wanted me not to bother the captain.

And whether or not she was left-handed.

The firehouse was like a big warehouse. Living quarters upstairs, with lockers and offices and trucks all downstairs. A large kitchen sat off to the side, and people scurried about, readying the trucks for the parade. Various aromas of coffee, eggs, oil, and gas wafted through the air.

"Can I help you, miss?" the big, hunky firefighter who'd rescued Fiona from the tree asked as his boots hit the floor.

He'd just slid down the pole in true heroic fashion. Here stood a real hero, not space-cadet wannabe heroes like the Dynamic Duo. He had a dark brown flat-top buzz cut, chiseled cheekbones, and the sexiest set of lips I'd ever seen. Not to mention his muscles filled out his uniform perfectly.

I could see why women swooned in the presence of firefighters. There was something so dashing about a man in a uniform of any kind. I took a moment simply to admire him, trying to think of someone to set him up with.

I couldn't get matchmaking off my mind these days, since my dating life was on hold for the time being. My gaze reached his face. His lips twitched in an obvious effort not to smile, but he just stood at attention, waiting patiently.

Feeling the flush hit my cheeks, I held out my hand. "I'm Sunny Meadows. And you are?"

His large palm wrapped warmly around mine as he leaned in and said, "Single."

I let out a goofy laugh and then pressed my lips together as I reluctantly pulled my hand from his. Smoking hot or not, there was only one man I wanted to put my fire out. "I, um, was actually looking for" — the woman who'd come to my house walked out of a room in the back — "her," I finished, shooting him a parting smile as I headed toward her.

She spotted me and stopped walking, setting her mouth in a hard, uncompromising line. "You again," was all she said.

"Yup, it's me. But unlike my house, I'm not on fire, and I promise not to set off any alarms. Girl Scout's honor, I swear." I held up two fingers and laughed.

She didn't.

"Okay, then." I cleared my throat. "Anyway, I just wanted to come by and thank you."

"For what? Doing my job?" She studied me, sizing me up, like she didn't quite know what to make of me.

"Well, yes, actually." I tried for another smile and a tone that would let her know I was sincere. My house Vicky meant everything to me, and if I'd lost her, I would have been devastated. Not to mention the terrifying thought of what could have happened to Morty, Granny, and Fiona if they hadn't put the fire out. "My granny and Fiona might be old, but my house is older. Not a good combination I'm afraid."

"Those two are something, all right," the woman grumbled, straightening her crisp uniform, her gray hair cropped short and not moving an inch.

"I know, right?" I held up my hands helplessly. "When they're not making trouble for the police, they're making trouble for everyone else."

She narrowed her eyes and snapped her rigid spine even straighter, which I hadn't thought possible. "That's why I handled the call. The police are trying to solve a murder. They don't need anything more to deal with right now, especially not the nonsense of two bored, bickering, insane old ladies."

The police or Captain Walker I wondered. "And that's why I am indebted to you," I said, which was true but wouldn't stop me from following all leads, including the one I had on her. "Can I have your autograph?" I held out one of the carnival flyers I'd found by the door and a pen.

She looked at me a bit strangely and then shrugged on an irritated sigh. "Apparently, the apple doesn't fall far from the tree," she muttered, taking the pen from my hand. She flipped the flyer over and held it up to the wall as she signed it with her . . . holy Mary, mother of God . . . left hand.

"Chief, the captain's waiting in your office," another firefighter, almost as hunky as the last, said as he walked by. Yowzer, they must all drink from the same God-gifted water fountain, I thought.

She handed the flyer back to me. "If that will be all, I have a parade to get ready for." She snapped a salute in my direction and marched off toward her office, which read CHIEF LINDA DRUMMOND.

She was left-handed, Captain Walker was in her office, and I had just found a new suspect. All in all, not a bad morning.

Not long after I left the fire department, I pulled into the parking lot of Mini Central Park. The day had already grown hotter with an early heat wave. I fanned my face, left the windows down in my bug, and then climbed out.

The Summer Solstice Carnival had long since shut down, but the fireworks display was set to go off over the swan pond at dusk. The parade hadn't started yet. It was supposed to happen right after lunch at one.

It was only noon.

Hopefully, I would catch Quincy Turner in his office. I really wanted to ask him about his Parks and Rec charity getting passed over for the carnival proceeds, and Bernadette's petition.

The park was pretty much empty, except for a few die-hard people who had already set their blankets and chairs and coolers up on the lawn as close to the swan pond as they were allowed. I spotted my parents talking to Harry.

I stayed far away from their spot and kept

walking. Hazel sat on a blanket, waiting impatiently, judging by her fidgeting and dirty looks. Smiling, I waved, but she just looked away, so I kept walking. I needed to finish what I'd come to accomplish before Mitch arrived.

I walked by Chuck, Abby, and third-wheel Mimi. She stuck pretty close to Abby's side, especially when she was in town. Ida Ray stopped and spoke to her for a few minutes, which was a good sign, but then she kept walking and joined another group on their blanket. Mimi gave them a sad wistful look, but then her phone rang and she walked away to answer it.

If Mimi would just learn to loosen up, she might find someone special so she wouldn't be alone. Since I had to wait to start dating, I was still in the matchmaking mood and thought, *I really need to find her a man.* But that would have to wait as well. I was on a mission.

I waved to them as well and kept walking.

Quincy's office was located just off the swan pond. I walked into the building that housed a front desk with all sorts of brochures on the area and things to do. Divinity's very own welcome center tourist spot. Quincy's office was in the back with the

210

door slightly ajar. No one was in the main office.

Instead of ringing the bell, I started walking toward the back and saw him through the crack in his door. I noticed he was on the phone and heard his raised voice. Knowing it wasn't any of my business, I stopped and started to turn around, until I heard what he said.

"I don't know what else to say. I've told you over and over that I'm sorry, but what's fair is fair. Bernadette never should have done what she did. She's a fraud. I deserved every penny she paid me for not telling the whole town, but it's still not nearly enough."

My jaw dropped. Quincy Turner was the blackmailer? Then who on earth had written the threatening notes to stay away from Captain Walker? The handwriting had definitely been female. Something told me that note wasn't related to this at all.

Quincy sounded downright frustrated and bitter as he continued. "Bernadette started the petition, but Ozzie put a stop to that in a hurry. I tried to stop him, but he runs in scary circles."

He paused and listened while the person on the other end of the line said something.

"It's not my fault she turned to them. Anyone in their right mind knows that's crazy. I have to think about myself. Times are tough. My business is still struggling. That auction money should have been mine. I have what I want. I suggest you find another way to get what you want and leave me alone or I will follow through and let everyone know what a fake Bernadette really was." He slammed down the receiver and rubbed his temples.

I took a moment to digest what I'd just heard. Quincy must have found something out about Bernadette that would damage her reputation somehow. I suspected it wasn't something personal since she didn't care what people thought of her. The only thing she cared about was her business. He must have threatened to expose Bernadette, for what I still didn't know, and that's when she started the petition to get the charity recipient changed back to them. When that didn't work, he'd made her come up with the money somehow.

What I didn't understand was where Bernadette had gotten the money, and who had she turned to that was crazy, and most important, who had Quincy been talking to just now? Even more strange, how had Ozzie put a stop to the petition? Murder?

So many questions . . .

Once I'd waited a few minutes to give

Quincy a chance to compose himself, I knocked on his door. Pushing it open wider, I was surprised at the mess. Papers were scattered about and clutter reigned. No wonder his business was in trouble. There was no organization whatsoever.

"Look, I said —" Quincy spotted me and rubbed his wrinkled brow. "Can I help you?"

What I knew of him, he had seemed like a nice enough guy. But with the cuts to his funding from the state, I knew he was desperate to keep his organization alive. And desperation made people capable of anything, even blackmail.

"My name is Sunny Meadows." I held out my hand.

"Oh." He eyed me like I had the plague. "You."

"I'm not here to cause any trouble, I promise."

He grunted. "Neither am I. Funny how no one believes me, either." He looked up at me with a defeated expression.

"I'm really sorry that your charity didn't get chosen to receive the auction and bake-off funds, but Animal Angels is a worthy cause as well."

His expression turned hard and angry. "Says you."

"Says everyone."

"Have you met the guy who's running the operation?" he asked.

"Well, not in person, but I've met his assistant. She seems nice."

"Ah, but you've never met Ozzie Zuckerman himself. If you did, I'm sure you'd have a change of heart."

"How do you mean?"

"There's something off about that man. Let's just say he has friends in low places," Quincy grumbled. "Am I bitter? Hell yes. I admit it. But that's not why I'm saying this. That man is about as warm as a rock. Not adopting those rescued dogs to folks in town and hanging out with shady riffraff. Mark my words, that man is not what he claims to be."

"Well, then, who exactly is he?"

His eyes met mine and held. "Finally, someone is asking the right questions."

"Thank you for your time, Mr. Turner. I hope things turn around for you." Whoops, I hadn't meant to add that last part. The last thing I needed was for him to find out I had overheard his conversation. Until I figured out what he had on her, I didn't know if he was dangerous.

His eyes widened with horror.

"You know, with the charity and everything. Oh, shoot, look at the time. The fireworks are about to start." I backed out of his office. "Happy Fourth of July."

I ran outside before I'd completely spilled the beans that I'd been spying on him. Making my way through the crowd of people, I ran smack into Mitch. He grabbed my bare shoulders to steady me.

"There you are," I said, nearly out of breath.

"Here I am." His gaze ran over the length of me. "Where are you coming from in such a hurry?"

"Trying to find you. I didn't want to be late for our date."

"Ah, our date. You've been so mad at me lately, I didn't think you would show."

"Mad, yes. Unreasonable, no. I'm not about to miss an opportunity to finally go on a real date with you." I softened a little. Not to mention I'd say just about anything at this point to take his mind off where I'd just been.

His full lips twitched. "Is there dessert involved?"

I patted his T-shirt-clad chest, giving him a little smile of my own. "Silly man. Dessert comes after dinner. This is just fireworks." Even though it was warm out, he still wore jeans. Other than when he worked out, he rarely wore shorts. Not that I was complaining. He filled out his jeans oh-so-nicely.

"That's what I thought." He sighed, looking frustrated and hungry and adorable all at once. But then his expression changed to one of his usual suspicion. "Your car is parked in the other direction. Mind telling me why you're coming from this side of the park? There's nothing back there but Quincy Turner's office, and I know you wouldn't be talking to him since he's a suspect in Bernadette Baldwin's murder. Would you?"

"Of course not," I scoffed, but looked up at the sky. "Nice night for fireworks, huh?"

He hesitated and then finally said, "I'll let your changing the subject slide since you've had a hell of a day."

I slowly lowered my gaze to his. "Thanks. I appreciate that. See, you *do* know how to treat a woman. You're just a bit rusty, is all." I tweaked his arm, and he grabbed my hand and intertwined his fingers with mine.

"Oh, I know how to treat a woman." His intensely magnetic eyes held me captive. "I've simply chosen not to date, until now."

"What changed your mind?"

"You." He caressed my cheek softly with his other hand.

"Oh." Warmth filled my every cell. Man, he was good.

"I heard about the fire. Is everyone okay?"

"Everyone's fine, thanks to Chief Drummond. I stopped by the fire department to thank her. By the way, did you happen to know she's left-handed?"

"No." He shrugged. "What does that have to do with anything?"

"She warned Granny and Fiona to leave Captain Walker alone." I waited for his reaction, anticipating him to be surprised and congratulate me on an awesome discovery.

"That doesn't surprise me," he said nonchalantly, not surprised in the least. I never had to worry about my ego getting inflated around him. "She worries about him," he added.

"Exactly." I poked him in the chest. "The threatening note that someone gave to Bernadette warned her to stay away from Captain Walker or else. And the note was written by someone left-handed. I think it was Chief Drummond. I think she cares about the captain." Whoops, I hadn't meant to mention the note. I bit my lip when he paused, and then he finally spoke.

"I don't even want to know how you saw that note, and of course she cares about him, but not in the way you think." Mitch poked me back playfully.

"What do you mean?" My shoulders

drooped with dread over what he might say.

"Captain Walker and Chief Drummond are cousins. Their fathers are brothers, and they both followed in their footsteps. They've always had a close bond because of it."

"Darnit." My shoulders slumped farther. "Every time I think I'm close to clearing Granny's name, something happens to blow my theory right out of the water."

Mitch lifted my chin with his fingertip. "You're not supposed to have theories, Tink."

"I can't help it. I'm not getting in your way, I promise. I'm just trying to add to the investigation. I can't sit back and do nothing. I just can't." I blinked back tears.

He cursed under his breath and stared up at the sky with a strained expression as though at war with himself. Finally, he lowered his gaze like he'd made a decision. "All right. You win."

"Excuse me?" Hope filled me. Was he saying what I thought he was saying?

"I'll tell you everything I know, but you first. What else is buzzing around in that pretty little head of yours?"

"Not much," I said, and immediately regretted it.

He smirked, and I smacked him.

"I walked right into that one. I meant not much regarding the case. You were right. I did go see Quincy and overheard him on the phone." I told Mitch everything I'd found so far.

"I think you're right. Quincy had something on Bernadette and then blackmailed her. But blackmail doesn't necessarily mean murder."

"I agree it wouldn't make sense for Quincy to kill Bernadette after she paid him off. Maybe the crazy people she went to get help from killed her," I added desperately. "Maybe even one of her staff did. She was broke. That must have been why Bernadette fired her staff the morning of her murder."

"Not bad," he said, and I swelled with pride. "It would make sense that she couldn't afford to keep them after giving away all her money. Although, I didn't realize she had money to give away." He pulled out his notebook and jotted down some notes.

"Told you we make a good team. You're just too stubborn to admit it."

"I'm the stubborn one?" He arched both brows until they disappeared beneath his hair as he stared at me. "You're funny."

"Don't forget I'm cute, too." I laughed.

"Sunny, I doubt I could forget anything

about you if I tried." He shook his head on a grin and then looked at his notes, all business once more.

"Anything else?" I asked, hoping he'd stay true to his word and share back.

"We still don't know who wrote the threatening note regarding the captain. Quincy obviously wrote the serial killer–style note as you put it. I'm following some leads regarding Ozzie Zuckerman. I got a tip from an anonymous informant, and some ideas from, well, somewhere else. Let's just call it a hunch from an unexpected source." I opened up my mouth, but Mitch held up his hand. "Before you pounce on me, I need to figure a few more things out, and then we'll talk. Deal?"

"Deal." I threw my arms around him and pounced anyway, hugging him tight as I stood on his feet to reach him better.

He hugged me back, and I felt the chuckle deep within his chest. Biting my lip, I tried not to grin from ear to ear like a love-struck buffoon.

"In the meantime, let's try to enjoy ourselves," his deep voice rumbled beneath my ear. "We *are* supposed to be on a date, after all."

"That we are. And you are such a dashing fellow." I lifted my head and kissed him on the lips, then turned around, wiggling against him until he wrapped his arms around me. I peeked up at him. "Just so you know that kiss wasn't dessert, it was just a crumb."

He chuckled again, staring down at me with an expression I couldn't quite read. "You're a nut."

"Oh, just admit it." I faced front once more, afraid to see his expression as I finished with, "You're nuts about me."

He rested his chin on the top of my head, not saying a word, but holding me a bit tighter. I melted in relief. Guilty by omission. At this point I'd take whatever I could get. I let out a dreamy sigh and leaned back to enjoy the show.

13

The next afternoon Granny Gert pulled three twenty-dollar bills out of a freezer bag of money and handed it to Raoulle, the hair stylist. "Thank you so much."

He took them a bit too quickly in my opinion and gave her a naughty smile, which he had to know would only encourage her further. Damn, he was good.

"I'm thrilled Tracy let you make a house call just to wash and set my hair. I miss the salon, but if I set off this darn ankle bracelet again, a certain someone will get so angry." Granny jerked her head in my direction, and my jaw fell open. "She's so touchy these days," she said in a loud whisper even though I was standing right beside her. "Must be hormonal if you get my drift."

I gasped, feeling my cheeks heat as I glanced at a smirking Raoulle. "Granny Gert!"

"Well, it's true," she said loud and clear

and then looked at Raoulle with pure mischief shining bright in her snappy brown eyes. "I have a great cookie for that, you know."

"Granny, I'm sure Raoulle needs to go."

"Not really," he said, grinning devilishly.

"My hair looks better than Mt. Saint Blue over there." Fiona patted her hair as she checked her image from every angle in the foyer mirror. Then she wrote a check for seventy dollars, making sure Granny saw, and handed it to Raoulle with a flourish.

"My hair is not blue, you ninny. It's a beautiful *natural* white, not some phony bologna color like yours. You're just jealous that mine is still thick and lustrous while yours is thinning." Granny snatched her freezer bag once more and pulled out another ten and a five, fluttering her eyelashes at Raoulle.

At least she'd taken the falsies off, but still. She was going to go cross-eyed if she didn't stop that. But I had to admit, I was thrilled the subject was off me. "The way you set and roll my hair is worth every penny," she twittered.

Fiona harrumphed, grabbing her purse and fishing out a twenty. "My hair is not thinning, Gertie. It's tame and has a style, something you lack." She smoothed it back with her perfectly manicured hands. "You're the one who's jealous. My strawberry blond color is gorgeous, and the way Raoulle applies it is extraordinary. The man has skills," she purred, winking at him in an exaggerated way.

"Stop, please. You two lovelies are gonna make me blush." Raoulle waved his hand through the air with a technique more dramatic than both of them put together. "You know I'd do anything for you guys."

Good Lord in Heaven, did he flutter his eyelashes back?

I thought about what he'd said. He'd do anything for them, all right. Like take their money. At the rate they were going in trying to outdo each other, they'd be broke before he hit the sidewalk.

"I think you've done enough for one day." I gave him a meaningful look that didn't involve winking or fluttering eyelashes. It said, *Not on my watch, pal.*

He sighed, his grin fading and eyes growing serious. "Oh, all right." Then he leaned toward Granny and said in his own loud whisper, "Definitely hormonal." Then he sailed out the door before I could say another word.

"Now that we've taken care of that, I have work to do," I said, heading toward my sanctuary in desperate need of respite. Some normalcy. My life back.

"Actually, you don't, dear," Granny said, sounding sorrowful.

I stopped and slowly turned around to face them. "What do you mean?"

"Your afternoon appointment cancelled," Granny said, and I was ready to hand her the shovel and wave the white flag. I surrender. Just bury me in the yard, six feet under, because I would never survive waiting for this case to be solved.

"It's no wonder they cancelled. They probably didn't want to be under the same roof with a criminal," Fiona chimed in, jerking her head in Granny's direction. "If you know what *I* mean."

"You should talk," Granny sputtered, looking completely aghast. "You're the one who keeps screwing up and getting us into more trouble."

"Stop!" I glared at them both. "I can't take any more of the Granny and Fiona Show. It's nothing but reruns, and I've had enough. I thought you two had a truce. Aren't you supposed to be trying to figure out who killed Bernadette?"

"Yes, but Fiona Schmona is no Sherlock Holmes. She has no idea what she's doing." Granny wiped her hands on her apron. "She honestly thinks my car is haunted. Can you believe that? That's all I'm saying about that."

"What's wrong with that?" Fiona plopped her hands on her cotton Bermuda shorts. "It can happen. This house is certainly haunted, and that cat of yours is just plain scary. He's not very friendly."

The shutters shook and a strong wind blew through the open windows, blowing my curtains around.

"See what I mean?" Fiona shuddered, wrapping her arms around herself. "If I have to stay here all summer, I'll never survive." She rubbed her chest and winced.

"This house has charm, and quit acting like you have chest pains. The only pain around here is you," Granny snapped.

Fiona stopped abruptly and dropped her hand, standing up straighter. "Like your theory is any better."

"Bernadette wasn't that old, and she wasn't married. She could have had a lover. Maybe she broke it off with him, and so he killed her. It makes a lot more sense than a haunted car," Granny scoffed.

"I can't imagine Bernadette being nice to anyone long enough to have a lover, but I do think she had a secret," I said.

"You do?" they both chimed in at the

same time, sounding stunned.

I filled them in on all that Mitch and I had discovered so far. "So, yes, maybe Quincy killed Bernadette in a bitter rage over not getting the auction money, even though she paid him something. According to him, it wasn't nearly enough."

"Or whoever she got the money from killed her for not paying them back. Or maybe whoever was on the phone killed her out of revenge for being a fraud. I can't blame her. I certainly took Phillip for all he was worth for being a fraud. He promised until death do us part, but he left me. Trust me, I felt like killing him," Fiona said, then she paused dramatically before she added with gusto, "I heard Quincy flashed plenty of big bills in town this morning. I think he has more than he let on."

"How did you hear that?" Granny eyed her suspiciously. "You haven't gone any-where, have you?"

"Obviously Raoulle talks more to me than you." Fiona gloated.

I still stood there in shock. Quincy had blackmailed Bernadette, taken all of her money, complained that it wasn't enough, but was flashing big bills around. Was he blackmailing someone else now? Like maybe the anonymous person on the other end of the phone? Quincy didn't have an alibi for the night Bernadette died. His actions now only made him look more guilty. And I still didn't know how Ozzie had put a stop to Bernadette's petition.

"Maybe you should do a reading for Bernadette, Sunny." Granny interrupted my thoughts.

"And she thinks *I'm* no Sherlock." Fiona snorted. "Kind of hard to do a reading on a dead person, there, spanky."

"Not necessarily," I said, warming to the idea. "I think you're onto something, Granny. Cover for me."

"Where are you going?" Granny asked, looking alarmed.

"To find something of Bernadette's. I don't know why I didn't think of this before. If I can find something that was near and dear to her that she used often, then I just might be able to get a read on her."

"Well, that's easy," Fiona said. "She lived for those darn turnovers. I bet her kitchen has some stories to tell." She let out a bawdy laugh.

"Exactly," I said, wagging my eyebrows at her as I added, "Watson."

She beamed. "I'll take that. I always thought Watson had more fun, anyway."

Granny rolled her eyes. "Isn't breaking

and entering illegal?"

"I'm not going to break or take anything. I just need five minutes to hold her kitchen gadgets, ask what happened, and then read the cards." I stepped into my sanctuary, grabbed my tarot cards, and fanned them up in front of them both like a magician as I said, "Simple as that."

Why couldn't anything be simple these days?

I had parked down the street, waiting for the crowd to leave Sam's Bakery so no one would see me sneak into BB's Baked Goods. It was Friday afternoon. People kept coming and going at a steady pace, picking up bread for dinner, desserts for after, pastries for breakfast . . . you name it, they bought it. With BB's closed for the time being, Sam was the only bakery business in town.

One dark four-door sedan with tinted windows had been parked out front the entire time. What in the world were they waiting for? I couldn't wait all day. Mitch and I were supposed to meet at his place later tonight, and he was supposed to fill me in about the lead he was chasing on Ozzie.

Sneaking around back, I gave the Dumpster a wide berth. I'd rather die than inhale that stench or feel those creepy crawlies ever again. Slipping on my hospital gloves, I tested the back door, but it was locked. I tried one window that was also locked. Finally, I found one window she must have left unlocked the night of her murder before she left to carry her turnovers up the hill to Trixie's. Somehow it had been overlooked and never relocked.

Thank goodness for small miracles.

The sun was hot and bright in the sky so there was no need to turn on any lights. *Although, I'd love to turn on the air conditioner,* I thought, as I pulled the neck of my T-shirt away from my skin. It was hotter than a firecracker in there. The place had been closed up since Bernadette's death. But turning on the AC or opening a window would draw attention to the fact that someone was inside the bakery.

So I crouched down low and searched her kitchen the best I could. The air was stale and suffocating, but I pressed on, taking in everything around me. I saw utensils and dishes and ingredients that might work. But then I spotted a rolling pin that looked like it had been used a lot. Hopefully to roll out the dough for her turnovers.

I swiped the rolling pin and made my way to the back of the kitchen and set my tarot cards and the rolling pin on a counter away from the front windows. I didn't have time to prepare my space like I usually did. Carefully taking off my gloves, I picked up the rolling pin and closed my eyes, breathing deeply and relaxing my body. I emptied my mind of all thoughts and focused on the object I held in my hands.

This was definitely Bernadette's special rolling pin. I could feel her energy vibrate through it, almost as if it was a living extension of her. In a way it was, since her bakeshop was her baby. It had been used a lot. I frowned. A strong negative vibe rolled off the pin as though the results were anything but positive. Something wasn't right here, but I couldn't quite place what.

I supposed the point was moot since BB's was closed now. I had to wonder what would become of the place since she didn't have any family. I made a mental note to check with the bank and see what I could find out. Maybe it would shed some light on what was off. In the meantime, I had to focus on trying to find out what had happened to Bernadette.

Tuning in to my Higher Self, I asked the universe to guide me through my reading. To allow me to connect to Bernadette's spirit. Opening my eyes, I set the rolling pin down. Deciding on a one-card spread, I picked up my tarot cards and shuffled them one time.

I'd already heard how she had died and what had happened right after her death. But no one knew what exactly had happened in the moments before, the moments leading up to her death.

"What happened right before Bernadette Baldwin was murdered?" I asked out loud.

I drew one card and turned it over, laying it down on the table before me. XV The Devil card stared back at me. The Devil card meant Bernadette had made a choice, completed an action, or was involved in a situation that was contrary to her best interest. It often involved being bound by something or addicted to something. Being bound to or controlled by anything holds one back, and they cannot make any forward progress on their quest in life.

I looked off in the distance as I thought about what the card might mean. Suddenly, my gaze filtered into tunnel vision — the same thing that always happened when my psychic abilities took over. I was in Bernadette's body, looking out through her eyes and feeling what she felt at the time.

She carried her box of turnovers as she left her shop and headed down the street toward the hill that would take her to Trixie's house. She was running late, but I could feel the confidence she had in those particular turnovers, like she knew for a fact they were the best around. I could also feel her desperation to succeed.

Her determination to win.

I felt the hair on the back of my neck stand up as hers must have when she heard the sound of a car's engine rumbling along behind her. Glancing over her shoulder, she saw a dark sedan. The same one that I saw parked out front of Sam's only moments ago.

Staying focused, I concentrated on what Bernadette had felt. A fear more powerful than anything I'd ever felt slammed through me. She hurried her pace, almost reaching the bottom of the hill now. Looking behind her, she saw the car stop. Two large men climbed out and took a step toward her.

I'd seen them around town at the carnival, at Papas, and even at the fireworks. I had taken them for tourists in town for the Summer Solstice Carnival and the Fourth of July holiday week. Divinity had a lot of tourists pass through in the summertime because of its quaint atmosphere, its great fishing, and its numerous antique shops.

I took another look at the men. There was

nothing simple about the way they had made Bernadette feel, or me for that matter. Utterly and completely terrified.

She started to run and —

Sucking in a sharp breath, I jerked out of my trance and ducked. There was a noise in the front of the store, like someone was picking the lock. Quickly snatching my tarot cards, I left the rolling pin on the counter and slipped into a food pantry, closing the door in the nick of time. The air was even more stifling inside the pantry, and the smell of stale food nearly gagged me.

"You search out here. I'll take her office in the back. She had to have hid it somewhere," said a male voice I didn't recognize.

Hid what? I wondered.

"Hurry. Everyone else has cleared out, but that chick's car is still down the road. She has to be close by."

That chick? I swallowed hard.

"Don't worry about her. We'll take care of her later. Boss will kill us if we don't do what he asked first. Now move."

I held my breath as they made short work of tossing Bernadette's store. She was being bound and controlled by the devil, all right. What in the world had she gotten herself into? Who was their boss? And even scarier . . . who was the chick they were talking about?

The man in the main part of the store where I was searched cupboard after cupboard, getting closer and closer to where I hid. Something bumped the door to the pantry I hid in. I shook all over and held my breath, terrified I was going to die.

Good Lord, I was having a breakdown.

"Hey, I think I found something," said the voice from the office. "Come see."

I nearly collapsed with relief as I heard heavy footsteps thump away. I waited a beat, cracked the door open, and then slipped out of the pantry. The door to the office was open, but two pairs of very broad shoulders and wide backs faced me.

I tiptoed on wobbly legs and finally reached the back door. Not giving a hoot at the moment that I'd left my hospital gloves by the rolling pin, I unlocked the back door and ran all the way to my car, not looking over my shoulder even once.

When I unlocked the door to my bug, I threw myself inside and slammed it shut. I waited a beat to see if they followed, and then realized the stupidity in that. My tires screeched as I stomped on the gas and peeled away from the curb.

Looking in my rearview mirror, I realized no other cars were on the street other than the dark sedan and my bug. My throat went bone dry. Guess the *chick* they'd been referring to was me. One question screeched through my brain even louder than my tires had.

How exactly did they plan to take care of me?

14

I parked down a side street and waited. It didn't take long until the dark sedan drove by. As discreetly as I could, I tailed them. I had been halfway home when I realized they wouldn't stop until they found me. It certainly wouldn't be hard. No one looked quite like me, and no one had a car like mine.

I refused to live in terror.

Evening was fast approaching, and I was supposed to meet Mitch later. I glanced at my watch. I still had time. I needed to find out who they were and what Meathead 1 and Meathead 2 were up to. So I stayed far enough away and tried not to lose them. They headed out to the outskirts of town, and worry tried to wiggle its way into my brain. I thought about what was out this way, and the only thing that came to mind was the big monster truck rally at the fairgrounds called Monster Jam.

Sure enough that's where the sedan pulled into.

I followed them into the packed parking lot. They didn't strike me as the kind of people who were interested in watching monster trucks jamming to loud music as they thrilled the crowd by driving over other cars and smashing into each other. When they pulled around in back, my suspicions were proven right. They weren't here to watch. They were meeting someone.

But who?

I parked and kept to the shadows, weaving my way in and out of cars. They entered a back door. After a minute, I followed suit. We were in the back where the trucks were being readied and the drivers were awaiting their turn.

I stopped short. Ozzie Zuckerman was talking to a driver in a humongous truck with wheels that were taller than my head. I saw him slip the man something and then they shook. After a minute, the man climbed down from the truck and headed off to the men's room. Meanwhile, Ozzie headed for the stands.

He didn't get far.

The two men from the dark sedan blocked his way. The look on his face and his body language were identical to what Berna-

238

dette's had been in my vision. One of the men pulled a gun, and Ozzie held up his hands, looking like he was pleading with them about something. He pointed to the truck and talked rapidly. Meathead 1 lowered his gun, and Meathead 2 led the way to the stands.

I saw a chance, and I took it.

Jogging over to the truck, I glanced up and read the name. Thunder Thighs. Of course. I shook my head and climbed inside. More like huffed and puffed and struggled my way up the humongous wheels into the cab. No wonder they'd named her Thunder Thighs. She, by far, had the biggest wheels of any of the trucks.

I only had minutes before the driver returned. I started searching the interior, looking for anything that would tell me who the driver was.

No luck.

I was just about to climb down when I spotted a piece of paper on the floor. I bent down and snatched the paper off the floor and then read it.

Throw the rally. Let Destructo last longer than Thunder Thighs. I'll split my winnings with you 50/50.

So Meathead 1 and Meathead 2 obviously wanted something from Ozzie, and they had wanted something from Bernadette as well. Quincy was right. Ozzie was definitely shady and not someone I should interfere with. *Too late.* I gulped, my throat going dry.

This was a very bad idea.

A horn blared, and everything happened at once. The driver came out of the bathroom, Meathead 1 and Meathead 2 spotted me in the driver's seat, and all the trucks started their engines. Having no choice and fearing for my life, I ducked behind the driver's seat just in time. He slipped inside and slapped on the helmet in the seat beside him then turned the key in the ignition.

The truck roared to life, and the two men started running toward the truck. Thank God they were too late. The driver slammed the gearshift into drive, punching the pedal with his foot. I'd never ridden in a monster truck before. In fact, I'd never even been to a rally before. I wedged myself behind his seat as best I could and wrapped my arms and legs around anything secure as I held on for my life. It was so loud, and with his helmet on, the driver couldn't hear me bouncing around as we flew out the doors into the arena. Adrenaline pumped through my veins as my body went into sensory overload.

Engines roared and trucks drove over the

tops of cars that were lined up, crushing them like soda cans. Other trucks crashed into each other like bumper cars. I didn't know where my driver was going to go or what he planned to do next. I swallowed a scream when I saw Destructo headed straight at us. The note had said to throw the race, but the driver had to make it look good. He jerked the wheel to the right and slammed on the brakes, doing several three-sixties in the dirt.

The crowd went wild.

My head spun. He kept barely avoiding Destructo, who kept relentlessly chasing us. We were supposed to willingly let him crush us? Yeah right. Not if I could help it. I had to think of something. My driver drove around the outside of the track, looking for a way out.

Destructo cut us off again, hitting us in the tailgate. We fishtailed, and the front of our truck flipped up as we bounced along doing a wheelie on our lovely thighs. My driver recovered, veering toward the center of the arena. I might be young, but I was certain I was headed for a massive heart attack.

I blinked. Where had that jump come from?

We hit the ramp and went airborne over

the tops of several cars, almost clearing the lot, until I screamed bloody murder and popped up out of the back.

"What the hell?" My driver's head whipped around, and he stared at me in complete shock, not paying any attention to his driving.

"Look out!" I screamed, pointing ahead, but it was too late. We didn't quite clear the lot, and the impact made my teeth chomp together, forcing us end-over-end several times until we finally came to a stop upside down. I'd always envied gymnasts who could flip about on the mat, doing somersaults and handsprings.

Not today. In fact, I didn't think I would ever envy them again. My driver groaned, and I kept fading in and out of blackness.

I was aware of the Jam coming to a halt when my driver didn't climb out of the truck. The trucks rocking along to the ear-piercing music stopped, and the music died. My ears would never be the same. I couldn't move if I tried. My stomach was still lodged in my throat. I heard footsteps outside the door of the truck. Oh, God. Meathead 1 and Meathead 2 or Destructo's driver had come to get me at last. When someone yanked the door open, I screamed again.

"Tink?" The gun pointing at my driver's

head stayed put, but a pair of sharp angry eyes nailed me dead on. "What the hell are *you* doing in there?"

"She's crazy," my driver snapped, sounding a lot less groggy now. "She could have killed us."

"Shut up," Mitch ground out. "I'll get to you in a minute."

"Thank God it's you, Mitch." I sniffed back tears. "Wait, why are you pointing your gun at him?"

"You weren't supposed to be in here. Remember my lead? This is part of it."

"Your lead. Right. I, um, was . . ." I sighed. "Let's just call it bad timing."

"Story of your life." He grunted. "Are you hurt?"

"No, just scared."

"You should be. You have no idea what you're messing with. Sit tight. I'll get you out of there."

Not like I can do anything else, I wanted to say, but thought that maybe letting my stress talk wasn't such a good idea under the circumstances. And I had a pretty good idea what I was messing with.

"No worries. I'm not going anywhere," I said instead. "Hurry, please."

He hauled the driver out of the truck and handed him off to his backup, I assumed.

Minutes later, Mitch returned with help, and soon I was free. After climbing out of the truck, I thought for sure I'd have a lot of explaining to do. I glanced around, but the police had taken the driver away, and Ozzie and the meatheads were nowhere to be found. Go figure. The sun had set, and the crowd had dispersed. I was sore and tired and starving.

Mitch had anticipated I would be too shaky to drive after I was freed. He'd called for my car to be towed back to my house, and he drove me home in silence, also anticipating I'd be in no shape to go back to his house. When we pulled in my drive-way, the Dynamic Duo was standing out front looking frazzled.

"Oh, thank goodness," Granny said. "I was worried sick when you didn't return from your little B and E."

Mitch narrowed his eyes. I started to speak, but he shushed me. "Go on," he said to Granny, who was oblivious as usual.

"It's okay, Detective." Granny waved him off. "Sunny said it would be okay because she didn't take anything."

"Did she now?" he said, a muscle in his cheek pulsing.

"She sure did," Granny kept going. "She just needed to touch something of Bernadette's so she could read her tarot cards. You know, for clues, seeing as how things aren't progressing quickly enough for us all."

I groaned. Granny had no filters whatsoever. The words coming out of her mouth sounded so much worse than the reasoning in my head. Now Mitch would assume I didn't think he was capable. No way was I bringing up Ozzie and the meatheads tonight, and so far he hadn't said anything more about the driver. He couldn't blame me if he wasn't willing to share his lead, either.

"Is that so?" Mitch hardened his jaw as he looked at me.

"Sure is," Fiona butted in. "I was here when the whole thing went down."

"I would hope so," Mitch said.

"Oh, you, where else would I be with this silly contraption on my foot?" Fiona laughed as though he were joking. He just stared at her in a no-nonsense way, and she started rambling on. "Then when Sunny's car showed up without her, we panicked."

"Can we just go inside?" I asked wearily. "I'm about to collapse."

"Hanging upside down in a smashed monster truck with a known felon less than an hour ago will do that to you," Mitch pointed out with a scowl.

"Oh my stars, what in the world were you doing in a monster truck with a person like that?" Granny asked.

"Oh, Lordy, my heart." Fiona fanned herself. "I told you vehicles are haunted. Bernadette's spirit probably forced poor little Sunny in there to get back at her for touching the stuff in her store and doing a reading on her."

"You really are a nincompoop." Granny waved her away and rushed to my side. "Come on, dear. I'll make you some cookies and tea."

"And I'll bake you a pie." Fiona chased after us.

"I'll settle for some dinner," I responded.

"We're not done talking, Tink," Mitch hollered after me.

"You are tonight," Granny said over her shoulder in her own no-nonsense tone as she hooked her arm through mine. My sweet granny had a spine of steel when it came to her family.

"I second that," Fiona added just as firmly from the other side of me, hooked arm and all.

I smiled. If only one good thing came out of this whole fiasco of a day, this was it. They'd agreed on something for the first time in ages. Hallelujah . . .

There was peace in my house at last.

The peace didn't last long. The next morning I headed out to the farmer's market. I'd been more than happy to pick out some fresh produce just to escape the new round of bickering regarding the best way to take care of me. I was fine today. The sun was shining, the breeze was blowing, and the smell of cut grass and flowers filled the air.

"What happened to you?" Mimi asked, glancing at the bruise on my forehead, then going back to examining a tomato for ripeness.

"Would you believe I ran into a door?"

"Nope. Word around town is you were riding in one of those crazy monster trucks in the rally last night." She looked me over and shook her head. "Doesn't really seem like your thing if you ask me."

It never ceased to amaze me how fast gossip spread in a small town. "Never know what you might like if you don't try new things, right?"

"With some criminal? You gotta be more careful of the people you hang out with. It sure doesn't look like monster trucking liked you." She snorted. "I'd stick to telling fortunes if I was you."

"I think you're right. Speaking of fortunes, what do you see in your future?"

"Why?" Her brow puckered. "I don't see nothin'. You do know I'm not the psychic one, right?"

"Yes, I just mean, what are your hopes and dreams?"

"I gave up on dreams a long time ago," she grumbled. "Nothing ever works out."

"I could do a reading for you if you'd like."

"No need," she said firmly.

"Wouldn't you like to see if there's romance in the air for you?"

"You've done gone and lost your mind, woman. Men are the enemy."

"Don't you ever get lonely?"

Her face clouded for a moment, but then she hardened her features like she always did. "Nope. Don't need a man in my life, that's for sure. Men only bring trouble. And I don't let many people in close. It hurts too much when they betray you. Family is all a person needs to be content, but they don't always have time for you, either. And friends come and go."

I knew she was talking about Abby not having much time for her now that she was married to Chuck. And Bernadette had been about her only friend, but now she was gone, too. That made me think of my vision and how afraid Bernadette had been of the Meatheads. They'd been there just before she'd died, and I couldn't help but wonder if they were responsible in some way.

"I gotta go," Mimi said, breaking into my thoughts. "I'm having lunch with Ida."

"Huh? Oh, okay. Have a nice day." I was glad she'd made another friend, and I decided to give up on the matchmaking idea.

She just grunted and kept walking, leaving her tomatoes behind. I hadn't meant to upset her. I'd simply wanted to help her. Nothing I tried to do worked out lately. Maybe it was time I did what Mitch said and butted out. I paid for my purchases and headed home.

Good Lord, what were they up to now?

I parked my bug on the road because my driveway was full of cars. Music and the sounds of people laughing and talking came from behind my house. I walked around back and stopped short. Granny manned the grill, flipping burgers and feeding what looked like the entire town. While Fiona had set up badminton, boccie, and croquet. Must be she was in charge of the social events.

"You didn't tell me you were having a

barbecue," Jo said as she bit into a burger beside me.

"I didn't know I was," I responded, still holding my bag of produce. "This is all the Dynamic Duo's doing."

"I can't really blame them. I know I wouldn't be able to stand being confined to the house. I'm sure they're bored."

"No wonder they sent me to the farmer's market. I better get this over to them."

"When you're done, come join Cole, Sean, Zoe, and I. We're up next in badminton."

"Sean and Zoe?" I raised a brow at Jo.

"She still hasn't caved, but that's not stopping Sean from trying." Jo laughed. "See you soon," she called over her shoulder as she walked off to join them, her auburn ponytail swinging jauntily behind her.

I made a beeline for the grill.

"Granny, what is going on?" I asked as I handed her the bag of produce.

"What?" she responded with feigned innocence, wearing mint green polyester pants, a cream-and-green-striped shirt, and her standard plastic rain cap since the wind had picked up a bit. "People have to eat."

"You're supposed to be on house arrest, not playing hostess. This isn't your own personal country club, you know."

"Told you she'd say no," Fiona said, coming up behind us. She had on sunflower yellow pedal pushers, a polka dot blouse to match, perfectly matched sandals, and a wide brimmed hat.

"And you" — I pointed at her — "this isn't social hour."

"It's summer. It just seemed like such a shame to let all those fun games I found in the shed go to waste. They've been rotting all winter, begging for someone to play with them."

"Hmmm, is that what they told you?" I crossed my arms over my chest.

"Why, do you think they can talk?" Fiona asked, looking around warily.

I threw up my hands. "No, they can't talk. I'm just saying I don't need to get into any more trouble with Detective Stone."

"That man needs to loosen up a bit," Fiona said. "He's way too uptight if you know what I mean." She elbowed me in the ribs with a wicked grin.

I ignored her and scanned the yard to see who was here. None of the police were here, thank God. They'd probably start their own petition to get the women thrown back in jail for not taking their situation seriously.

The Sewing Sisters were here, playing boccie, with the exception of Hazel and

251

Harry. They were probably on a date somewhere. Abby and Chuck were here, but
Mimi was not. She was having lunch with
the widow Ida Ray. Even my parents were
here. I could hear my mother above everyone else, complaining about the inn's coffee.

The café was my mother's favorite place.
She said the café was the only place in town
with decent coffee. As much as she loved
the quaint inn they stayed at, she constantly
argued with the owner on how he should
run the place. Especially his espresso bar.

Pulling my gaze away, I took a closer look
around. There was no sign of Ozzie, the
meatheads, or even Quincy. I didn't think
they would show up here, but that didn't
mean I still wasn't nervous they'd come
after me.

"Looking for someone?" a deep voice said
from behind me.

I whirled around, slapping a hand over
my chest. Mitch stood there, wearing jeans
and a T-shirt as usual, and taking my breath
away like he always did. "Don't do that,
Mitch. You scared me more than seeing the
Devil card in a reading for myself." I
breathed slowly, willing my heart to quit
pounding.

"You should be scared," he said. "Do you

have any idea what would have happened to you if those two thugs had gotten ahold of you?"

"Thugs?"

"They're loan sharks, Sunny. Ozzie is up to his eyeballs in debt. That's why he was betting on the monster truck rally and trying to rig the outcome in his favor. That driver is known for his shady dealings. You ruined that for him. You might have made him crash, but you did so on your own. Destructo didn't take him out."

"How did you know about that?"

"I was on the verge of catching Ozzie in the act and arresting him, but someone ruined my chance."

"I'm sorry. I didn't mean to interfere with your investigation; I really didn't. But when I was at BB's Baked Goods, doing a reading on her rolling pin" — Mitch arched a brow, but I ignored him and kept going — "by the way, something is *off* in Bernadette's kitchen, but I'm not sure what yet. Anyway, those thugs broke in, looking for something."

Mitch pulled out his notebook and flipped through it for a minute, then studied me. "You thinking what I'm thinking?"

"Bernadette had to get the money from somewhere to pay off Quincy."

"Exactly, but we can't prove anything with Quincy yet. And I have nothing specific on Ozzie yet, but I'm positive there's more to both their stories."

"I think so, too. I just hope those thugs stay away. I heard them say they would take care of me later. Maybe I should buy a gun."

Mitch arched a thick black brow in a way he knew annoyed me. "Not a good idea, especially with your present company. Just be smart, lock your doors, carry your pepper spray, and for God's sake, stop putting yourself in dangerous situations." He touched my cheek until I looked at him. "I have enough to worry about, Tink."

I relented a little and covered his hand with mine. Just when he made me angry, he did or said something really sweet. I sighed. "You're getting better."

"With what?"

"Your words."

He laughed. "Come on. We have a badminton game to win."

I smiled. "You're on."

15

Saturday night Mitch actually accompanied me to bingo. I promised Granny I would play in her spot since she couldn't go. I couldn't believe Mitch actually agreed to go with me. He really was trying to make us work, even in the difficult situation we found ourselves in.

I worried about Granny. We weren't getting any closer to solving Bernadette's murder and clearing her name, yet she was living in la-la land. So blasé about the fact that she might go to prison. Then again, Granny was the ultimate optimist. Not *dealing* could just be her way of actually dealing with the whole situation.

"Hey, Captain. How's the table tonight?" Mitch asked as we sat at Captain Walker's table. It was hot and stuffy in the community center, with numbers being called out and murmurs echoing throughout the room.

"Hopefully your luck is better than mine," Captain Walker replied, rubbing his bald head, then scratching his goatee.

"Granny always wins. I'm hoping some of her luck will rub off on me," I chimed in.

"How is your grandmother?" the captain asked me, the sincerity and worry evident in his eyes.

"You know Granny. Always chipper no matter how dire the situation." I tried for some of her optimism, knowing it's what she would want me to do. I worried enough for the both of us.

"And Ms. Atwater?" he asked, looking equally concerned and worried about her as well.

"When she's not sparring with Granny, she's stirring up some kind of trouble. The two of them together are one big handful. Basically, I have no life."

"You can say that again," Mitch grumbled.

I gave him a sympathetic look and an apologetic shrug.

"Say what again?" Harry asked as he escorted Hazel around to the other side of our table. "Mind if we sit?"

"Not at all," Captain Walker said.

Hazel smiled coyly at him, shaking her brown curls a bit and pushing her glasses up her nose. He blinked, gave her a distracted smile, and then looked back at his card and checked his nearly empty board.

Harry grinned at me, flashing a nice set of teeth in his still-handsome face. "Nice to see you again, Miss Meadows. I couldn't help but overhear the detective. How are things going for your grandmother and Ms. Atwater? I haven't seen much of your parents out at the inn to inquire about them."

"Why don't you come by and see them yourself?" I said, praying he'd take me up on it. "I'm sure they'd love the company. They get so bored, and boredom equals mischief with them."

Harry hesitated, looking as though he was actually considering it, but then said, "Maybe soon." He shot a look at Hazel and the captain. "I've been busy with other matters these days."

Interesting. "Well, the next time you have a minute, swing by and I'll introduce you. This whole unfortunate ordeal is not easy on any of us, but thank you once again for your help in getting them released into my custody."

"Glad to be of assistance." He sounded sincere. "Let me know if you need anything else. Judge Navarra and I have gotten to know each other quite well since I've been in town."

"Believe me, you'll be the first person I contact if it comes to that. Hopefully, we'll clear their names and find the real killer soon."

"That's always been my motto." He was such a nice guy, but a strange look crossed his face right before he added, "Justice must be served."

Hazel ignored Harry for the next hour, flirting nonstop with Captain Walker. The funny thing was that Harry didn't seem to mind. Maybe it was because anyone with eyes could see the captain wasn't interested in her.

"Bingo!" Hazel yelled in delight, clapping her hands.

"Good for you," I said.

"Congratulations," Mitch added.

"Do you have a pen?" she asked me. "I am going to frame this card. I never win anything." I handed her a pen, and she wrote the date down and then signed the card with a flourish. She ran up front to claim her prize, Harry trailing at a distance behind her.

Captain Walker slapped his card down on the table. "I give up." He saluted us both and then left the building.

I turned to Mitch. "Did you see what I saw?"

"Her signature?"

"Yup. Looks familiar, doesn't it?" I stated.

"Actually, yes." He studied me. "Did you notice anything else?"

"Hazel Kissinger is left-handed."

"Bingo," he said, and then added, "You're getting pretty good, Tink."

"I've always been good, Detective." I winked. "You've just never seen me in action."

"The night is young," he said on a low sexy voice, his eyelids lowering to a sleepy bedroom look.

"And we still haven't had a real date. Not to mention the case is cold, remember?" I gently reminded him, regretting our decision to wait for dessert as much as he seemed to be.

"How could I forget?" He groaned. "You're killing me, Tink."

Harry and Hazel returned to the table. "Where did the captain go?" she asked, looking disappointed.

"Lady Luck deserted him, so he called it a night," Mitch said. "Can I see your winning card?"

"Sure thing." Hazel thrust it at him proudly.

"Nice handwriting," I said. "You have a very distinct flowery style that's easily recognized, I imagine."

Her beaming face slipped a bit, and her gaze darted briefly to Harry. His sharp gaze was locked on Mitch, and then she took her card back. "Thank you," was all she said.

"Huh. I think you're right, Sunny," Mitch said, rubbing his jaw thoughtfully. "In fact, I've seen handwriting just like this recently. The person was left-handed, too. Coincidence?"

"Hmmm." I pretended to contemplate, then said, "I think not."

"She was with me," Harry said in a calm, cool, and ruthless judge-like way, putting his arm around Hazel's shoulders. I recognized the look because it was the same one my mother used when she was about to play hardball.

"Excuse me?" Mitch asked.

"I know what you're getting at, Detective. Yes, Hazel acted on an emotional impulse and wrote the note to Bernadette, warning her to stay away from the captain. But that's all she did. After the captain dismissed her so callously, her affections turned in other directions. The night of the murder, she was with me."

"But I thought you two just started hanging out," I said in surprise as I studied Harry in a whole new light. And based on Hazel's actions tonight, I would say her affections were still pointed straight in the captain's direction.

"I met Hazel my first night in town, and we've been friends ever since. Friendlier as of late. And with that, I think we'll call it a night. If you have any further questions, you can speak to my lawyer." His hard gaze landed on me. "I know a good one." They left without another word, leaving me with another question.

Why on earth was a man like Harry involved with a woman like Hazel?

Sunday after church I paid a visit to the Divine Inspiration Inn on Inspiration Lake. Today was cloudy, with the threat of a summer thunderstorm looming in the distance. Once again, Harry was MIA. He was probably off somewhere with Hazel, working out their alibis.

The inn was a large pale-green-and-white Victorian house with an enormous wraparound porch. A bit like Vicky, but much newer and nicer. It sat back from the road on a private lot of land, with a large backyard filled with wicker furniture and tables.

Down by the lake sat a long dock where

people went fishing or jumped off to swim. And a row of quaint cottages ran along the edge of the lake, with their own private beach that housed kayaks, canoes, rowboats, and inner tubes.

I could see why my parents were so enchanted with this place. It was full of elegance and charm, yet filled with plenty of things to do. And plenty of people at the moment, including my parents. I took in the scene before me.

A tall man in a white suit with sandy blond hair slicked back, like something straight out of *The Great Gatsby*, wandered around making sure the guests were satisfied. He stopped short when he saw my mother and, while his smile remained firmly in place, it stiffened somewhat.

He had to be Pierce Theodore, owner of Divine Inspiration.

"Vivian. Donald." He bowed slightly at the waist. I heard him say as I came to a stop before them, "I trust your stay here has been pleasant?"

"It's been satisfactory." Mom leaned in and added, "It will be pleasant the day you take my advice and get a decent espresso bar."

"Some fine cigars would be a nice addition as well," Dad chimed in, rubbing his stomach. "There's nothing like topping off a day with a quality cigar and top-shelf liquor."

Peirce stiffened, nodded once as though he didn't trust himself to speak, and then wandered off to his other guests.

"Mom. Dad." I bowed slightly, just like Pierce had, and then chuckled. "Don't you two think you're a bit hard on Mr. Theodore?"

"Certainly not, darling." Mom dusted imaginary lint off the front of her suit, in full lawyer mode now. "This inn has so much potential to be a five-star establishment, but Mr. Theodore has settled for four and a half. I'm just trying to push him a bit. One should always strive to do their best."

Dad grunted, glancing in my direction, but didn't say a word. Probably because he knew I was their ride to my place for their weekly session with Granny and Fiona. I'd told him in the past that if he kept insulting me, I'd stop speaking to him. Just because my profession wasn't his cup of tea didn't mean I wasn't doing my best. I was happy. That was all that should matter.

"Where's Mr. Dingleburg?" I asked, changing the subject while I still could.

"Off somewhere righting the world, no

doubt. Now there's a man who is a success in life," Dad boomed, bringing us right back around.

Grrr.

On the drive to my place, I filled them in on what Mitch and I had discovered thus far.

"Well, you'd better step it up," Mom said from my backseat. "We can't clear either of their names based on that."

"You're not getting in Detective Stone's way, are you?" Dad thundered from beside me. He wasn't even a lawyer, yet he also wore a suit and played the part of Mom's sidekick.

Lord help us all when they both retire.

"Of course I'm not getting in Mitch's way," I lied. "And you don't have to shout. Your voice echoes in here."

"It wouldn't if you'd spend some money and buy a real car. I can hardly move in this contraption." Dad squirmed. "My suit is wrinkling."

"A car with air-conditioning that works would be nice," Mom said, holding a scarf around her head. "My hair will never be the same. And I'm starting to perspire. That just won't do."

"We're here," I said, silently thanking the Lord for small miracles. As soon as we stepped out, the heavens opened up and it began to pour.

I bit back a laugh as Mom shrieked, attempting to run in high heels. "Donald, do something."

"I've got you, darling." He scooped her up and she wrapped her arms around his neck as he carried her, his strides much longer than hers. They were both laughing by the time he set her down, but when they saw me, they cleared their throats and smoothed their clothes.

"Too late. I saw you." I smirked.

"I don't know what you're talking about." Mom marched toward the front door and led the way inside. Dad followed hot on her heels, not saying a word, but his lips twitched several times as he passed by, and he shot me a rare wink along the way.

I shook my head with a grin. In my heart, I knew they cared about me as much as they cared about each other. They were both just too proper and stubborn to ever show it.

As soon as we got inside, it stopped raining and an eerie feline rumbling purr sounded from close by. My parents looked around warily, then took Granny and Fiona into the study to go over some things. I was making myself a cup of iced tea when Morty appeared in the kitchen, carrying a small stuffed dog in his mouth. I stared at him in surprise.

I'd tried to tell Granny that Morty didn't play with toys, but she'd ordered it for him anyway after all the signs he'd given that he liked dog toys. Fiona had topped her with a whole litter of stuffed puppies, of course. Trying to outdo each other even further, Granny had indeed made dog biscuit–shaped cookies out of cat food, and Fiona had managed to make a cat-sized ankle bracelet like theirs. A ball of string or a rubber mouse would have been the logical choices, but there was no talking to either of them when they were on a tear.

Up until now, Morty had never so much as given any of their "toys" a passing glance. Now he had Granny's stuffed dog in his mouth and stood before me, just staring at me. I reached down and tried to take it, but he pulled back like he wanted to play tug-of-war.

"This is a first." I looked at him oddly, tugging it back. He must actually like toys after all, but tug-of-war? "You're not a dog, you know."

He stepped back, made sure I was watching, and then proceeded to shred the dog to pieces with his razor sharp teeth and claws, no booties or bow ties in sight today.

I gasped a bit, startled. "Morty, that wasn't nice. If you didn't like the toy, you didn't have to play with it. Granny is going to be upset with you."

I swear it looked like he heaved a sigh before turning his nose up at me and leaving the room.

What on earth had gotten into him? I wondered.

Fiona walked into the kitchen first and yelped, hopping a good foot. "Sweet Jesus, what is that?"

"Morty's toy." I picked up the shredded dog and quickly hid it in a cupboard before Granny could see it. I would throw it out later when she wasn't around.

Fiona shuddered. "I need a drink."

"I have iced tea."

"Perfect. And, honey, make mine a Long Island Iced Tea. It's five o'clock somewhere."

"Uh . . . you do realize there isn't actually any tea in the cocktail. It just looks like it. Not to mention it's complicated to make. I don't have half the ingredients it would take."

"Whatever, honey. Just put something in it. I'm not fussy."

"Okay." I shrugged and searched my cupboards for anything that might work. I

267

was a beer drinker. Finding an old bottle of vodka, I held it up, and Fiona nodded in approval. I poured a shot in her glass of iced tea and handed it to her.

Fiona proceeded to add a generous amount of sugar and lemon then took a sip. "Sweet tea with a kick. Perfect."

I saluted her and chuckled, trying not to shudder. I'd stick with my beer.

Granny came out next. "If I didn't have the stretch marks to prove it, I'd swear that child is not mine," she mumbled.

"What was that?" I asked, knowing exactly what she'd said but wanting to hear it again to reassure myself that I wasn't the only one my mother drove crazy.

"Oh, nothing dear." Granny was too nice. She retied her apron and said, "I was just wondering if you had the time."

"Sure." I smiled in sympathy. "It's two P.M. Why?"

"I'd say it's time for some afternoon tea." Granny nodded, heading toward the tea-kettle on the stove.

"I've got my tea right here." Fiona held up the half-empty glass and winked as she sat at the table.

"Figures." Granny shook her head and put the kettle on.

"What can you tell me about Hazel,

Granny?" I asked, sitting across from Fiona.

"Hazel Kissinger the Sewing Sister?" Granny eyed me curiously.

"That's the one."

"What do you want to know?"

"Anything. Everything."

"Well, she's in her sixties. Sings in the church choir. Never been married. I heard she had a new beau named Harry."

Fiona grunted. "I never did like men named Harry."

"I don't know. This guy seems really nice. Except, it's weird. I don't think they like each other. It turns out Hazel is left-handed, and her handwriting matches that on the threatening note that someone gave to Bernadette, warning her to stay away from Captain Walker."

"You're kidding!" Granny said.

"Don't act so shocked. Anyone who isn't blind can see Hazel is sweet on the captain." Fiona snorted. "Except maybe him."

"That's not the part I'm surprised about. I'm surprised she had the guts to write a note like that to Bernadette. She's so quiet and reserved. She doesn't seem the type."

"Writing her threat in a note was probably easier than saying it in person, I imagine."

"Do you think she killed Bernadette in a

jealous rage because the captain paid more attention to her?" Fiona asked.

"The note did say we, so that's why Bernadette thought the two of you were threatening her."

"Why, that's nonsense," Granny sputtered.

"Not nonsense. Brilliance," Mom said as she and Dad entered the kitchen. "If Hazel killed Bernadette and framed the two of you, then all three of you would be out of the picture. She would have been a shoo-in to win the bakeoff, and then the captain would have to notice her."

"Does Detective Stone know this?" Dad asked.

"He was with me, and besides, Hazel has an alibi," I said.

"Who?" Fiona asked.

"Her new boyfriend, Harry," I said.

"Wait, that's not possible. Judge Harry . . . I mean . . ." Mom's gaze darted to Fiona's intense one.

"What do you mean Judge Harry?" Fiona asked. "What's his last name?" She watched my mother closely, who flushed pink and squirmed for the first time since I could remember.

"Dingleburg, why?" I answered.

A loud crash sounded as Fiona's glass hit

the floor, shattering into a million pieces. We all jumped and stared at her. Her jaw hung open, and her face looked frozen.

"Donald, darling, call 911," Mom yelled. "I don't think she's faking this time. I think she's had a stroke."

"Harry?" Granny sputtered, locking eyes with Fiona.

"Harry!" Fiona ground out, livid anger replacing her shock.

"Would someone please tell me who Harry is?" I asked, thoroughly confused.

"Judge Harold Phillip Dingleburg," Fiona spat and glared at my mother. "Why didn't you tell me?"

"Tell you what?" I asked, even more confused. My mother had said she didn't know who Harry was, which was obviously not true. "I repeat, who on earth is Harry?"

Granny took a breath and finally said, "Harry is Fiona's ex-husband."

16

Two hours and several sweet teas with a kick later, Granny, Fiona, and I were still sitting around my kitchen table when the doorbell rang. My parents had already left to follow up on some things. Mitch was busy checking into a few more leads of his own. Meanwhile, the rest of us were still trying to wrap our brains around what had just happened.

"I got it," I said to the women. I jogged to the front door and opened it without thinking. A gust of wind swirled through and then settled. I just stood there and stared. "Harry? Or should I call you Phillip?"

"My middle name is Phillip. Fiona never liked the name Harry or Dingleburg. That's why she called me Phillip, and she kept her maiden name of Atwater."

That's what Granny had said. Scandalous for their era, to which Fiona had given her the raspberries and just kept drinking. "Did you know she was in town when you came here?" I asked suspiciously.

"Yes. I followed her."

I started to close the door.

"Wait." He stuck his foot in the doorway. "Hear me out. I always thought Fiona liked Phillip because it was closer to Frank, and by keeping her maiden name she could still feel single. I was a fool. I made a big mistake in leaving her." He scrubbed a hand through his distinguished gray hair, looking more frazzled than I'd ever seen him. "Can I come in please? Just give me five minutes to talk to her."

"Answer me one thing. Are you dating Hazel?"

"No. There's never been anyone for me other than Fiona." The sincerity in his voice rang through loud and clear. "Five minutes. Please?"

I pushed the door open wider and stepped back. "I can let you in, but know this: I can't make her talk to you."

"Fair enough."

He followed me into the kitchen, and Fiona dropped her second glass of the day.

"Oh, dear." Granny rushed to clean up the mess.

"What the hell is he doing here?" Fiona spat.

"I'm here to explain," he said tentatively.

"I don't want to hear anything you have to say." She looked away and crossed her arms stubbornly. Suddenly, her face looked alarmed. "You didn't tell the kids about me, did you?"

His face softened. "No. I would never do that without talking to you first."

"Wait. Then how did you know I was here?"

"I followed you."

She gasped. "You did what? You had no right. You're the one who left me."

"And I've regretted it every day," he said softly.

Her chin wobbled, but she clamped her jaw tight and sat up straighter. "You missed your chance. I won't let you hurt me again."

"Fi, don't be like that. And if you remember, you hurt me, too."

"Don't call me Fi. Besides, I heard you've already moved on."

"Hazel and I are just friends. We met when I first arrived, and then she was worried because she did something stupid by writing that note to Bernadette, so she came to me for advice. That's all. And in return, she kept tabs on what you were up to for me. I couldn't come into town because I knew you'd spot me, so I was biding my time at

274

the inn, figuring out how to convince you to take me back. That's when Bernadette was murdered, and you and Gertie were arrested."

"You know my granny?" I asked, fascinated.

"We all went to high school together. I'm just glad I was here to talk to Judge Navarra on their behalf." He leaned against the counter in the kitchen, and no one offered him a chair or anything to drink. No one dared based on the way Fiona was looking at him.

"You're the one who convinced him to let us go on house arrest under Sunny's custody?" Granny asked dreamily.

He nodded. "It was the least I could do."

"Awww, Harry, that was so sweet of you," Granny twittered.

Fiona glared.

"Were you really with Hazel the night of the murder?" I asked.

He looked at Fiona, who raised her brow at him as though asking, *Do you swear to tell the truth, the whole truth, and nothing but the truth?* He sighed. "No, I wasn't. We both needed an alibi," he confessed.

"Why would you need an alibi?" Fiona asked, sounding somewhat placated.

"I didn't want anyone to think I tried to

set you up to take the fall for something you didn't do, out of spite and revenge."

"Did you?" she asked, narrowing her eyes.

"Why would I come clean, knowing it would put me at risk now?" He stared at her with a tortured look on his face. "I talked to the judge for you."

Her shoulders didn't look quite so stiff now. I thought for a moment she would give in, but then she looked away as she said, "I do believe your five minutes are up."

"What do you mean, he's not here again?" Jo asked Yvonne at Animal Angels early Monday morning.

We'd arrived before opening hours because we were supposed to finally meet with Ozzie. Jo had asked me to come along because I had information against Ozzie that might help persuade him to let them adopt the dog. I didn't plan to blackmail him, but I figured my presence alone would be enough to make him squirm.

Cole was on his knees, trying to coax the big fawn-and-black Great Dane dog from the back of his pen with a dog biscuit and soft words.

"We were supposed to meet with a couple interested in adopting another dog from here," Jo added.

"We'll take him," Cole said, not moving his gaze away from the dog. "I don't need to talk to anyone. I want him." And just like that, the dog settled down as though he could understand him. The dog's gaze locked on Cole's as well, and he crept forward inch by inch until he accepted the dog biscuit from Cole's hand.

Jo looked at Cole, and her whole face softened.

"I'm so sorry," Yvonne replied. "Mr. Zuckerman found another family outside of town who wants this same dog, too. In fact, they are supposed to pick him up later today."

"Like hell." Cole surged to his feet, and the dog didn't even flinch. "Biff is ours." The dog stood to his full, impressive height and let out a deep woof.

"Biff?" Yvonne asked.

"Short for Bigfoot," Cole said firmly. "Point is, he's named. He's mine. End of story."

"Has this other couple even come to see Biff?" I asked, interjecting before Sasquatch could run off into the woods with him like a caveman.

Yvonne shook her head. "I've never seen them before. Unless Mr. Zuckerman brought them in after hours when I wasn't here."

"Can you do me a favor and give me a call just as soon as you hear from Mr. Zuckerman?" I asked. "I want to talk to him before he gives that dog away."

"He'll have to go through me before I let him give Biff away," Cole stated in a fiercely determined and menacing tone. "I'm not leaving."

"Cole." Jo rested her hand on his arm.

He relaxed a little at her touch, and a wisp of a smile crossed his lips. The dog let out of a soft whine. "It's okay. I promise," Cole said to Jo while laying a hand on the dog's massive head. "You go to work. I'll be fine right here." He glanced at Biff and then back at her. "He needs me."

She pressed her lips together, blinking back tears, and then nodded. "Okay." He was going to make a great dad, I thought, willing my own tears to dry up.

"Call me if you hear anything, Sunny," Jo said to me.

"I will. And don't worry, Jo. We'll figure this out. Won't we, Yvonne?"

Yvonne straightened with a backbone I hadn't seen before and nodded once with a sniff. "I'm good at stalling. You just keep your cell phone charged and ready."

"Sounds like a plan."

I left Animal Angels and drove around

town for the next hour, checking all the possible spots where Ozzie might be. He wasn't anywhere in town, that was for sure. I tried calling Mitch, but he didn't answer, so I sent him a text.

A while later, Yvonne finally called me. "Ozzie showed up with a couple of guys I've never seen before. They certainly didn't look like family men. They were big and scary and . . . they took the dog." Her voice hitched.

"What do you mean? Where was Cole?"

"He's at Doc Wilcox's but don't worry. He's okay. Just a bit bruised. His pride is hurt more than anything, but he's a mess emotionally. I tried to stop them, but Ozzie fired me and kicked me out. I called the police, but Ozzie left with Biff and his thugs before they got here."

There were only two guys I knew of who could overpower Sasquatch. The meatheads. I had checked the hotel and even the inn after my encounter with them at the monster truck rally. No one with their description had ever stayed there. I had hoped they'd left town.

Suddenly Yvonne's words registered. "Did you see or hear where they were going?"

"When Ozzie kicked me out, I didn't leave. I hid behind the shack and called 911.

I heard him say something to the big scary guys about them taking Biff to the campsite, and that he would meet up with them later."

Even Yvonne was calling the dog by the name Cole and Jo had given him as though it was already a fact. The dog was Cole's, plain and simple. We all knew it. I had to find a way to stop them.

"Thanks, Yvonne. You did great." I hung up and headed for the only campgrounds I knew of. The ones at Divinity Beach. No wonder there was no record of the meatheads in town. Smart move of them to choose a campground instead of a hotel.

As I drove, I called Jo and she confirmed Cole was okay . . . yet not okay. I assured her I would do everything I could to get Biff back. She warned me not to because she didn't want to see me get hurt, too. I told her I had backup. Then I called Mitch again. But once again, there was no answer.

I couldn't stop worrying about Cole. The poor man had been through enough after losing his first wife, which he blamed himself for. Now he'd lost the dog on his watch. If he and Jo lost Biff for good, I was afraid Cole would never be the same.

The meatheads were loan sharks. What on earth could they want with Biff? Mitch couldn't get mad at me this time. I'd tried to ask for his help, but I couldn't wait. Biff needed me. Jo and Cole needed me. I would not let them down.

I arrived at the beach and headed toward the campgrounds. It was still pretty early, so things were just getting started. The sun was bright with the promise of a glorious beach day, the temperature rising quickly. Campers were stirring, the sounds of voices and the smell of bacon and eggs and coffee filling the air. I had no idea where I would find them, but I had to at least try.

I made my way along the edge of the campsites, looking for a massive dog. There were campers and tents strewn about on various lots. No sign of a Great Dane anywhere. I had almost given up when I noticed a path that led around a corner to a private lot. Following that path, I struck gold.

Biff was tied to a tree by a camper, and a dark sedan was parked beside that. He crouched down low like he was scared to death when he saw me. I approached him slowly, cooing all the way, with one eye locked on the camper.

"It's okay, Biff. I'm not going to hurt you, buddy," I whispered. He whined at the word *Biff*, already recognizing it. He really was Cole's dog.

"You be a good boy, and I'll get you out of here."

Biff seemed to understand I was there to help him. He let me touch the rope that was knotted around a tree, but I couldn't get it untied. Taking a deep breath, I let my hands trail along the rope until I reached his collar. He actually let me near his humongous mouth.

It took a lot of twisting and tugging, but I finally got the rope untied. Biff surged to his massive feet, standing nearly as tall as I was. I gripped his collar tighter, when the door to the camper opened. Biff took one look at his captors . . .

And the race was on!

"Get her," Meathead 1 yelled.

"I'll get the car; you go on foot," Meathead 2 bellowed, his voice fading in the distance as Biff pulled me along like a rag doll.

"Whoa, boy. Slow down. Easy, now," I huffed, out of breath as I held on for dear life.

One of the meatheads was closing in fast.

Biff ran full speed, zigging and zagging around trees, darting through campsites, and leaping over burned out fire pits. I had long since lost my flip-flops, and my feet were stinging from pinecones, needles, pebbles, and Lord knew what else, but no way was I letting go. I fell a couple of times and skinned my knees as Biff dragged me along, but I managed to get back up while still hanging on.

People hollered at us, but I had no idea what they were saying. I just kept shouting, "Sorry," in between my yelps of pain and words of encouragement to Biff.

After taking a roundabout path, we finally reached my car. It took everything in me to dig in my heels and pull Biff to a stop. He stood there, fit as a fiddle, barely breathing hard, while my tongue hung out a good inch and my sides heaved as I struggled for air.

I fished the keys out of my pocket and opened the door to my bug. Biff barely squeezed inside, leaving just enough room for me to climb in and lock the door just in the nick of time.

Meathead 1 came barreling through the trees, and Biff cowered, whining once more.

Poor baby.

"Don't you worry. I won't let that big ape hurt you anymore." I started up my car, and the big burly thug pulled out a gun. This time I was the one who let out a whine as I threw my car into drive, stomping on the gas.

Dirt and gravel kicked up and shot out

from beneath my tires as I roared down the campground road much faster than the posted fifteen miles per hour suggested. Just as we reached the main road, the dark sedan appeared in my rearview mirror.

I pushed the pedal as far down as it would go, but they were still gaining on me. We had almost reached the main part of town when the sedan slammed into the back of my bug. I gasped, struggling to keep my car on the road. I had just regained control when the sedan slammed into my car again.

My poor bug couldn't take much more. I fishtailed and then spun in a one-eighty, ending up in the ditch. The sedan stopped, and the meatheads got out. My doors were locked, but that wouldn't do much good against a bullet.

"I'm so sorry, boy," I said with a sob and rubbed the top of Biff's head.

Pride filled me when he found the courage to bravely stand over me and growl out the window.

One of the meatheads pulled his gun and aimed it at my car. I wrapped my arms around Biff's neck and closed my eyes as my body shook all over. This was it. I was going to die, never having told Mitch how much he meant to me.

A shot rang out, and I screamed.

Scuffling and shouting came from outside my window. It took me a moment to realize I wasn't dead. I pried my eyes open and couldn't believe what I saw. Mitch was kneeling on the back of one facedown, bleeding meathead, handcuffing his wrists. Meanwhile, a slightly roughed-up Sasquatch shoved the other handcuffed meathead into the back of the squad car.

Biff whined and pawed at the window, wagging his tail as he stared out with eyes only for Cole. I hit the unlock button and leaned over to pull the door open. Biff shot outside and lumbered over to Cole, standing on his hind legs with his front paws on Cole's shoulders. Cole laughed with tears in his eyes and rubbed Biff's fur everywhere he could reach. When the dog dropped back to the ground, there was no leash necessary.

He wasn't about to leave Cole's side.

My driver's-side door opened, and Mitch reached in and lifted me out. I half laughed and half sobbed as he buried his head in my neck. I wrapped my arms around him and hugged him tight.

"You're gonna put me in an early grave, Tink," his deep voice rumbled against my skin.

"I called you this time, I swear. I just couldn't let Cole and Jo lose Biff."

285

Mitch leaned back and searched my eyes like he wanted to say something but then planted a kiss on my lips instead. It didn't matter. That kiss said it all.

He gently set me on my feet. "You're a good person, Sunny."

"How did you find us? And why didn't you answer your phone?"

"By the time I read your text message, I had also received messages from Yvonne and Jo and Cole. I didn't answer earlier because I was arresting Ozzie and the man who was supposed to adopt Biff. Turns out Animal Angels is a front for a dog-fighting operation."

"You're kidding! That's awful."

"Ozzie was in major debt and owed a lot of money to loan sharks. The proceeds from the charity auction were enough to get Animal Angels going. The real money was going to come from selling the dogs to bad people involved in a whole underground dog-fighting ring."

"What's going to happen to Animal Angels now? Those dogs still need good homes."

"Yvonne's taking over. She was doing most of the work anyway."

"That's perfect. Those animals are lucky to have her."

"You're lucky. After you ruined Ozzie's

chance of winning money from the monster truck rally, and then you stole Biff, both he and the loan sharks wanted you dead."

I swallowed hard. "Well, that's not good."

"Now do you see why you had me so worried? Thanks to Morty, I was able to put a stop to Ozzie's plans. Biff was going to be his first sale, and the money was going to pay off the loan sharks."

"But Biff's not even mean."

"Trust me" — Mitch's eyes met mine with the hard truth — "he would have been by the time they were through with him."

I shuddered at the mere thought of what they would have put that poor animal through, then Mitch's words registered. "Wait, how did Morty help you?"

"All the clues he's been sending. First, he dropped a dog biscuit at Granny's feet, and then a puppy collar at Fiona's feet. When he dropped the Summer Solstice Carnival flyer with Animal Angels featured on the front at our feet, I knew something was up. Then you told me about Morty standing by the flyer on the back of the fire truck."

"And the stuffed dog he shredded," I finished. "He was trying to tell me about the dog fights, and once again, I misinterpreted what he meant." I shook my head. "No wonder he was so frustrated with me and acting so strange lately."

"Must be why he turned to me for help." I gaped at Mitch, and he said, "Shocking, I know. The biggest clue was when, from out of nowhere, he showed up in my car one day with Ozzie's business card. I looked down at the card for a mere second, but when I looked back up, he was gone. Between all that and the text messages from Yvonne, Jo, Cole, and you, I managed to find you in time. I'm just glad you're safe now."

"Thank you." I touched Mitch's cheek. "I'm just glad it's over."

"Just because Ozzie was arrested doesn't prove he killed Bernadette. I have a feeling this investigation has only just begun."

17

Tuesday morning Granny pulled her freezer bag out of the freezer and fished fifty dollars out. "Oh, my, Wally. What a workout. Good thing today's laundry day." Granny fanned her flushed face and perspiring brow with the bills. She wore yet another flamboyant homemade, seventies-style, yoga-pant concoction even though it felt like ninety out already.

"It was great for me. You sure do know how to Wallycise your clients, sugar," Fiona purred, still half out of breath, and then tucked sixty dollars into the waistband of Wally's shorts like he was one of the Chippendale dancers. She had donned another ultramodern, yet super-loud, yoga outfit and was perspiring nearly as much as Granny Gert.

"It was better for me," Granny said. "I'm sweating more. Here, feel my head."

"Ewww, that's nasty," Fiona responded.

"At least I perspire like a lady. You look like your sweat glands opened up and puked a week's worth of fluid out."

"Ladies, it was a pleasure working with both of you," Wally's smooth, velvety voice rumbled as the white of his teeth blazed next to the milk-chocolate silk of his completely dry skin. He was obviously enjoying every minute of their company. "Nothing wrong with a good sweat. It means you're working hard." He winked.

Morty looked from Granny to Fiona to Wally and finally to me. The women didn't know how to dress themselves any better than they dressed him. At least today he was blessedly au naturel since they'd obviously expended their energy in trying to outdo one another and left him alone for once.

Morty let out what sounded like hissing laughter, Wally did a double take, and then Morty disappeared faster than a blink. Before Wally could comment, Granny started rambling on again.

"Here's an extra ten for making me have to use the rinse cycle twice." Granny fluttered her lashes as she patted her scarf-covered white curls.

"Forget the rinse cycle. Here's another five for the spin cycle, darling." Fiona tossed back her brightly colored, bandanna-wrapped head and twittered like a cockatiel.

Good Lord.

I opened the front windows wider, but there was still no breeze. Nothing but hot, sticky, humid air. I hated being cooped up all winter, but right now I'd give anything for air-conditioning, I thought, feeling irritated. I wasn't sure if it was the heat or the lack of progress on this blasted case.

"Same time same place on Thursday?" Wally asked with a thumbs-up to the ladies and a sympathetic smile in my direction.

"Oh, go on with you, now." Granny patted his bulging bicep, letting her hand linger. "You know we'll be right here. We're not going anywhere anytime soon with this little accessory strapped to our ankles."

"Well, then, I guess you won't have an excuse to say no," he said and patted her hand. "Exercise is the key to longevity."

"Then count me in," Fiona chimed in, not about to be left out.

Wally gave her a pat as well and then left.

I sighed. Granny was right. At the rate we were going, it would be a while before we solved this case. I glanced through my notes and tried to take stock of where we stood.

Ophelia Edwards might have injected a laxative in Fiona's pie to make her lose the bakeoff because she wanted her job as president of the Knitting Nanas, but that didn't make her a murderer. The maid had confirmed her whereabouts, thereby giving her an alibi. She was no longer a suspect.

Hazel Kissinger was left-handed and had admitted to writing the threatening note, warning Bernadette to stay away from Captain Walker. She had purposely used *we* in the note, hoping Bernadette would assume it was Granny and Fiona who wrote it. Love made you do stupid things, but Mitch had told me last night that Hazel's neighbor confirmed she saw her pulling into her driveway at the time of the murder. So Hazel was no longer a suspect.

The employees Bernadette had fired all had alibis as well. That still left Harry, but I couldn't imagine him trying to set Fiona up for murder out of revenge. He genuinely seemed to want her back, and he had been instrumental in getting the judge to agree to let them out on house arrest. Yet Harry didn't have an alibi. He said he was driving around looking for Fiona that night.

Then there was Quincy Turner. He'd been angry that the carnival committee had passed up his Parks and Rec Program in favor of the Animal Angels Organization, and he'd admitted to blackmailing Bernadette for her being a fraud after her petition didn't work, but he wouldn't say how she was a fraud. And I still didn't know who the person was on the other end of the phone the night of the Fourth of July. I had a feeling he blackmailed that person for more money to keep quiet. If only I could find out who that person was, then I was sure I would discover what was worth that much money to keep quiet.

Ozzie Zuckerman had threatened Bernadette physically to get her to back off from the petition. He needed the auction money to pay off the loan sharks he owed. He could have killed her to stop her from making any more waves. Or the loan sharks could have killed her. They had been looking for something in her office, and Bernadette had to have gotten the money to pay Quincy from somewhere.

Her business had been struggling not that long ago, but then suddenly, she seemed to be doing okay. Like she had gotten an influx of cash from someplace. If she used the new source of money from her business to pay off Quincy, she might have turned to the loan sharks for some quick cash to put back into the business or risk having to close. Desperate people did crazy things sometimes. In the end, she'd had to close anyway.

I just had to find a way to prove that one of the remaining suspects killed Bernadette Baldwin, so Granny and Fiona could be set free. But I had no clue where to begin. My cell phone rang. I glanced at the caller ID.

"Hey, Romeo, how are things going with Zoe?" I asked Sean, crossing my flip-flop-clad feet at the ankles and fanning my bare shoulders beneath my tank top.

"They're not. Every time I ask her out, she still says no. My wee little heart can't take much more abuse."

I laughed. "Right. I'm sure you're absolutely broken up over this."

"Actually, I have to admit, it does kind of sting, love," he said in a tone more serious than any I'd ever heard him use.

"Then take my advice and quit asking her out. Just talk to her. Get to know her. I'm sure she'd like that." I knew I would, if I ever got to have my own date with Mitch. The few moments we had alone recently were spent talking about the case.

"I've tried," Sean said. "I've told her all about the bar, and Wally's World, and everything I could think of about my life. How I live, what I do, what I'm into. She doesn't seem to care."

Men were so clueless.

"Because you're talking all about you.

294

Stop talking and start asking questions. Find out how *she* lives, what *she* does, what *she's* into. Start listening. You're too used to women being enamored of you. It's time you do the admiring for a change. You might be surprised by the outcome."

"Huh. I never thought of it that way. Thanks, lass. You just might be on to something."

"Glad to help. I do know a thing or two about women, but you still owe me after my Dumpster diving and your lack thereof."

"That's actually why I'm calling."

I set my feet on the floor. "If you think I'm climbing back into another stinky Dumpster or anywhere else, you're out of your ever-loving mind."

"As I recall, Dumpster diving was your brilliant idea. Not mine. But no worries. There are no smelly Dumpsters involved. Only construction ones."

I puckered my brow. "What are you talking about?"

"Now that Wally's back from his personal training session with the Dynamic Duo, I don't have to cover the gym anymore. I'll pick you up and fill you in."

"I'm game for anything that gets me out of Crazyville."

"See you in five."

■ ■ ■ ■

"What on earth does Cole West have to do with Bernadette Baldwin's murder?" I asked Sean as we arrived at the West Construction site.

"We were going over wedding stuff when we got talking about Zoe. He said she wanted to order the cake from BB's Baked Goods, but now that it was closed, she had to order it from Sam's Bakery. Seems to me Sam's is doing a great business now that he doesn't have any competition left in town, don't you think?"

I shrugged. "I guess so. But how does that make him a murderer?"

"Let's go talk to Cole. He has all the details."

"Okay." I followed Sean across a gravel parking lot, through various construction vehicles and non-smelly Dumpsters. Didn't matter, I still gave them a wide berth. We reached the main office, when the door swung open and Biff bounded outside, jumping around excitedly and looking like a normal, happy, healthy dog.

Like he should.

"Hey, boy." I gave his head a good rub, and he let out a deep woof, then shook all over and ran back to the door, never letting Cole out of his sight for too long.

Cole jogged outside in work boots, jeans, and a T-shirt while carrying a hard hat. "Hey, Sunny. Did Sean fill you in?"

"A little, but not completely. What's going on?"

He looked around, always wary and never completely trusting of anyone except Jo. He and Biff really were one and the same. "Let's go inside where we have privacy."

"Sounds great," I said, and meant it. The trailer that served as an office had air-conditioning. I took a moment to stand in front of the fan and close my eyes. "This is Heaven."

"I can see that," Cole's deep voice said with a chuckle.

"You need a moment alone, lass?" Sean asked, the teasing note in his voice firmly back in place.

"Nope. I'm good."

"You're good, all right. Lucky Mitch." Sean wagged his brows.

I smacked him. "Behave. That's the kind of stuff that gets you in trouble with women." I focused on Cole. "Sean said you had important information regarding Sam?" I sat in a chair next to Sean across from Cole's desk.

Cole sat on the edge of his desk, facing us. "A while back, before the murder, Sam came to me asking for an estimate on a job."

"What job?"

"Knocking down the wall between his bakeshop and BB's Baked Goods."

"Why would he want to do that?"

"I asked him the same thing. He said Bernadette's business was hurting, so he was going to see if she wanted to merge their businesses. He wanted solid numbers on what it would cost before he approached her. When I didn't hear back from him, I contacted him to see what was up. He said Bernadette wasn't in the market for a partner and had said no."

"Really," I said. "Did he seem angry about it?"

"More frustrated than anything," Cole went on. "Sam said as competitors, neither one of them was doing that great. But if they merged, it would be a win-win situation. Bernadette wouldn't listen, and now her shop is closed."

"And Sam is making out like a bandit," Sean added.

"Sam once said he never gambled because it was too risky. When Bernadette had said no to merging, maybe he killed her to ensure all the business went his way," I said.

298

"Maybe it's time we talked to him and found out," Sean said. "You up for a little good cop, bad cop again?" he asked me.

"You read my mind."

We thanked Cole and headed into town to talk to Sam. Ten minutes later, we were enjoying a slice of cinnamon raisin bread on the house in a corner booth of Sam's Bakery. Sam sat across from us, dressed all in white with a tall chef's hat on the top of his big round head. He was a pudgy man with tufts of white hair around the sides and back.

"This is delicious, Sam. You seem to be doing well for yourself," I said around a mouthful in full good cop mode.

"I do okay." He nodded proudly.

"I see that," Sean chimed in, using a tone that said he was born to play the bad cop. "Looks like you doubled your customers since BB's closed. Lucky you."

Sam's smile slipped a little. "I don't like what you're implying. I'm not going to say I'm not happy that business has picked up, but no one enjoys benefiting from someone else's death."

"Since she turned you down in merging your businesses, her death was the only way you really could benefit, now wasn't it, lad?"

"Where did you hear that?" Sam narrowed

his beady eyes, and his round face nearly hid them from view.

"You didn't like Bernadette much, did you?" Sean went on.

"It doesn't matter if I liked her or not. I would never kill anyone."

"Where were you on the night of her death?" Sean asked.

"None of your damn business," Sam exploded. "I don't have to tell you a thing."

"You're right, you don't," I said, knowing it was time for me to step in with more good cop. "We're just trying to figure out what happened. That's all." I handed him my card. "If you can think of anything at all, please give me a call."

Sam took the card. "Look, all I wanted was to merge our businesses so we would both benefit. Bernadette might not have been the nicest person, but she usually had good business sense. I knew she was hurting for money, yet she said no. It didn't make a bit of sense. Am I happy my business is booming now? Hell yes. I'm human, Miss Meadows, but I'm hardly a killer."

My gut told me there was more going on here than borrowing money from loan sharks. My gut was never wrong, and I had a hunch I knew what it was. Time to put my background to good use and call on the socialite within.

Just before closing, I hit up the bank. We only had one in town. I did all my banking online, so I didn't know the bank manager personally. That worked in my favor perfectly.

I adjusted my wide-brimmed hat, smoothed my summer white suit, and teetered along on spiked heels. Holding my head high, I walked with an air of authority. Basically like my mother and all the people who ran in her social circle.

After asking to speak with the manager, I headed to the waiting room in the back and waited for him to call me in. After what seemed like forever, he finally did. I went into his office and closed the door.

Holding out my hand, I shook his way too soft, limp one and said, "I'm Sylvia Eleanor Meadows of the New York Meadowses. Lovely to make your acquaintance, Mr. Vladamir."

"How can I help you today, Ms. Meadows?" He folded his long frame behind his desk and adjusted his round spectacles over dark bushy eyebrows.

"You have such a lovely little town here," I said, testing the waters to make sure he didn't know who I was.

He smiled with pride shining bright from his eyes. "We're quite proud of our town. Divinity is full of charm and elegance and class. A wonderful place to live and raise a family. Are you married?" He eyed me subtly.

"No, I'm not married . . . yet." I smiled coyly. "You should be proud of your darling town. Although, I do have to say the newspaper headlines are a bit alarming." I folded my hands in my lap.

"Ah, yes, well, I can assure you we normally don't have crime in Divinity. At least we didn't use to. Lately, it's as though a cloud has formed, and we can't seem to get out from beneath its mist of doom and gloom. Too many newcomers who don't belong here, is what I say." He huffed, mumbling something about quacky fortune-tellers and crazy old ladies wreaking havoc.

"Hmmm, you don't say," I replied, knowing he was talking about Fiona and Granny and myself. I stiffened my spine and made my smile even brighter.

"Never mind all that negative nonsense," he said. "You seem like a high-caliber person. The exact kind of people Divinity needs. Are you planning to stick around for long?"

"That depends."

"Anything I can say to persuade you to stay?"

"Well, actually, I was wondering, now that the owner of BB's Baked Goods has had such an unfortunate demise, will the bank foreclose on her business? I am interested in relocating my business."

He frowned. "But BB's Baked Goods is not for sale."

"It's not? I was told the owner didn't have any relatives. Wouldn't the property revert back to the bank?"

"Not if she had a partner."

Sam had said Bernadette had told him no. "So, you're telling me that Bernadette Baldwin had a business partner?"

He checked his books. "That's right. Just a few months ago, but legal just the same."

I gave him my most charming smile. "Any chance you could divulge the name of her partner?"

He leaned forward as he said, "I would if I could, but I can't."

"Can't or won't?" I put on a pout, but I wasn't about to flutter my lashes. That was pushing it.

"Can't," he assured me. "The partner was a silent partner and chose to remain anonymous."

I sat there stunned, my lips parting in my

shock. If Sam wasn't Bernadette's partner, then who the heck was? Or was Sam lying? And how did they feel about Bernadette giving all the money away to buy Quincy's silence? Mad enough to kill her and become the sole owner? And when, if ever, did they plan to reopen?

"Are you okay? You look like you might faint," the bank manager broke into my thoughts. "I know you must be disappointed, but I have other properties that would be suitable for a business. What kind of business did you say it was?"

I pulled off my hat and looked him square in the eye as I said with relish, "Fortune-telling."

He choked and gaped at me. "But I thought —"

"I know exactly what you thought. Toodles, Vlad. My friends call me Sunny. In your case, don't bother calling me at all."

I kicked off my shoes and walked out the door in my bare feet with my head held high.

18

At the end of the week, I had just about given up on trying to figure out who Bernadette's silent partner could be. I'd even gone for a walk on the trails behind Mini Central Park to try to clear my mind, but it hadn't done any good.

The day was gorgeous, not a cloud in sight.

I had to face facts. I needed help. Time to call Mitch and my parents and have a family meeting. I pulled into my driveway to find half the town there again. What on earth was the Dynamic Duo doing this time? I parked my bug and made my way through the crowd of people only to stop short and gape.

Half of Vicky's contents were strewn about across the lawn with a huge sign posted in the front that read, YARD SALE! Figured. It was the weekend, and the Dynamic Duo was bored. Still, none of this stuff was theirs to sell.

Granny stood behind a table, serving fresh-squeezed lemonade while Fiona stood by a money box, ready to handle the sales. You couldn't even read half the prices because they kept crossing each other's out and remarking them.

"I came as soon as I could," Mitch said from behind me.

I whirled around. He stood there, slightly out of breath since he'd just come from his weekend jog in his NYPD shorts and T-shirt. The scar from breaking his leg was barely visible beneath the hair that had grown back and the tan he now sported.

My parents were close behind him as they power walked in their matching tracksuits. "What are they up to now?" Mom asked, sipping daintily at a bottle of water.

"They've put us off schedule. I have a tennis match with Harry before lunch," Dad thundered.

"Wait, what?" My brain fogged with confusion. "Who called you?" I asked Mitch.

"You texted me a 911 text," he said, eying me as though I'd stayed out in the sun too long.

"No, I didn't."

"Darling, you texted us the same message," Mom said. "Really, Sylvia. Texting is so impersonal. You should have called."

"Are you feeling okay?" Dad asked, putting the back of his hand to my forehead. "Experiencing any memory loss?"

"I feel fine." I moved my head away. "Look, I don't even have my phone on me. I forgot it in the house when I left to go hiking through the trails at the park."

"Well, if you didn't text us, then who did?" Mitch asked.

"Yes, our first sale!" Fiona squealed.

Before she could exchange money with Ida Ray, who had her eye on an antique chest of drawers, dark clouds rolled in and thunder boomed. A flash of lightning lit up the sky and streaked to the ground not ten feet away. Big fat raindrops pummeled the ground and everything standing on it.

Ida shrieked and ran for her car, as did everyone else. Meanwhile, we all bolted inside, soaking wet and dripping on my hardwood floors. No sooner had everyone left, and I was positive all of Vicky's things were ruined out on the lawn, than the clouds blew away as quickly as they had come.

I ran back outside to bright sunny skies, and even though my clothes were still wet, all of the yard-sale items were completely dry. The others followed close behind me. Mitch walked up beside me and looked around, his lips parting but no words emerging.

Morty dropped my cell phone at my feet, glared at Granny and Fiona, scowled at Mitch, hissed at my parents, and then disappeared.

I picked up my phone and looked at my parents and Mitch, but no one would voice what we were all thinking. It was pretty clear who had sent them the text from my phone. And with the look he'd just given Granny and Fiona, you didn't need a set of cards to read his message.

Don't mess with his stuff!

"Tea anyone?" I asked, leading the way back inside.

They followed me quickly, with Fiona mumbling something about cars not being the only thing haunted around this place. Once we were all sipping our iced tea on the front porch — after that display, no one wanted to go anywhere near Morty — I told them about what I'd discovered and asked them what they thought.

"That widow Ida Ray has plenty of money," Mitch said. "She lets everyone know it, too."

"Yes, but she's no spring chicken. I doubt

she'd want to work," Mom said.

"No, but if her husband is gone, she might be bored and want to start a new adventure," Fiona said. "A new investment could have been exciting for her. And she was a regular at BB's Baked Goods. I'm sure she wouldn't want to see it close down."

"And she wouldn't want anyone to know she was a partner in case the adventure didn't work out. Some people make rash decisions and then regret them later," Granny chimed in, pointing her finger at Fiona behind her back.

"I think at least talking to Ida would be worth it," I said, and Mitch made a note in his notebook. "She might not have liked the way Bernadette handled her money and killed her so she could be the sole owner."

"Since we're sharing," Fiona said, "Harry invested a large sum of money into something hush-hush a couple months before I left for my trip."

"Now, how do you know that?" Granny asked. "You were already divorced. I think you're just being spiteful." She tsked.

"I am not. The kids told me." Fiona hoisted her chin a notch. "Harry tried to talk to me a couple times before I left, but I wouldn't listen. They said he got wind I was setting off on a grand adventure. Maybe he

309

decided to have an adventure of his own. He certainly had enough money to do so. That would be a more believable reason for him to be in town than some ridiculous notion about him trying to win me back."

"You really don't have any faith in me whatsoever, do you?" asked a male voice from the other side of the porch.

We all startled because no one had heard him approach. Harry stood with his hands in his shorts pockets, shaking his head at Fiona.

"Then tell me. What did you invest that money in?" she asked.

"I can't tell you yet," he said. "Can't you just trust me?"

"Been there. Done that. It didn't work out so well," Fiona replied. "I think I'll pass this time around."

"Hi, Harry," Granny said with sly smile. "I trust you'll stay for lunch."

He tipped his hat to Granny. "I'll take a rain check, Gertie."

Fiona gasped. "You will not."

"He will, too," Granny countered. "Last I checked this was my house, not yours. Besides, you already had your five minutes. Now, it's time for mine." She twittered at Harry. "And if you're really nice, I might even give you ten." She let out a trilling giggle.

"It's a date," he said, ignoring a fuming red-faced Fiona. "Right now I have to beat your son-in-law in tennis."

"Well, that shouldn't be too hard," Granny muttered.

"Mother," Mom snapped.

"It's the truth." She lifted her hands, palms up. "I tried to tell him there's a cookie that will make him better, but he doesn't believe in that any more than he does Sunny's gifts."

"Now I know where Sunny gets her foolishness from," Dad boomed. "Thank goodness it missed a generation. Come on, Vivian. You have work to do, and I have a match to win." Mom had to walk quickly to keep up with an irate Dad.

Harry tipped his hat and left as well.

"On that note, I have a case to solve, and you have a mess to clean up. See you when I see you, Tink." Mitch leaned in as though to kiss me, noticed the ladies staring, and cleared his throat instead. He glanced at the yard and scratched his head. "Have fun with that."

"Oh, I'll have fun, all right." Granny and Fiona could clean up their own mess and apologize to Morty. I, on the other hand, had work to do of my own.

Let the games begin.

"I really hate games. I'm no good at them,"
I said as I sat on a barstool Saturday night
in Smokey Jo's, sipping a beer. Mitch was
working late, and I was on my own . . . date-
less . . . listening to seventies folk music
and feeling sorry for myself.

"Then why play them?" Jo asked as she
wiped down the counter.

The bar wasn't that busy for a Saturday
night. Just a few regulars like Abby and
Chuck. Mimi and Ida had joined them for
dinner and cocktails at one table. Harry sat
at another by himself, no Hazel in sight.

Smart man.

And even Quincy Turner sat alone, nurs-
ing a mixed drink over his dinner. A few
others were scattered about, and the rest
were probably at a restaurant with an
outdoor patio since the nights were getting
longer and the weather was gorgeous.

"I have to be sly because no one will talk
to me since I'm not *officially* on the case," I
grumbled, not even trying to hide my
frustration. "I stopped by Sam's earlier
today, and sure enough, Ida was there." I
had filled Jo in on the yard sale, the freak
thunderstorm, and our latest silent partner

theory. "Ida is a crotchety old woman."

"She and Mimi make a great pair." Jo laughed. "At least they have each other now. Maybe it will soften them up a bit."

"No kidding." I grunted. "Anyway, Ida might brag about how much money she has, but word around town is she's tighter than the skin on my mother's face. Yet there are also rumors going around that she opened up her purse strings wide lately. I tried to steer the conversation in that direction, but she told me in no uncertain terms to mind my own damn business. Then she accused me of souring her stomach, and she left."

"What about Sam? Do you really think he could be the silent partner?" Jo asked.

"He says no, but something seems off with him," I responded.

"How so?" Jo shook back her thick auburn curls and tightened her apron, looking at me with genuine interest. She had such a way of making people feel like she was really interested in what they were saying, even when she had so much going on in her own life.

"I'm not sure," I said. "He just seems uncomfortable when talking about Bernadette, and he rarely makes eye contact. I don't know. Maybe I'm reading into it." I took another drink of my beer. "How are the wedding plans going?"

"Your mother has been amazing. She has such a sense of style and class. She's given me some great advice."

I frowned. "*My* mother? I mean, I get the style and class part, but you actually enjoy her company?"

"You've been really busy lately." Jo shrugged, hesitated, and then said in a quiet voice, "Don't you think you can be a bit hard on her sometimes?"

"Seriously?" I scoffed. "Weren't you listening all the times I've talked to you about her?"

"Yes, and I understand she can be controlling and demanding and a pain in the butt at times. But sometimes I think you're the one who's not listening," Jo said gently. "She's proud of you, you know."

"Excuse me?" I choked on a sip of beer. "I repeat . . . *my* mother?"

"You'd be surprised. I have a sister like her. Some people just have a hard time expressing their feelings. That doesn't mean they don't feel them."

A certain cynical, grumpy detective came to mind. Why was it I could forgive and forget and read between the lines when it came to him, but I couldn't do that with my parents? "Touché," I said grudgingly, then asked, "How are the rest of your plans coming along?"

Jo's face clouded over. "Zoe is a godsend, but nothing that I want is working out. Maybe Cole and I should have had a longer engagement. At this rate, we're going to have to get married in a barn because that's all that's available."

"I'm sure it will all work out just fine. Like you said, why wait? You and Cole both love each other and are ready now. That's all that matters."

Jo twisted the dishrag in her hands, looking uncharacteristically nervous. "I guess."

"What's wrong?"

"Nothing. Everything. I don't know."

"Are you having cold feet?"

"God no," she stated emphatically. "But I'm afraid he'll change his mind."

"No way," I responded just as emphatically. "You haven't seen the way he looks at you." I reached out and squeezed her hand. "I have."

"What if he thinks I won't be a good mother?" She looked on the verge of tears.

"Are you crazy? What makes you think you won't make an amazing mother? You're one of eight kids. You've seen it all. I, on the other hand, am an only child. I have no clue what I'm doing around babies."

"I thought being a mother would be easy, but Biff is a handful. He only listens to Cole, and he's making a mess of our house. I snapped at him this morning, and the poor thing looked like he was scared to death."

"Cut yourself some slack. Biff is a different situation. He's been abused, remember? He still needs you to be stern, and he knows you love him. He'll come around."

"Cole might not, though. He got angry with me, and we had a fight. We haven't spoken since." Her voice hitched. "We never argue. What if we start arguing about everything? Money, kids, politics, whatever."

"Welcome to life," I said gently. "Cole fell in love with you while arguing. He loves your fire and passion and willingness to speak your mind. That's what makes you the perfect match for him."

"Tell him that."

"You don't have to. I already know," Cole said from behind Jo in a deep soft voice and then wrapped his big strong arms around her and whispered in her ear, "I'm sorry, baby."

Jo twirled around and threw her arms around his thick neck and kissed him square on the mouth. "Me too."

He used his thumb to swipe away a tear that had rolled down her cheek.

"Just so you know," she added, "I'm too old to change. I'm not going to stop speaking my mind or occasionally losing my temper with both you and Biff."

"And I'm not going to stop pointing out when you're wrong or loving you anyway. As long as you don't stop loving me, it's all good. Deal?"

"Deal, you big lug." She punched him playfully on his shoulder, and he swatted her on the bottom.

"That's my girl," he said softly. "And for the record you're stuck with me for life. I'll never change my mind about you or us, Jo. Get used to it." He tweaked her nose and then headed back into the kitchen with Sean.

"You good now?" I asked.

"I'm great now. God, I love that big ape," Jo said dreamily.

"I'd say the feeling's mutual." I smiled, happy for her but a bit sad for me. "You're lucky."

Jo snapped out of her dreamy state at my tone of voice and looked at me sympathetically. "Your time will come, Sunny. You'll see."

"Yeah, if life ever gets back to normal. I feel like trouble follows Mitch and I wherever we go."

"Maybe that *is* your normal."

"Lord, I hope not."

"Hey, it's what drew you together in the first place." She threw my words back at me.

"That's what I'm afraid of," I replied with genuine concern.

I thought about that. What if the reason we were attracted to each other stemmed from working together on a murder case? The element of danger. The excitement of a new lead. The adrenaline rush of saving each other. The satisfaction of solving a crime.

What if we weren't *us* without the drama?

I didn't want to think about that. Our time together was precious right now because we didn't get much of it. What if we had lots of it, and we discovered we were boring? We wouldn't have anything to argue over or talk about. It's not like I could talk about work. He still didn't completely believe in what I did, or who I was. And when I wasn't consulting with the police on a case, then he wasn't free to talk about it with me.

What was left?

"Stop stressing and have another beer," Jo said, sliding a draft in front of me as though reading my mind.

I took a sip and the hairs on the back of

my neck stood at attention. A strong sensation that someone was watching me crept up my spine. I didn't want to give myself away, so I looked in the mirror behind Jo and scanned the room but didn't see anyone new. *Huh.* Although, I did lock gazes with Quincy, and his face hardened with anger.

Anger directed at me.

"What's next for the case?" Jo asked, changing the subject away from Mitch and I, distracting me like a true friend.

"I guess I try to figure out who the silent partner is and what Sam is hiding."

"Speak of the devil." Jo looked behind me.

I turned around and saw Sam. He came in alone and sat in a corner booth. A minute later Quincy stood, looked around, and then he joined him.

"I didn't even know they knew each other. I'm sure they knew *of* each other, but I had no idea they were familiar enough to have dinner together."

"Me either," Jo said. "Then again if Sam is the secret partner, it would stand to reason that Sam might know about the blackmail and want his money back from Quincy. Maybe he was the person on the other end of the phone that night of July fourth."

19

Sunday morning, the entire town seemed to be at church. *Must be more than a few guilty consciences going around.* Mitch sat beside me, listening to the sermon, while I people-watched. Several people avoided eye contact with me.

When mass was finished, Mitch and I wandered outside. I had to park down the street by the curb. Mitch had met me there and parked out back in the parking lot. I'd been late, and I should have known better. Sacred Heart's parking lot filled early on Sunday mornings in Divinity.

"I made some calls yesterday," Mitch said as we stood by the curb, in the road, waiting for the people to clear out before we drove home.

"And?" I asked.

"Turns out Ida has a son in Boston. She found out he's a pretty bad alcoholic. He lost his job, his wife divorced him, and his kids don't want anything to do with him. When he tried to commit suicide, Ida intervened. She's been paying for him to go to rehab for the last three months. That's the investment she doesn't want anyone to hear about. She wasn't even in town the night of the murder. She was visiting her son in Boston."

"Great. So she's out of the picture." I sighed, feeling exhausted. "At least we still have Sam as a possibility for the silent partner angle. I think he lied, but Quincy knows the truth. He could have been trying to get more money out of him in exchange for keeping quiet. We need to find out what he had on Bernadette."

"That's a possibility. I planned to talk to Sam today, but I didn't see him in church. I'll pay him a visit this afternoon at the bakery."

"Great, it's a date. I haven't had lunch yet." I grinned.

He frowned. "Sunny, we talked about this. You do all the thinking you want, but I will do the investigating. I will keep you informed on everything just like I promised. You have to trust me on this one."

"I do trust you." I bit my bottom lip and ran my fingertip down the front of his dress shirt. "We just haven't spent any quality time together, is all."

He groaned and wrapped his hand around mine, flattening my palm to his chest for a minute, then lowering them both. "You don't play fair," he said in a husky voice.

"I never understood the saying all's fair in love and war. There's nothing fair about love and war. It's called fighting for what you want." I bit my lip.

We just stood there, holding hands and staring at each other, when someone shouted, "Watch out!"

I turned my head and saw my bug rolling down the street, straight in my direction. My mouth parted, and my limbs felt paralyzed. It felt like an out-of-body experience, and I could suddenly relate to how Bernadette must have felt.

At the last second Mitch picked me up and held me against his chest as he hurled his body backward. He landed flat on his back with me facedown on his chest, which had cushioned the blow. My car rolled by at a good enough clip to have flattened me if it hadn't been for my hero.

"As much as I love the feel of you against me, Tink, I think you crushed my lungs," he wheezed. "Think you can get up now?"

"I'm so sorry." I scrambled off him and helped him to his feet. Running my hands all over his chest, I asked, "Are you okay?"

"I'm okay." He stilled my hands. "But I won't be if you keep doing that."

"Oh, sorry. And thank you so much. You saved my life."

He cupped my cheek, then ran a hand through his thick hair, and over his whiskered face. "How the hell did that happen?"

"I have no idea." I looked down the street to where my bug had come to a stop, half on the sidewalk and half in the road. Thank God it hadn't hit anyone else, and there didn't seem to be any damage. "I have my keys, and I always put the emergency brake on. There's a slight decline to this street, but nothing like the hill in front of Trixie's house, and I parked there the other day, no problem. It shouldn't have rolled like that."

"Come on. I want to check something." Mitch led the way across the street to my bug. He opened the door and looked around. I peeked over his shoulder, of course. Sure enough the emergency break was off and the gearshift had been knocked into neutral. "Sunny, you're crowding my space."

"Sorry." I backed out of my bug. "There's no way my car did that by itself."

He pulled himself out of the car as well and looked at me. "Exactly. This is why I didn't want you involved in this investigation, Sunny. You're getting too close. I hope now you will back off." His tone was frustrated and no nonsense and definitely grumpy. "Someone did this on purpose. The question is who?"

My cell phone rang.

It was a number I didn't recognize, but I answered anyway. "Hello?"

"Hi, Sunny. This is Dr. Wilcox."

My stomach jumped to my throat as I immediately thought of Granny Gert. "Is anything wrong?"

"Your grandmother is fine. It's Ms. Atwater who called the paramedics."

"Oh. Let me guess. Another false alarm."

"Actually, no. She was having severe heart palpitations and was positive she was having a heart attack. Because they are on house arrest, I made a house call."

"I really appreciate that, Doctor. Is Fiona okay?"

"She's fine. I gave her something to calm her down. She experienced a severe case of anxiety, but she should be fine so long as no one gets her riled up anymore."

"Anymore?" I asked suspiciously. "What in the world brought this on?"

"Not what." He hesitated. "Who. The answer would be Granny Gert. Apparently she was having a lunch date with Harry, and the stress was too much for Fiona to bear."

"I see." I set my jaw.

First someone tried to kill me, and then Granny nearly killed her friend — no matter what they said, it was plain to see they enjoyed sparring with each other. It was probably the most excitement that either of them had had in ages. But I, for one, had had enough.

"Since they were released under your care, it was my duty to call you," Dr. Wilcox said.

"Thank you."

"You're welcome. And, Sunny . . . don't be too hard on them. They've been through a lot."

"Don't worry, Doc. I know exactly what they need."

"What were you thinking, Granny?" I asked with hands on my hips as I stood in the foyer of my house.

Mitch had dropped me off and called in the CSI group to go over my car from top to bottom. I'd promised him I would stay home for the rest of the day so he could do his job without worrying about me. I'd agreed for once, but only for today. No way would I put myself on house arrest with the

Dynamic Duo.

I'd end up in the loony bin for sure.

"I was only trying to help the nincompoop," Granny said. "How was I supposed to know she was telling the truth for a change?" Granny's snappy brown eyes didn't look so snappy anymore. They were filled with genuine concern. Good. She needed to worry a little so maybe she would think before she acted impulsively next time.

"How is you dating her ex-husband helping her?" I asked.

"It wasn't a date; it was lunch. And I thought maybe it would make her jealous. Remind her of how she used to feel about Harry. It's plain as day she still feels that way. She's just too stubborn to admit it."

"And you." I pointed my finger at a sheepish Harry. "When will you stop playing games and just tell Fiona you love her?"

"I told her I wanted her back, but she wouldn't listen. What more can I do?" He looked so worried and lost and helpless, I believed every word he said.

I softened a bit. "She wants to hear that you love her, not just that you want her back. What more can you do? Fight for her, that's what. Instead of playing silly games like trying to make her jealous, shower her with affection and words of love."

"I've sent her a bunch of gifts, but she sends them right back." He paced the foyer. "Stubborn woman."

"She doesn't want your money; she wants your time. Don't you see this is all a test? She wants to make sure you're serious and that you're not going anywhere. She wants to make sure you mean what you say." I looked him in the eye. "She wants to make sure you won't hurt her again."

"Boy, I really messed up, didn't I?" His shoulders drooped.

"Yes, you did. But she will be fine, and you didn't do anything that can't be fixed. But right now, you need to leave," I said firmly. "Think about what I said."

"I will, and thank you." He nodded. "I know exactly what I'm going to do."

"What's that?" I couldn't help asking out of curiosity.

"Exactly what I planned to all along. My investment, remember?" A determined look entered his eyes. "I'm going to give her the trip of a lifetime, even if it means carrying her over my shoulder until we get there." He left without another word.

"That's so romantic," Granny said wistfully.

"I know you miss Grandpa and only wanted to play matchmaker for Harry's sake. And I know you like Fiona no matter what you say. But you're still in trouble. You guys aren't kids anymore. This could have been much more serious than it was. You have to start thinking first, Granny."

"You're right, and I'm sorry." She patted my hand. "It can't have been easy with both of us under your roof. I do appreciate everything you've done for me, sweetie. I promise to try and get along with Fiona, even if it kills me. One way or another, we'll be out of your hair soon."

"Don't worry, Granny." For the first time, I could see she really was worried. I'd been right that Granny's defense mechanism was to act like nothing bothered her so everyone else wouldn't worry. I hugged her. "We'll figure it all out. We always do."

"I know, dear. I'm not worried. I think I'll take a little nap now." She hung up her apron and headed for the stairs, looking like she had the weight of the world on her shoulders.

So much for not being worried.

Later that day I sat in my sanctuary ready to give Abigail Webb a reading. Abby had called, asking if I could do a reading for her. I usually didn't work on Sundays, but I was going stir-crazy confined to the house and worrying about Mitch. What if someone had been trying to kill him instead of me? We'd both been standing in the road when my car had rolled.

The doorbell rang, and I let Abby in. We'd had our share of differences in the past, but now that she was happily married to Chuck, she'd stopped obsessing over Mitch and acting crazy. We'd sort of come to a tolerable acceptance of one another. Pushing her feelings aside for me, she did respect what I did for a living.

Abby still looked great from the makeover her cousin had given her — full-bodied brown hair with short sassy bangs. "I appreciate you accommodating me on such short notice," she said.

"My pleasure," I replied. "Follow me, and we'll get started." I led the way into my sanctuary.

I parted the strands of crystal beads that served as a door and entered the small, cozy, pale blue room with her right behind me. The scent of my aromatherapy oils filled the air, and new age music poured quietly out of the speakers of my stereo. My tropical fish tank bubbled in one corner of the room while my unlit fireplace occupied the other.

I had scattered various green plants and

herbs about, and my fortune-telling supplies sat on shelves in yet another corner.
My favorite part of the room was the constellations that covered the ceiling in a
fabulous depiction of the universe that
glowed when I dimmed the lights.

"Hold out your hands so I can see what
type of fortune-telling tool will work best
on you," I said.

Abby did as I asked, and I held her hands
and closed my eyes. I pictured each tool in
my mind's eye, and when I thought about
tarot cards, her hands warmed and tingled.
I opened my eyes and smiled.

"You're a tarot sort of girl."

"I am?" She blinked.

I nodded. It was always like that for me.
Each person I did a reading for was different, and a certain feeling would come over
me when I touched upon the one that would
work best for that particular person at that
time. It didn't mean other tools wouldn't
work on them, it simply meant that tool
would work best for that particular situation.

"Allow me to prepare my space and ready
myself." I gestured toward the old-fashioned
tea table in the center of the room, and she
sat down. Once I had gathered my tarot
card supplies, I joined her.

The first thing I did was cover the table with a silk scarf. This protected the cards' energy from any undesirable vibrations. Next I placed some elemental symbols around the table. I chose a stone to represent the earth, a seashell to represent the water, a candle to represent fire, and incense to represent air. Finally, I used fanning powder on the cards because it made them feel wonderful, not to mention it was great for keeping them from sticking together.

I ate a piece of chocolate and offered one to Abby. Then I centered myself by breathing deeply, trying to pull the energy into my core. This helped me to focus, letting go of all other thoughts, and be fully present during a reading. I grounded myself by picturing a connection to the earth and its stable calming energy as I connected to the universe, inviting divine wisdom to flow through me.

"Do I have your permission to connect with your Higher Self?" I asked.

A wide-eyed Abby nodded as though unable to speak in her fascination of all that was happening.

"Place your hands palms up please."

She did as I asked. I placed my own hands palms down over hers until they were slightly touching. Then I closed my eyes as

I tuned in to my Higher Self. I asked the universe to connect us and keep the connection as it guided me through the reading, then I removed my hands and opened my eyes.

"Think about what you want to know, and when you're ready, ask your question out loud."

Abby puckered her brow in concentration, and then said, "I've been through a lot in my life, but I'm finally happy. I have almost everything I've ever dreamed of. I'm so afraid I'm going to wake up, and it will all be gone. I guess I just want to know what the cards see for me."

"Okay, then. I will use a three-card spread with the first card representing your past, the second card representing your present, and the third card representing your future." I shuffled the deck of cards three times, and then laid three cards facedown.

I flipped over the first card, and the VI The Lovers card of the Major Arcana cards stared back at me. I smiled. "This card is the Lovers card. It represents your past, and it means you made a decision that made your heart glad. It's complex and deals with the union of opposites."

"Kind of like me and Chuck," Abby said excitedly.

"Exactly. When you made the decision to get married, it made you feel good and certain and strong, but also scared and vulnerable. Just like falling in love feels. You chose the decision in your heart, and all is right in your world."

"Yes, it is." She beamed. "What does the next card show?"

"Well, let's see," I said. I turned over the second card, and the Three of Wands of the Minor Arcana cards stared back at me. "The Three of Wands is in the position of your present. This card represents active waiting. You are waiting for news of something. But you aren't just sitting around. You're making plans for what to do if the outcome is in your favor, and what to do if it is not." I looked at her with raised eyebrows. "Does this mean what I think it does?"

She bit her lip, nearly bursting at the seams. "I wanted to keep this hush-hush, but I am just so excited. I haven't taken a test yet, but I think I might be pregnant because I'm late. So cross your fingers and don't tell anyone. I want to surprise Chuck."

"I won't breathe a word, but I can do better than cross my fingers." I walked around the table and knelt before her. "Do you mind?"

She shook her head slowly, warily.

"It's okay," I said as I gently laid my hand on her stomach and closed my eyes. Focusing, I felt a warm vibration. It was faint and barely there, but there was a definite hum. Opening my eyes, I said, "You might want to take that pregnancy test when you get home." I winked.

Her jaw fell open as I walked back around the table and sat down once more. "You mean . . . ?"

"I can't say for certain, but I'm ninety-nine percent sure."

She jumped up and started to leave.

"Wait. You still have one more card."

"That's right." She sat back down but couldn't stop fidgeting in her excitement.

I flipped over the last card and thought, I should have let her leave.

"You look funny. What's wrong?" she asked when I hesitated.

"Well, this card is positioned to reveal your future. It's the Five of Cups." My eyes met hers. "This card represents the experience of loss and grief. It represents a period of mourning."

Abby gasped. "Am I going to lose the baby?"

"I don't know, I just —" My body jerked as my vision channeled into tunnel vision.

"What's happening?" I heard Abby ask in the back of my mind, and I held up my hand to silence her before she broke my trance.

I spoke out loud, saying exactly what I was seeing. "I am standing inside someone else's body, but I don't know who. I feel the person's anger and frustration. The person is facing you, and you're clutching your stomach and backing away while shaking your head in disbelief. You are outside of your trailer, backing toward your front door when you trip and fall backward. You cry out in pain as the person lunges forward to —"

"No!" Abby screamed, yanking me back to the present. "I change my mind. I don't want to know. I can't. Just stop. Please." And then she bolted out of my house, leaving me behind and stunned.

What just happened? Who was after Abby? Who was angry with her? Could Chuck be angry about the baby? Did he even want children? There was a definite loss involved. Either she would lose the baby, or Chuck would leave her. She'd been so happy, but then I'd made her miserable. She was right. She had been through a lot, but I was afraid her troubles were just beginning.

It was times like this that made me want to quit.

20

Five hours later, dusk was settling on Divinity. I knew I was supposed to stay put. I had promised Mitch. But I couldn't stop thinking about Abby.

The reading I'd given her just didn't make sense. Chuck was so happy to be married to Abby. I couldn't imagine him not wanting kids. And it wasn't like Abby had an ex who would be angry that she'd moved on with Chuck. For years she'd been obsessed with Mitch. He certainly wouldn't be unhappy that she'd moved on with her life.

Who else could possibly be angry with her?

A wild thought occurred to me. It was a long shot, and I wasn't even sure it was possible. But it was the only thing that made sense. I called Chuck at the hotel and asked where Abby was. He said she was home because she wasn't feeling well. He didn't act like he knew why, so I didn't say a word about the baby. I did however ask him some other questions. His answers filled in so many blanks for me. For both Bernadette's murder and for my reading with Abby.

I just realized that last card in Abby's reading regarding the sense of loss in her future, the Five of Cups, had to do with the number five. That could mean five minutes, five hours, five months. I looked at the clock. It was almost five hours since I'd done her reading. And the vision had taken place in the evening.

I sucked in a breath.

That meant I had exactly ten minutes to get to Abby to stop whatever was about to happen. "Granny, Fiona, Morty," I shouted. All three appeared. Granny looking rested after her nap, Fiona looking less stressed after her sedative, and Morty looking like, well, Morty.

Aristocratic, and mysterious, and up to something.

"I have to go to Abby's. If Mitch calls, let him know where I am. I tried his cell, but there's no answer as usual."

"Oh, but, dear, won't he be mad?" Granny asked.

"Yeah, sugar, I thought you were supposed to stay put?" Fiona seconded.

"This is an emergency. I have my cell if I

need it. Just sit tight and don't get into any more trouble, okay?"

They glanced at each other sheepishly, then both said, "Scout's honor," at the same time and then, "Jinx." They laughed.

Oh, boy. Those two as allies instead of enemies might be even scarier.

I turned to Morty to tell him to keep an eye on them, but he had already vanished. Oh, yeah, he was definitely up to something. I had seen that look in his eyes before, but I didn't have time to worry about that right now. It was nearly dark.

Hurrying to my car, I quickly made my way to Abby's trailer. I pulled up but didn't see anyone. Parking my car in her driveway, I hurried to her front door and knocked. If I could get her to listen to me, I could get her to safety. I felt it was the least I could do after my reading had upset her so much.

I walked back several steps when she opened the door and stepped outside. The sun was setting, but it was still hot and steamy out. She faced me with her arms crossed, walking forward to meet me.

"Thank God I got to you in time," I said.

"What do you mean?" she asked warily. "I don't think I can handle any more bad news. "I took the test like you said, and it's positive. I'm pregnant. But now I'm too afraid to tell Chuck. You've got me thinking I'm either going to lose the baby, or Chuck is going to leave me."

"I know, and I'm so sorry about that. That's why I'm here. Chuck isn't the one you have to worry about."

Abby's eyes widened and she started to walk backward, shaking her head in stunned disbelief.

"I haven't even said anything yet," I said, carefully walking toward her so as not to startle her further. She looked like she was frail and vulnerable and ready to snap.

She tripped and fell and cried out in pain, just like in my vision.

"Abby, wait, you're going to hurt yourself." I reached for her to help her up. She was acting so strangely.

Her eyes widened even more, and she looked at me in horror as she screamed, "No!"

Something hard crashed into my skull from behind me, and my world went black.

I pried my eyes open, and the pain slicing through my skull nearly did me in. As carefully as I could, I blinked to clear my vision and looked around. I was tied up and sitting on a brand-new wicker chair on a renovated porch with a fresh coat of paint.

The last time I'd been on this porch, the wood was weathered and the wicker was ancient. A revelation hit me. Abby hadn't been looking at me in horror. She'd been looking at the person behind me. I raised my eyes and wasn't surprised in the least at the person who stood before me now.

Mimi Pots.

She held a shotgun, but she was dressed in nice clothes, not a housecoat like the first time I'd met her, and she had a full set of false teeth with no chewing tobacco in sight. Abby stood, wringing her hands beside Mimi and pacing.

"And here I thought Abby was the one in danger. That your anger and frustration were directed at her. I had no idea they were directed at me." I studied Mimi in confusion. "Why?"

She shrugged. "You were getting too close. I wasn't worried about Detective Stone. All men are morons. But you . . . you're smart. It was only a matter of time before you figured this whole thing out."

"I knew Abby's cousin had given you a makeover for the wedding for free, but I should have realized that didn't include a new car and the renovations on your trailer. I was just glad to see you were coming around town and trying to make friends."

"I thought winning that jackpot in Atlantic City was the best thing that ever happened to me," Mimi said. "It wasn't much money, but it was supposed to be my fresh start."

I studied her. "You were Bernadette's silent partner, weren't you?"

Abby looked stunned.

"Why Bernadette?" I asked.

"I don't trust easy, and Bernadette was my friend. I'm tired of just getting by and wanted to do something. I didn't have a lot of money left over, but I had enough to partner up. Except you know I don't like the limelight," Mimi said. "Those gossips around town got nothing better to do than yammer on, twisting things about. Even changing my looks didn't make a difference to them. They were still uppity know-it-alls."

"Then why did you keep hanging around town?" I asked.

I figured if I kept her talking, I could think of a way out of this mess. If only I could free myself, I could call for help. I tried to make eye contact with Abby, but she just kept pacing and shaking her head like she couldn't process what was happening.

"I had to keep my eye on my investment. Bernadette might have been a sound businesswoman, but she wasn't well liked. She always felt like an outsider in her own town.

That's why she could relate to me, I guess. She was nice to me. We —" Mimi cleared her throat and repeated, "We were friends."

"What happened?" I asked quietly.

"A stupid man up and ruined things once more." Mimi scowled.

"Are you talking about Quincy Turner?" I asked. "Were you the one on the phone that day?"

"He done lost his mind when Bernadette put the bug in your granny's ear about how Animal Angels needed the money much more than the Parks and Rec organization did." She scowled.

"Is that when he started blackmailing her?" I interjected as I kept working the rope behind my hands.

Mimi's face hardened. "The stupid man started snooping around and following Bernadette." She kept talking as though she were ranting to herself and had forgotten I was even there. "I told Bernadette that someday she was gonna get caught buying her turnovers from that small Amish farm way out of town. You can only pretend to bake them after hours for so long before someone catches on."

I gasped. "Bernadette's famous prize-winning turnovers weren't even hers?" The negative vibes that had rolled off her rolling pin suddenly made perfect sense.

Mimi blinked as though realizing what she just said, then she shrugged, waving her gun around. "BB's Baked Goods would never survive the scandal if everyone knew Bernadette was a fraud. They'd see our whole business as a fraud, and I couldn't let that happen."

"What happened?" I asked, hoping to keep her talking.

"I convinced Quincy to give Bernadette a shot to change the carnival board's mind. The main thing he wanted was the auction money. So Bernadette started the petition to change the charity recipient back to the Parks and Rec Program, but then Ozzie threatened her with violence if she didn't back off."

"Quincy asked for money next, I take it?" I asked.

"You'd be right. He's no fool. But Bernadette didn't have any money." Mimi huffed out a breath. "Except mine. She paid him off but didn't tell me because she knew I'd be furious. Instead, she got involved with those loan sharks to try to pay me back before I found out."

"Is that when you killed her?" Abby stopped pacing and asked Mimi with a note of agony as though she dreaded hearing the answer.

"Land sakes, child. I didn't kill Bernadette. She might have done some stupid things, but she was my friend. I found out just in time and confronted her. I convinced her not to take the money from the sharks. It wasn't worth the risk." Mimi shook her head.

"Especially after I discovered their boss was none other than my husband who went out for coffee fifty years ago and never came back," she went on. "He finally came back when he heard I won some money, and since we never officially divorced, he figured half the money was his. Damn fool didn't know it wasn't much money at all, but he wouldn't have cared anyway. He considered everything his. But I took care of him."

"You're the informant who tipped Detective Stone off before the monster truck rally, and now they're all in jail." I had to hand it to Mimi. She'd grown a backbone over the years, and this time around, she wasn't letting her husband get the upper hand.

"Damn right I am," Mimi ground out. "They were after me because they couldn't find my money at BB's, and I had convinced Bernadette to stay away from them. They didn't know she gave it to Quincy, and that

I didn't have any left after my new car and the repairs on my trailer. They wanted what they considered theirs, and I knew they wouldn't stop until they got it. That's why I rarely went anywhere alone. I was losing everything, but I'd rather die than let that monster win again. We had to fire the staff and close our doors. The bakeoff was our only shot."

"Only, Bernadette had new competition this year with Granny and Fiona, didn't she?" I asked, still working the knot.

"That's right," Mimi growled. "Bernadette was worried, and frankly, so was I. We planned to hire a new staff at lower wages, and if she won the bakeoff as usual, it would bring in all sorts of new business. We would be fine. I had things I could sell if I needed to. But then she died."

"What happened?" Abby asked, looking on the verge of hysteria.

"It was a horrible accident." Mimi shook her head and pursed her lips like she was fighting back tears.

"An accident?" I asked, my eyebrows sky-high. "You're kidding."

"Do I look like I'm joking?" Mimi spat. "That blasted granny of yours and her sidekick Fiona were ruining everything. I couldn't let them win the bakeoff. All I was trying to do was make it look like they were cheating."

Mimi picked up her shotgun and cocked it. "I put Granny's cookies and Fiona's pie in that beast of a car your granny drives. But your granny is a horrible driver. The dang fool woman left her keys in the car, and the stupid thing was in neutral. When I shut the door, it rolled forward. I tried running after it, but it was too late."

"You mean to tell me no one was in the car when it hit Bernadette?" I couldn't believe what I was hearing.

"That's right." Mimi nodded. "The car was empty, other than the cookies, the pie, and their purses."

"No wonder no one hit the brakes. There wasn't anyone driving at all. This really was an accident and not a murder," I muttered, trying to make sense of it all. The whole thing was such a senseless tragedy. I finally looked her in the eye and said sadly, "You should have called the police and told them everything. You would be in far less trouble if you had."

"What do you take me for, a fool? I was so upset when I saw Bernadette under that car that I did call the police."

"You were the anonymous caller," I said in wonder, but then creased my forehead.

"Why did you say Granny and Fiona were in it together?"

"I figured it was all their fault anyway." Mimi nodded once. "Someone needed to pay for what happened, and it sure as shoot wasn't going to be me. I didn't want Bernadette to die in vain, and I couldn't let her business die with her. Our business."

Mimi slapped her chest. "I've done without my whole life. It was time I got something in return. I figured once this whole thing blew over, I would talk to Sam and see if he still wanted to partner up. I need to be successful for when Abby's baby comes along. But you're a Little Miss Smarty-pants. You're the only one who knows the truth. I like you, Sunny, but I have no choice. You have to go."

"Mimi, this is crazy. You're not a murderer. You can't do this," Abby said. "What about me? I know what happened. Are you going to kill me, too?"

Mimi looked confused. "Of course not. We're family. When Chuck leaves you, which he will because they all do, then you can move in with me and we can raise the baby together." She looked like a battle was raging within, but then she must have pushed down her doubts and made up her mind. "This is war. There are always casualties in war. It's just the way of the world. It's time you toughened up and learned that."

"Chuck won't leave me," Abby said, standing up straight and firm. "You're not getting anywhere near my baby, Mimi. You're not the woman I thought you were."

Mimi actually gasped and jerked as though Abby had slapped her across the face. Her voice wobbled as she said, "You can't mean that. Bernadette's death was an accident. I told you that."

"But everything else you did wasn't. And killing Miss Meadows certainly won't be." Abby looked at me, broke down, and then sobbed. "This is the loss you were talking about, wasn't it? Because I'm definitely in mourning."

"You're acting like I'm dead, child," Mimi said.

"You are to me," Abby responded coldly.

Pain and remorse flashed across Mimi's face, but then fury and anger took its place. "You did this," she spat, pointing her shotgun at me. "You and that granny of yours. Men are supposed to be the evil ones. Not women. You're a traitor to your own kind." A wild look filled her eyes, and I could tell she wasn't all there anymore.

"Mimi, stop," Abby pleaded, laying her

hand on Mimi's arm. "If you turn yourself in now, we can get help for you. There's still time."

Mimi jerked away and pushed her toward me until she stumbled into the other wicker chair. "She's brainwashed you with all her woo-woo talk. It's like a cult, and she's the ringleader. Once she's gone, your mind will clear. You'll see. Then you'll realize everything I've done, I've done for you. For us. I don't care what you say. We *are* family. Because if we're not, then I've got nothin'. I can't let that happen."

She hefted her shotgun up to her shoulder, pointed it at my chest, put her finger on the trigger, and . . .

Suddenly, Mimi's house started to shake violently. She stumbled about on the porch, and her shotgun went off, hitting a hanging basket of flowers. Colorful petals filled the air like confetti, and I was reminded of Mitch holding me in his arms as we watched the fireworks on the Fourth of July.

Another bout of shaking jarred my teeth, while Abby clutched a wicker chair for dear life. I bounced around helpless since my hands were tied behind my back.

"It's an earthquake!" Mimi shouted when a loud crack sounded and the porch beneath her feet split open and gave way. She screamed and fell through, dropping the gun on her way.

The house settled instantly, and Morty appeared as if from out of nowhere about ten feet away.

Mimi stood chest deep, trapped between the porch floorboards. The rest of the porch remained intact, with just that one section damaged. The gun lay just out of reach, as if taunting Mimi and letting her know she had failed.

Mimi stared at a slightly puffed-up and glowing Morty. He gave her the same look he'd given Granny and Fiona when they had tried to sell off Vicky's belongings in a yard sale. You didn't mess with anything that belonged to Morty, and from the moment I'd met him, his message was clear: I belonged to him.

Mimi's eyes grew wide and crazed as though he was sending her some message telepathically. Quite frankly, nothing would surprise me when it came to Morty. "Keep him away from me," she shrieked. "He's the devil, I tell you. I can see it in his black eyes."

"No worries, Mrs. Pots. Where you're going you won't see much of anyone for years to come." Mitch stepped onto the porch and glanced at me to make sure I was okay.

It was just enough time for Mimi to wiggle her arms out of the porch and grab the shotgun.

"Look out!" I yelled.

Mitch spun around and kicked the end of the gun just as she pumped the shotgun and fired off another shot. It shattered a window of her house, and Mitch dove onto the porch, wrestling the gun from her hands and hurling it into her yard. He didn't waste any more time and handcuffed Mimi before pulling her out of the hole.

Once he had her secured in the back of his squad car and had called it in, he re-appeared on the porch. Abby had already untied me, but I wasn't the one Mitch was looking at. He stared at Morty for a full minute, and then saluted him as if to say, *Thanks, partner.*

If I didn't know better, I'd swear Morty nodded at Mitch, and then turned away to regally disappear into the woods.

"Where's he going?" Abby asked.

"Wherever he wants," Mitch answered with a note of newfound respect in his voice.

"Whatever," Abby said, looking confused and sad and just plain worn out. "I'm going home to call Chuck."

"No problem. I'll send someone over later to get your statement, Mrs. Webb."

"Thank you, Detective." Her eyes met mine briefly. "And thanks for everything, Miss Meadows. I'm sorry you had to go through all that."

"It's okay, Abby." I smiled at her. "Good luck with the baby and tell Chuck congratulations for me."

"I will." She waved and slowly made her way back to her trailer, cradling her stomach every step of the way.

Mitch and I were left alone for the first time. I looked at him as he stared at the woods. "Will wonders never cease?" I said in awe. "Does this mean that my two favorite fellows are finally friends?"

Mitch raised a brow as he looked back at me. "I wouldn't go that far. Let's just say we have a better understanding of one another, and a bit more tolerance." He studied me with a hard look in his eyes. "What you did, on the other hand, I'm not tolerating well at all. You're making me completely gray. I thought I told you to stay put."

"You did." I took a step toward him and bit my bottom lip.

"And you didn't listen as usual," he said with less bite to his voice as he watched me take another step.

"But I did call you." I stopped before him

353

and wrapped my arms around him, resting my cheek on his chest. "You didn't answer as usual."

"I was a little busy," he said, wrapping his arms around me and resting his chin on the top of my head as he talked. "Turns out Sam wasn't the silent partner, but I can see you figured that out. He just happens to be profiting from being the only bakery in town these days. And he met with Quincy because he's still looking to expand his business. He made the same offer to Quincy that he made to Bernadette, wanting to partner up and sell his baked goods in the park. Once he found out that Quincy had blackmailed Bernadette, he pulled out of the deal. I'm sure he'll make an offer to buy BB's from the bank now that Mimi has been arrested. Quincy's been arrested as well for blackmail."

"What's going to happen to the Parks and Rec Program?"

"The town said they wanted someone who can bring new life into the park. Turns out Jo's cousin Zoe, the party planner, is interested."

"That's great," I said. "She'd be perfect. I'm sure she would plan all sorts of events in the park that would bring in more than enough money to keep it going."

"I think so, too." He smiled, and an awkward silence filled with tension fell between us.

"So, how did you end up here?" I asked curiously.

"Morty, if you can believe it." Mitch chuckled. "That crazy cat showed up outside Sam's Bakery window. I figured something was up, so I followed him. He kept appearing and then disappearing, as though leading me to something. When I lost sight of him, I called your house. Granny filled me in, and here I am."

More policemen showed up, and Mitch stepped back to look me in the eye. He pointed his finger at me. "Don't move. I mean it this time." Then he jogged off to give them instructions regarding Mimi. A minute later, he reappeared by my side.

"Wait, don't you have to go with them?"

"I told them something really important came up."

"What could be more important than bringing Mimi in?"

"Dessert." He scooped me into his arms and headed for his car with long purposeful strides, adding, "Case closed."

"But what about dinner?" I asked, already breathless as thrills of excitement zipped through me.

"Sometimes rules are meant to be broken, Tink. Like having dessert first."

"Why, Detective Grumpy Pants, that's very naughty of you."

His heated gaze met mine. "You ain't seen nothing yet."

"I always did like a bad boy."

"Then you're gonna love me." His head lowered and his lips touched mine. My heart flipped over in my chest, and I knew without a shadow of a doubt . . .

I already did.

EPILOGUE

"Well, ladies, Judge Navarra threw out all charges. The case has been dropped, and you are free to go," Mom said as we sat on my front porch one week later on Sunday afternoon.

"Well, it's about time. The first thing I'm going to do is get a pedicure and maybe a massage." Fiona rubbed her bracelet-free ankle. "I owe you."

"I know." Vivian smiled.

"Thank you, Vivian. You did a wonderful job like you always do. I'm proud of you," Granny Gert said.

Mom blinked. "Thank you, Mother. It was good seeing you again. Things haven't been quite the same since you've been gone."

"Of course they haven't. She has no —" Dad started to boom.

"Donald," Mom snapped, giving Dad a look that said, *I can yell at my mother all I want. You, not so much.*

"Yes, dear," Dad said in a much quieter voice.

"That's my girl," Granny said with a wink.

Mom rolled her eyes.

And I couldn't help but laugh . . . a little.

"It's so nice to have things back to normal again," I said.

Now everyone needed to get the heck out of Dodge and take the drama with them. Four weeks of the Granny and Fiona Show was enough to drive anyone mad.

"I'll drink to that." Fiona raised her sweet tea with a kick in celebration.

"I'm sure you will," Granny chimed in but with much less bite. "I have to say I'm actually going to miss you, Fi."

"Right back at ya, Gertie." Fiona smiled, then gave Harry a saucy grin. "But I have a vacation to take with a man I like to call Harry."

"You do?" Harry asked in stunned surprise.

"I do now. Phillip was a stuffy man from my past who worked way too much to give me the attention I deserved. That's why I always tried to make him jealous and think I still had feelings for Frank. Crazy fool could never see how much he had come to mean to me."

Harry looked stunned and a bit hopeful.

Fiona hoisted her chin a notch. "But that's all in the past. I'm ready to start fresh with the fun and exciting retired Harry standing before me now. Maybe he won't be so blind. Do you still have a ticket with my name on it?"

"Always," he said and covered his heart with his hand. "And trust me when I say I've learned my lesson. My eyes are wide open now."

"Good. It's a start." She nodded once and clinked her glass to his.

After gathering her belongings, Fiona and Harry said their good-byes and left my house.

"On that note, Viv, we'd better get home. You know how Sylvia doesn't like us to overstay our welcome." Dad stood.

"Dad, it's not like we won't see each other soon." I fibbed, thinking a nice long break was what I needed right now.

"Oh, darling, don't worry. We'll be back in a couple months." Mom joined him by the door.

"You will?" I asked, dread filling me at what I was about to hear.

"Of course, silly. Didn't know you? Your lovely friend Jo invited us to the wedding." Mom gave me a sly look that said, *Winning.*

"Now there's a woman who has a good head on her shoulders," Dad boomed.

And we're back.

"Great," I replied and hugged them both before they headed off to the airport in a taxi.

Just wait until I saw Jo again. I would never be able to cut loose and enjoy myself with them watching my every move. What did it matter anyway? I wasn't even sure I had a date since Mitch was busier than ever at work and was once again putting that before me . . . us. Even Zoe had agreed, if a bit reluctantly, to be Sean's date. He still had a lot of ground to cover with her, but we would work on that. Once again, I was the loner. I sighed.

Story of my life.

"Well, I'm exhausted. I'm going to go take me a little nap," Granny said. "Come on, Mortypoo. I need a snuggle buddy."

Morty shook his whole body, but the biggest bow tie she'd made for him yet stood firmly in place. He gave me a pitiful look.

"At least the booties are gone," I said in consolation.

He just hissed and then trotted after Granny.

I stood up and started to head inside when a voice spoke from behind me.

"Where do you think you're going?"

I pressed my lips together and closed my eyes before turning around slowly. Mitch stood on the porch before me, wearing a pair of basketball shorts and a damp T-shirt as though he'd just come from a run.

He looked great, but that didn't mean I wasn't still angry with him.

"You show up now?" I asked.

We'd had the most amazing night of our lives the previous Sunday, staying up together and talking about everything. Our hopes, our fears, our dreams. But never once did we talk about us. I wasn't even sure I knew what *we* were. We'd skirted around the issue for so long. Skipped the dating part and went right to dessert. And then we were right back to usual Monday morning: something always coming up to keep us from spending time together.

I was beginning to think my biggest fear was coming true. We really were only good together when there was drama happening around us.

"I don't know what to say," he said, shifting from foot to foot, not quite meeting my eyes.

"Don't bother. It's obvious you only wanted dessert. Now we're back to the same old routine. We're done. We're over. Case closed. There's really nothing left to say." I turned around and put my hand on the door. "I want more; you obviously don't."

Strong arms wrapped around me from behind and pulled me tight against a wide sculpted chest as though they didn't plan on ever letting me go. His deep voice whispered low in my ear, "I definitely want more, and there's everything left to say. Please don't tell me we're over."

I closed my eyes and pressed my trembling lips together. "I can't keep doing this, Mitch. It hurts too much. I don't even know what you want from me."

"Dammit!" He let go of me and stepped away.

I was afraid to turn around. Afraid to see his face. Afraid he would confirm everything that had been running through my head all week. But I did turn around, because I had to see him one last time before I ended it. Ended us. I faced him and looked into his tortured eyes, then opened my mouth to put him out of his misery.

His lips swooped down over mine before I could say a word. He pulled me in close until my body was pressed against his, and he poured out so many emotions in that one endless kiss. When he finally broke away, he tipped his forehead down until it rested against mine.

"I've been through so much, lost so many people I cared about, I swore I would never let this happen. Being with you scares the hell out of me. I tried to rationalize that I'm too busy at work to have a *real* relationship. I tried to stop thinking about you. I tried to ignore you. I tried to run you out of my system. You're right. I didn't want you. I didn't want any of this."

I pulled away from him. "Wh-what are you saying?"

"That fate doesn't give a damn about anything I want." He cradled my face in his big hands and kissed me so tenderly on the lips, tears rolled down my cheeks. "But it sure as hell knows what I need. I need you, Sunshine Meadows. So much it hurts."

"What does that mean?"

His eyes searched mine and softened, unguarded and pouring out everything he was feeling. I sucked in a breath as I saw it plain as day before he said the words that would change my life forever.

"I love you, Sunny. Will you marry me?"

For the first time in my life I was speechless. And then I began to really cry.

"Is that good or bad?" he asked, looking terrified of what I might say.

"I just wanted you to ask me out on

another date." I started laughing through my tears. "I think you're more afraid I'll actually say yes."

"Skipping to the end and doing things backward seems to be our thing. I'm not gonna lie. I don't know the first thing about being a husband. I just know I can't live without you."

"Well, then. I think it's time we did something about that, don't you?"

He narrowed his eyes. "Like what?"

"Move in together."

"Here?" he asked, looking around warily.

"Your apartment is way too small."

"But you haven't even said yes."

"And I'm not going to . . . yet. You've still got some making up to do, mister. And I still want to be courted. Not to mention there's another man in my life who has to give his blessing first."

"Well, hell, why don't I move a mountain for you while I'm at it," Mitch grumbled, and then blew out a breath. "You don't make things easy, Tink."

"What fun would that be, Grumpy Pants?" I stood on my toes and kissed him.

His face softened with love. "Fine. You win."

"Come on. Let's go check out your new living quarters."

"I'd say I thought you'd never ask. Problem is I was afraid you actually would."

"You big scaredy cat." I laughed and took his hand, pulling him after me, feeling hope for the first time in a long time. But Mitch was right. It would definitely take a miracle to get Morty to agree to let him stay. Good thing pulling off miracles just happened to be my specialty.

And I had a plan. . . .

The employees of Thorndike Press hope you have enjoyed this Large Print book. All our Thorndike, Wheeler, and Kennebec Large Print titles are designed for easy reading, and all our books are made to last. Other Thorndike Press Large Print books are available at your library, through selected bookstores, or directly from us.

For information about titles, please call:
    (800) 223-1244

or visit our Web site at:
    http://gale.cengage.com/thorndike

To share your comments, please write:
    Publisher
    Thorndike Press
    10 Water St., Suite 310
    Waterville, ME 04901

CPSIA information can be obtained
at www.ICGtesting.com
Printed in the USA
FFOW04n0926301113
2522FF